SUPERNOVA

THE COMMONS
BOOK 1

JESSICA MARTING

SHADOW PRESS

CHAPTER 1

Lily Stewart stared at the last zombie, shambling towards her little fortress. It mindlessly chewed on an arm pilfered from an innocent victim, red and black gore dribbling down its face. She looked over her weapons cache, willing a measly hand grenade to materialize. It didn't.

The zombie lost its grip on the arm and tossed it aside jerkily. It sped up. Damn it—they were now capable of *running*? She hadn't banked on that happening.

She let out a low curse. The zombie lurched forward with a guttural moan and stepped into her fortress. GAME OVER flashed across Lily's computer screen. THE ZOMBIES ATE YOUR BRAAAINS!!!

Lily sighed and closed the game, then brought up a list of the day's appointments for Lazarus Cryonics. There weren't a lot, at least as far as she could tell. Lazarus didn't seem to do too much business. There didn't seem to be a big market for it in southern Ontario.

But then, what did she know? Part of the reason Lily had taken the job in the first place was its welcome respite from the thick August heat, air-conditioning being a luxury her stingy she was a teenager, for one, and when she discovered the affair between her fiancé and best friend. She found out about their affair three months into it, when she had been expecting a proposal from Cameron. Lily and Cameron had built a quiet life for themselves in the basement apartment in her father's house, and she had expected that they would take over the family business when her father retired. Of course, that hadn't happened. He had taken one look at Katy shortly after moving in with Lily after university and that was that.

But those wounds had healed. Her former stepmother was still alive, now living in Vancouver. While she hadn't spoken much to Cameron and Katy, especially now that they were married, they were still living, too. Her father's death felt like an insurmountable ache that she couldn't get past. He was the one person in her life who had never let her down.

Back at the lab, the reception area was empty and quiet save for the whoosh of the air conditioner. She took her seat behind the desk and wasn't surprised at the lack of messages. She opened *Undead Uprising* and picked out her weapons for another go-round with the zombies. No machetes this time, since they ran out too quickly and were cumbersome besides. Hand grenades only required her to right-click and hit the space bar.

At five minutes to two, a tall, well-dressed man let himself into reception. "Hey," he said by way of introduction, then added, "Why does this place have to be middle of nowhere?"

"Good afternoon," Lily greeted him professionally. "You must be Mr. Claybourne."

The man took off his sunglasses, a pair that probably would have set Lily back a week's pay. Watery, red-rimmed hazel eyes sized her up from the other side of the desk. "I am. Who are you?" he asked.

She shifted uncomfortably in her ergonomically correct chair. "Lily. May I get you a bottle of water, Mr. Claybourne?"

"No thanks," he said. She felt him sizing her up, and looked away. She knew what he saw: She looked like she had grown up in the country in her simple blue linen dress and short-sleeved black cardigan. A mistake during the heat wave, but the air conditioning here was cranked up to Arctic temperatures.

The door off reception opened and Pitro and Zadbac stepped out. "*Min* Claybourne," Pitro said, bowing slightly. "We have been anticipating your consultation. Please come in." He held open the door.

"I don't want to get suckered into everything," Claybourne warned them. "I just want to be alive to see alien ass in a few hundred years." He followed the doctors through the door.

———

WHEN THREE O'CLOCK ROLLED AROUND, Andrew Claybourne hadn't yet emerged from the rooms off reception, and Lily had been eaten by zombies four times and bombed them to kingdom come twice.

She was giving notice at the end of the week. After today, she would be happy to book tanning appointments or sling beer at a dive. She was sticking to her new life plan—stay in Toronto and force it into becoming her home while working a job that paid the bills until she had enough saved up to go to teacher's college—but she couldn't deal with the doctors who cheerfully talked about death anymore. Cryonics was weird and creepy. Lily couldn't handle weird and creepy anymore.

She fired a couple of cannonballs at a horde of ravenous zombies and watched with satisfaction as they exploded into a mass of red and black gore. The screen blinked NEXT LEVEL.

A scream made her hand twitch, knocking the mouse off

CHAPTER 2

Ensign Taz Shraft was being punished. That was the only way to describe being assigned to cleanup duty with an hour to go until he was off shift, sorting through museum crap that had come unstrapped from their containers in the *Defiant*'s cargo hold. He would be here until midnight to get all of this done.

Of course, he did have a little too much to drink during the twenty-eight-hour stayover on Golfell Station a few days ago and made a clumsy pass at a woman who turned out to be his commanding officer's sister. Drunkenly hitting on Lieutenant Steg's sister could never bode well, especially when the lieutenant in question loathed Taz.

There was no sense of organization to the crates shoved in the cargo hold, bound for a new museum on Rubidge Station, nearly a week's journey from the *Defiant*'s current point. When he tried to argue that point to Lieutenant Steg, his superior had growled at him to take it to the captain.

So Taz had foolishly tracked down Captain Rian Marska to explain his plight. *Acting* Captain Rian Marska, he corrected himself, the former commander recently tasked with temporarily patrolling Commons space in between deliveries of science teams and spare parts and...museum artifacts. This was the worst delivery so far.

Captain Marska told him in no uncertain terms that he needed to get to the cargo hold and put the museum pieces back in some kind of order, any order, as long as they stopped breaking free of their bonds and crashing around in the belly of the ship.

There were definitely some problems with the environmental programs in the cargo hold. A few statues and crates had lost their gravitational pull and drifted towards the ceiling. And it was *hot* in here. Taz unzipped his uniform jacket and draped it on a huge figure of a Mulaskan wildcat, clipping his comm badge to his T-shirt.

He made the few adjustments he could from the utilities panel on the wall, cursing at his lack of access to the programs. He could fix the whole gravity problem in the cargo hold if given access to the systems, but Marska would never give him that chance. He grinned mischievously and deliberately adjusted it so a few artifacts crashed to the floor.

He couldn't find a fix for the heat though, so he sighed and set to work. He remotely controlled an antigravity jack to stack the largest of the crates. A third of the hold cleared, he came across a long sealed plastiglas case and shuddered. Taz hated the corpse displays in museums.

A label was affixed to this one: *EARTH HUMANOID, 21ˢᵗ CENTURY.* Inside he saw the perfectly preserved body of a woman who would have been pretty in a wholesome kind of way in life. She had long dark hair and a healthy glow to her fair skin that spoke of living on a planet with natural sunlight. She had been attired in a blue dress and short-sleeved black sweater when she died and was preserved.

Taz looked at the floor. He was the first person to admit he had few morals, but parading a dead body around to be gawked at crossed a line for him. It was downright creepy and certainly disrespectful. It wasn't as though anyone in the Commons hadn't seen a humanoid before. He would be careful with this one.

He directed the jack to the plastiglas coffin, intending to put it in the most secure corner of the hold where the artificial gravity always worked. Sweat poured down his back and seeped through his T-shirt. He considered taking off his pants, but that guaranteed a visit from the captain to check up on him, and would open the door to all kinds of questions he didn't want to think about.

The jack raised the coffin to his eye level and its lid lifted slightly with a small pop. With a sinking feeling Taz realized the preserving seal around it had pulled off, likely disintegrating because of the heat and being bounced around.

A dead body and near-tropical conditions made for a working environment even Taz wouldn't tolerate. He lowered the jack to the floor and looked around frantically for something that could act as a makeshift seal. He tried to press the lid back into place, but only succeeded in dislodging it further.

Oh, shit.

He looked at the body, at the face serene in eternal sleep, and wondered for a few seconds if she had voluntarily signed up for this.

Then her eyes opened.

"Fucking gods!" Taz sputtered. He instinctively backed away and crashed into a clothes rack displaying twenty-second-century Ragma monks' robes.

Zombies, he thought at first, as his panic rose. As a green recruit, he had ended up assigned to a mission on Corlon where a biochemical weapons plant had exploded. While the workers affected by toxic spores were technically still alive, they had lurched around and tried to bite each other's faces off. He had been ordered to aim for the head.

He also had an overactive imagination and a penchant for the cheesy zombie vids they showed at Rubidge Station's cinemas. This was more like a scene out of one of them rather than the Corlon disaster.

With shaking hands, he aimed his regulation laser pistol at the coffin, where muffled thumps pounded from the interior, followed by a weak, bewildered "Hello?"

Taz had never heard of a talking zombie. He lowered his weapon slightly, but didn't move towards the coffin.

The lid lifted, and the exhibit's—the woman's—head peeked out, her dark hair disheveled. She saw Taz, and her eyes took in the laser pistol. She looked at him with a beseeching plea in her eyes, which Taz now saw were green and more than a little dazed. Her mouth moved, as though struggling to find words. Finally, she croaked, "Please don't kill me."

Taz lowered the weapon to his hip but didn't holster it. He cautiously approached the coffin. "Who are you?"

She coughed, a dry, hacking sound, and spoke again. "Where am I?"

"Tell me your name." Taz thought about which sectors were pissed off with the Commons Fleet this year. At least three, he figured. What a brilliant way to infiltrate a ship: Make the spies appear like dead museum exhibits.

"Lily Stewart," the woman replied. "Can you help me up? My legs are numb."

Taz brought up the weapon again and aimed it at her heart. "Who do you work for?"

She managed to lift her knees and she wiggled her feet to get the circulation going. "I was working for Lazarus Cryonics," she said. "Please help me up. I need some water." Her eyes focused, and she saw the weapon trained on her, and held up her hands in surrender. "I'm not a threat, I promise," she said. "I don't even know where I am."

Taz peered in the coffin. Beside her was a small black

satchel made of an unfamiliar fabric. It was large enough to conceal a weapon. "Give me your bag," he said. "Lift it out and drop it on the floor."

She looked surprised. "My purse? You can have it, just please don't hurt me."

Taz had to give her credit for acting the part of a ditzy stowaway. Her eyes kept drooping and he saw the fine tremors in her hands as she lifted the bag and let it fall to the floor. Taz poked it with his foot, then bent down to turn it over with the barrel of the laser pistol. The bag's contents spilled across the floor.

"Hey!" she protested. "That's a new phone!"

A palm-sized device with a flat screen was on top of the debris that fell out of the bag. There was also a collection of old-fashioned metal keys, a paperback book, some tubes that looked like cosmetics, slips of paper, and a pink wallet.

There was something very wrong with this picture. Not just because a supposedly dead exhibit had resurrected itself, but because the charade was so well done. Whoever was employing her had done his homework. A bound *book*, for the gods' sakes!

She had hoisted herself up and pulled herself out of the coffin, gracelessly crawling to the floor. "Where am I?" she repeated.

Taz didn't reply. Instead, he tapped his comm badge. "Shraft to Lieutenant Steg," he said. "We have a live one in the cargo hold."

———

LIEUTENANT STEG WAS NOT HAPPY. But then, he was always a little pissed off about something. Acting Captain Rian Marska gave up trying to get an intelligible explanation for the security chief's blustering through his comm badge and merely waited for him to finish. The lieutenant shouted into Rian's comm set, interrupting his mediation between a pair of ensigns from engineering with demands for a private conversation. Rian heard the words "Shraft" and "idiocy" in the same sentence and immediately dismissed the ensigns. At least Steg's latest diatribe would be more interesting than settling a fight over who got the prime tables in the mess.

"I don't know how the stupid shit managed to get through the academy," the lieutenant sputtered. "Is this his idea of a joke?"

"If it is, I'll handle it," Rian replied smoothly. "What does he mean, 'a live one'?"

"He said something's still alive in the cargo bay he's supposed to be sorting through. The stupid shit—"

"*Language*, Lieutenant. I'll be right there."

The captain rose from his seat. He knew about Ensign Shraft's regrettable romantic entanglement with Steg's younger sister, although the gods only knew why he did. He did his best to remain professional and out of the *Defiant* crew's personal lives, often to no avail. He never expected a patrol ship captaincy would mean solving more human resources issues than anything else.

Ensign Shraft had the bare minimum of common sense to make a go of it as a Fleet officer. While he had graduated from the academy with a concentration in engineering, he had instead been assigned to communications on his first posting to keep him out of trouble. Rian had discovered the hard way after two days on board that Shraft's favorite things to do involved reprogramming bots for his own amusement and hitting on as many women as he could. He wasn't a practical joker though; Fleet wouldn't have tolerated that.

The captain was aware of the gravity issues in the *Defiant*'s cargo hold, which was why he had protested hauling the artifacts to Rubidge Station's new museum. Half of them were bound to be damaged by the time they were to be delivered, but Fleet said his ship was the only one with an empty hold passing through the station's sector in time for the opening.

He left his office off the bridge and took the lift to the cargo hold, meeting Lieutenant Steg as the security chief stepped off another. The lieutenant was scowling, of course, made more menacing by the faded scar across his forehead. The officer's uniform strained at the shoulders, a testament to his size and strength.

"If he's fucking around—" Steg began, but Rian cut him off.

"Brig," Rian replied curtly. "And what did I say about your language?" They stepped through the automatic door to the cargo hold and were immediately assaulted by the heat.

Ensign Shraft was standing at the other end of the hold, but crates blocked the view of the lower half of his body. His laser pistol aimed at something, and his gaze barely flickered from his target as his commanding officers entered. They stepped around the crates and Rian felt a little dizzy in the spots where the gravity wasn't holding tight.

A young woman sat on the floor on the receiving end of Shraft's weapon. Her back was supported by an open plasti-glas coffin, and her bare legs were set straight out in front of her, covered to her knees by a light blue dress. Her feet were tilted to either side, as if weighted down by the flimsy heeled sandals she wore. She looked queasy and confused, eyes glassy and unfocused, and more than a little terrified of the ensign's laser pistol.

"I'll be damned," Steg said.

"I think she's a spy, sir," Shraft intoned.

The woman shook her head, and raised a hand to it as if the movement hurt. "No, I'm not," she said softly. Her voice sounded scratchy and hoarse, like it hadn't been used in a long time.

"Who are you?" Rian demanded crisply.

"Lily Stewart," she said. "I can't get any answers from him—" she pointed at a shaking finger at Shraft—"and he won't give me back my purse or tell me who he is or where we are."

Rian was going to hold off on the introductions until he was sure of this woman's identity. She didn't seem to be a threat yet and was obviously under the influence of something so he didn't call for a full security team. "Ensign, lower your weapon."

Shraft reluctantly complied.

"Where are you from?" Rian asked.

"Toronto," she said, and gave a wheezing cough. "Well, I was born and raised in Courtice, but I moved to Toronto about six weeks ago."

The places were unfamiliar to Rian. "Where is this Toronto?" he asked suspiciously.

"Canada," she said, and even through her glassy-eyed haze, he caught her disbelieving undertone, as though he should have heard of that place.

"Canada?" said Steg. Sarcasm laced his words. Rian shot him a look.

"North America," the woman said. A shaking hand smoothed out the wrinkles in her skirt.

Rian's eyebrow shot up. He had only a passing knowledge of the Commons' oldest settlements, but North America sounded familiar. One of the former geographic areas on Earth. He turned to Shraft.

"Ensign, what exhibit is this?" he asked quietly.

"Earth humanoid, twenty-first century," he replied.

He remembered reading the cargo manifest before it was loaded into the hold back on the planet of Repub-1. One of the natural history artifacts listed had been discovered a couple of years prior on a forgotten, uninhabited planet in Earth's solar system. The only example of what was then a novel means of preservation in a pile of discarded remains.

Trepidation, then shock, left a sour taste in his mouth. It was too horrible and impossible to be true.

He didn't let his face betray his thoughts as he regarded the woman sitting on the floor. "What day is this?" he asked gently.

"I don't know," she said.

"Captain," said Steg, disgust in his voice. "I should call a security team." One meaty hand poised over the comm badge clipped to his collar, but Rian shook his head.

"What was the last day you remember?" he prodded.

She thought a moment, and her head lolled to the side and her eyes closed. She forced it back up, as though fighting to keep conscious. "August third, 2017," she said finally.

Rian took a deep breath of the humid air and forced himself to stay calm. He crouched down until he was almost level with her face. A pair of wide glazed-over green eyes stared back at him. He was either going to be delivering to her the worst news of her life, or he was about to make a huge security breach. "You're on the Commons Fleet ship *Defiant*," he said finally.

She blinked. "A ship? We're on the water, then."

"No, not exactly." Rian was unsure how to deliver this kind of news. His training had never prepared him for this.

"Then where are we?"

Might as well be honest. "Right now, the Keros Quadrant, a Commons-controlled area of space. We're on our way to Rubidge Station." He ignored Steg's snort at revealing that information to a stranger and focused on Lily Stewart in front of him.

"Space?" she said, her voice small and frightened.

If she was a spy—and Rian thought that looked like less and less of a possibility—then she was good at it.

"What day is it?" she asked.

This time Shraft spoke. "We use a six-day week. It's day four."

A very confused look crossed her face. She looked around at the odd objects in the cargo hold and the men standing before her. "What year is this?" she asked warily, her voice a little stronger.

"Give it up already," boomed Steg, and her shoulders jumped slightly. "It's 2867."

Terror filled her eyes, and her mouth dropped open. "No," she breathed. She rose unsteadily to her feet and swayed. "No, no, no!" She leaned against the coffin for balance and pointed at a pile of stuff on the floor. "My phone. My wallet," she said. "Give it to me." Shraft looked at the captain, and Rian nodded his permission. He picked up a folded-over pink bundle and handed it to her. She opened it and struggled with something inside before giving up and handing it over to him. "My ID," she croaked. "My credit cards."

Rian took the wallet and peeled out a few thin cards from slots inset in the leather. They were nearly plastered to the material and made a tearing sound as they were removed. They were made of plastic, with crude holograms inlaid into them. A few bore her name and picture and detailed the rights associated with the cards. Lily Stewart, resident of a long-ago city on a planet that now housed shipyards and its workers. Born on February 10, 1988.

The faulty coffin seal and fritzy environmental controls. Her total ignorance which seemed too genuine to be feigned. Her inability to stand on her own using muscles that hadn't moved in over eight hundred years, if this woman's primitive belongings were any indication. Either she was a hell of an actress, or, as Rian suspected, she was telling the truth.

He looked at the woman, leaning unsteadily against the coffin that had held her in stasis for centuries. She looked bewildered, stunned, and still drugged from whatever had been administered, and the confusion hadn't abated from her eyes, but thank the gods, she wasn't crying. Rian Marska had never known what to do with a crying woman, but when the drugs wore off and her fear returned, he knew he would have to figure it out.

He pushed that thought from his mind. "Lieutenant, pick up her bag," he ordered. Turning to Lily Stewart, he asked, "Can you walk?"

"Maybe," she said. She took a few tentative steps, wobbling on her heeled sandals. "My legs aren't working right. I feel like I'm going to throw up."

Steg and Shraft each took a few steps back. Rian rolled his eyes. "Take a few deep breaths," he advised. "I know it's hot in here and that isn't helping." He tugged on the collar of his Fleet-issued jacket. Sweat was forming at his temples. He held out a hand to steady her, and she sighed and fell into his chest, her knees buckling.

Rian caught her and bent at the knees, hooking his other arm around the back of her legs and picked her up. He cradled her to his chest and her head fell heavily against his shoulder. "Lieutenant, notify sick bay about their new patient," he ordered.

"Are you sure you don't want a security detail, sir?"

"That won't be necessary."

"Wouldn't it be easier to transport her to sick bay, sir?" Steg asked. "I can call the team and have them configure the beam."

Rian turned around to leave the cargo hold. Steg and Shraft followed. "If she's feeling sick now, it's going to be a hell of a lot worse after the transport. She's not used to it."

Lily Stewart lay limp in his arms. "I'm right here," she said sleepily. "You don't have to talk like I can't hear you."

"Apologies," he said.

They stepped into the corridor, greeted by a rush of cool air. "If you think you're going to be sick, tell me," Rian said.

"Did you just get your suit back from the cleaners?" came her muffled reply against his shoulder. Her breath tickled his neck and his skin prickled involuntarily.

"No," he said, and fought back a smile. Steg pressed the button for the lift.

"I feel better out here," she said.

"The environmental controls are a little off in the cargo hold," explained Rian. The lift doors opened and they entered. Rian ordered it to deck six, to the ship's sick bay. Understaffed, of course, but that was the usual state of things aboard this rust bucket.

"Controls? Like a thermostat?" she asked sleepily.

Rian caught Steg and Shraft's questioning looks and shrugged a little himself. "Sure," he told her, and she lifted her head from his shoulder.

"You can put me down now," she said softly. Rian obliged, and she leaned against the lift's wall, blinking against its bright light. "I'm really not at home," she said, dismay in her voice.

Please don't cry, Rian thought. *All I'll be able to do is stand here like an idiot.*

She didn't cry, just stared up at him, her green eyes large and glassy and lips parted in uncertainty, then at Steg and Shraft. The ensign couldn't wipe the look of incredulity off his face and Rian damned himself for not ordering him to stay in the hold. Steg raised a menacing eyebrow at her and she sucked in a harsh breath in response. She turned back to Rian. The look on her face tore at him, a sensation he wasn't accustomed to experiencing after sixteen years in the military. He had seen much worse.

He looked away. He would have to treat her as one more unusual occurrence he had to deal with. Besides the possibility of her being some sort of spy, however small, there was still the issue of his captaincy on the *Defiant*. He wanted a permanent captaincy and hadn't risen through the Fleet ranks as quickly as he had by letting damsels in distress distract him.

He chanced another look at her, at the terrified shock on her face. This was beyond distress.

The lift stopped at deck six, where the *Defiant*'s chief medical officer, Ashford, met them in the sick bay's foyer. He was a year or two away from retirement, silver-haired, and infinitely patient. He was also qualified to do his job, a trait that most of Rian's crew often lacked, and in the week he had been on board, he hadn't complained about his new posting. He watched the woman trailing between Rian and Steg. She took in her surroundings like a lost child. "Who's this?" Ashford asked. "Accident in the cargo hold? I have a bed ready as the lieutenant asked."

"An accident of sorts," Rian confirmed. "Steg, Shraft—return to your stations. Shraft, that means the cargo hold." He could almost hear the ensign swearing at him in his mind as he walked away. *Bloody Vu'saarns.* No matter what Shraft's personnel file said, Rian was still sure he harbored some kind of telepathic ability. Steg muttered something unintelligible and held out Lily's satchel between two fingers. Rian hooked the strap over his wrist and let it dangle.

"Who are you?" she asked the doctor.

"Doctor Orrin Ashford." As usual, the doctor was unruffled. "Who might you be?"

"Lily Stewart."

Dr. Ashford held out a mediscan unit and held it a few inches from her body. His eyebrows knitted together and he frowned.

"Captain, where did you find her?"

"In a coffin in the hold."

Ashford slipped the unit into his lab coat pocket. "Miss Stewart, how are you feeling?"

"Sick and thirsty."

"Unsurprising, but we can do something about both," he promised her. He gestured to a room off the foyer. "Bring her in here, Captain."

"You've been sedated," Ashford explained to Lily.

She shrugged clumsily. "I must have been, to be dreaming about this."

Both Rian and Ashford tensed at that statement but didn't contradict her. What was the point? The doctor ordered the lights on, and the illumination panels on the ceiling glowed dimly. He turned down the sheets on the bed in the center of the room and gestured to it. "Come over here, Miss Stewart," Ashford suggested gently. She stared at the bed for a moment and stepped out of her shoes, padding to it on bare feet.

"Captain, could you bring our patient some water?" Ashford asked. "There's a dispenser in my office."

Rian obediently went to the doctor's office, a small room at the back of the infirmary. He left the satchel on Ashford's desk and returned to Lily's room with a plastic cup of water. She gave a barely audible "Thank you" and took a few sips. She lay back down on the pillows.

"You need to sleep," Ashford said quietly.

"I just woke up!" she protested half-heartedly. But her eyes were rapidly closing. She murmured, "This is the weirdest dream I've ever been in." She gazed at Rian, her eyes taking in his face for a brief, lucid moment. A small smile played across her lips, and his heart constricted for a second. It had to be caused by the heat from the cargo hold.

Her eyes closed peacefully, and within seconds she was asleep.

Ashford and Rian left the room, the door sliding shut behind them and took seats in his office. Ashford activated monitors for her room that would keep him informed of her life signs and movements while Rian fidgeted in his seat. The mediscan would have told him things about his mysterious new patient. "Doctor?" Rian said expectantly.

He laid his mediscan unit on the desktop. "You say you found her with an exhibit for Rubidge Station?"

"Shraft did. She woke up in a coffin that was supposed to be from the twenty-first century." His curiosity was only getting stronger. "What did your scanner say?"

"Do you really think she's from that time?" Ashford countered.

"I think it's a possibility worth exploring," Rian replied carefully.

Ashford appeared to weigh his words before replying. "So do I," he finally agreed. "I'm going to do a full exam when she wakes up, but the basic scan I took told me a couple of things that may back up her story. But first, it picked up high tonismi levels, which prevents me from checking out as much as I like."

Rian started. Tonismi was a heavy tranquilizer that caused total paralysis that mimicked death, outlawed in the Commons and Kurran Empire. It was still favored by the Nym, a ruthless, cold-blooded people hell-bent on controlling the galaxy.

The doctor's words hit him like a physical blow, and he felt like an idiot. He deliberately kept his voice low and even, fury coloring his words. "So she's a spy for the Nym," he said tightly, tamping down his temper. "I didn't know they resorted to using humanoid women in coffins." This was a first for the Fleet. The Nym loathed anyone who wasn't one of their own. "I can't believe I have a Nym spy on my ship."

"I don't think you do," Ashford said patiently. "The tonismi is wearing off, and my mediscan picked up something else unusual that lends some credibility to her story."

Rian unclenched the fist he didn't know he had been making and nodded.

"Two things, actually. First, she's been immunized."

"Everyone gets immunized," Rian argued. "Coll particles. You don't have to go to medical school to know that."

"Captain, please. She hasn't been immunized against Coll particles."

Okay, that was a bit of a stretch, but not impossible. It was theoretically possible to live without that vaccine and not be a hacking, wheezing mess, but only if one avoided all interstellar travel. In the Commons, that was a necessity. The air recyclers on ships and stations emitted the miniscule particles, causing a perpetual mild flu. The symptoms could be averted with the vaccine.

"So she's from the Fringes then," Rian deduced, referring to the sparsely populated and somewhat reclusive worlds outside the Commons proper. There were those on the Fringes who never left their home planets.

Ashford waited, but Rian could tell his patience was thinning. "I'm sorry, Doctor, continue."

"She's been immunized against diphtheria and pertussis," Ashford continued. "The antigens are still in her bloodstream. I studied those diseases in medical school. They're extinct Earth diseases; they haven't existed in over five hundred years."

"You know this for a fact?"

"You've seen my personnel file. I was born on Earth. My father worked in the shipyard and my mother was a nurse."

Rian had never heard of the diseases, but he wasn't a doctor. "Go on."

"Her appendix is gone," Ashford continued. "It was cut out. She probably has a scar."

"What?" The lack of the Coll vaccine was possible. But no one had things cut out of them anymore.

"It was surgically removed using ancient techniques," the

doctor explained. "It's healed of course, but the mediscan picked up the internal scarring from the instruments the surgeon used. Someone sliced her open the old-fashioned way with a scalpel and cut out the appendix."

Rian's stomach turned over, and he blanched. The only kind of surgery he knew of involved simple, nearly painless laser procedures. Ashford leaned back in his chair and regarded him thoughtfully across the desk.

"Gods," Rian finally managed.

"Presumably, she was sedated for the surgery," Ashford returned dryly. "Two of her ribs have been broken in the past, and healed naturally. None of the bone tissue was regenerated. If she's a spy, whoever she works for made her suffer first." He regarded the captain thoughtfully across his desk. "Have you ever broken anything?"

"Yes, it's part of my job description. I broke my collarbone when I was an ensign. It was during the civil war on Naa'-natcha." Rian still had a scar, but some quick field medicine had tranquilized the pain so he could keep fighting, and the bone was regenerated in a few hours.

"Imagine living with that until it healed on its own."

"I don't want to."

He gestured to the bag on his desk. "Now, on to this." He held the mediscan unit over it, and it emitted a small beep. "It's detected tonismi residue in this, and the chemicals used for her preservation. Be careful."

Again, Rian damned himself for not thinking straight. He felt fine, so he wouldn't worry about any lingering effects of the drug, but he had no idea what was used to preserve remains in her time.

"I'll take a look at this, and put it in a decon locker," Ashford assured him. There was a bank of individual deconta-mination units for medical waste at the back of infirmary. "It's safe to handle for short periods of time." He poked around the bag and took out the crude ID cards, opened the pink wallet and spread some printed paper credits across the desk, along with her other belongings.

"Keys," Ashford said, jangling a ring of metal tags in his hand.

Rian sighed. "I'm not completely ignorant, Doctor. My sister uses keys in her home. Her daughter has figured out how to use the palm locks to get out of the house."

Ashford picked up the old-fashioned communicator that Lily called a cellphone. The unit was shut off, its screen dark. Rian doubted the thing would work, that whatever technology had supported it was long gone. He shook his head, trying to remain neutral until the doctor finished. The cosmetics in the slim tubes would have gone rancid, as well. He picked up a small slip of paper. It took him a moment to read it—the written language had changed over the last eight hundred-odd years—but was able to make out that it was a store receipt, issued for the purchases of tampons and Diet Coke, whatever they were.

"I'm still going to do a complete exam," Ashford said, and Rian set down the receipt. The doctor gathered up her belongings and stuffed them back in the satchel. "But based on my scan and the things we have here, I'm inclined to believe this woman really is from the twenty-first century."

"You're sure about this?" Rian asked.

"My mediscan doesn't lie," Ashford said.

"What about the tonismi?"

"When it wears off, we'll ask her," Ashford replied. "It should be out of her system within the next twenty-four hours, if not sooner. Tonismi is a fussy drug, and I don't want to risk anything by giving her something to counteract it."

"What about negative reactions? Allergies?"

Ashford shook his head. "If someone wakes up after receiving a dose, they'll live."

Rian tried to formulate a hypothesis for how a Nym sedative ended up drugging someone born 850 years ago, and came up with nothing besides her being a spy. He would have to wait until she woke, and notify Fleet in the meantime.

"I'm going to check on her," Rian said, and rose from his seat. "I'll send a transmit to the admirals—"

"The first of many," Ashford wryly interrupted.

"Likely. I also want to be informed as soon as she wakes up."

Ashford demurred and Rian went back to her room. The door opened when he pressed his palm into the lock and quietly stepped into the darkened room.

She was deeply asleep. Rian drew the blanket folded at the end of the bed over her out of an instinct he didn't know he had, wanting her to be comfortable. She stirred a little at the movement but didn't wake. He doubted she would be so docile when the drugs wore off.

"Captain," Ashford whispered from the doorway. "I'll notify you when she wakes up."

Embarrassed at being caught being kind to a possible spy, he left the room. But not without a last look at the bed.

CHAPTER 3

Lily woke in a darkened room, the narrow bed unfamiliar. Her new Dufferin Grove apartment had lots of windows. It was one of the reasons she had rented the place. Where was the sun? For that matter, where were the windows?

Her head throbbed when she forced herself to sit up. She threw off the blanket and found she was fully dressed save for her shoes, and she sat up, her bare feet dangling over the edge of the bed. She had ended up here somehow, and the events were slowly and hazily reconstructing themselves in her mind.

Lazarus Cryonics. Andrew Claybourne, his hand half torn off and his face smashed in. Zadbac and Pitro standing over him, about as irritated as if he were nothing but a housefly, then Zadbac chasing her into the street.

The orange bars caging her in on Wilson Avenue's sidewalk.

What the hell had happened after that?

She remembered nothing but terror giving way to heavy numbness as her body lost control of itself. Then she woke up in a plastic box, feeling like she had slept off a night of four-dollar tequila. Feeling a strange mixture of calm and panic when she broke out of the box, as though her body couldn't process what her brain was telling it, that the sweating man pointing a gun at her was real. She remembered feeling cold and heavy despite the cloying heat of the crowded room she found herself in, as though her body was protecting itself from the temperature.

Then she remembered being picked up and held by someone with startling blue eyes, who felt safe and spoke quietly, soothingly, and the feeling of safety being wrenched away when she heard the year *2867*.

This couldn't be. It had to be a dream. She must have met up with a couple of friends from her university days, friends she had been playing phone-tag with since she moved, and had a little too much to drink, and ended up in a hospital somewhere. It didn't look like any hospital room she'd ever seen, but stranger things had happened when tequila was involved.

There was some light offered by ceiling panels, and she found her sandals at the foot of the bed. She looked around for a light switch to brighten the windowless room a little but found nothing. Remembering Zadbac and Pitro, but not recalling the name of the bar or who she could have met up with the night before, she looked around the room in vain for something to use as a makeshift weapon.

If either of them were on the other side of the door, she would just have to pray and make a run for it. She didn't want a repeat of what happened last time she tried that, so she carried her shoes by the straps in one hand.

The door slid open sideways when she stepped in front of it, surprising her. It revealed what looked like a waiting room, shaped like an octagon, with doors and short hallways branching off the sides. She resisted closing her eyes against the bright light and the accompanying headache, and took stock of her surroundings. Through one glass-walled hallway she could see what looked to be an office, with a computer screen mounted on a desk.

She tiptoed into the waiting room and the door closed behind her. Lily hadn't been in a hospital with automatic doors to private rooms, but there was a first for everything. She looked to either side for a way out.

Before she could decide which direction to take, another door opened and a vaguely familiar man in a white lab coat strode into the waiting room. He looked to be past sixty, his thinning hair silver in the bright light overhead. He smiled warmly when he saw her. "Good afternoon, Miss Stewart," he said. "I came by to check on you. Your monitor said you woke up."

Monitor? What was more troubling to Lily was that she recalled hearing the friendly, reassuring timbre of his voice very recently in the context of her dream. "Hi," she said awkwardly. "You know my name, and I'm sure I was introduced to you before, but I've forgotten."

"I'm Dr. Ashford," he said. He spied the sandals in her hand.

"You're not going to kill me, are you?" There was no harm in asking.

"No. I think we should sit down and have a talk, though. My office is just through there." He gestured to one of the hallways off the octagon. "How are you feeling today?"

Lily slid her feet into her shoes and followed him. There was something about him that was very reassuring and told her she could trust him. She still wasn't going to let herself do so. Despite Zadbac and Pitro's creepiness she hadn't expected them to do what they did. If nothing else, maybe there was something she could use as a weapon in his office. In response to his question, she said, "I have a headache."

"Are you hungry?"

"No."

He led to her to the office she saw through the glass walls. He sat behind the desk, and motioned for her to sit. There were a few chairs in front of it, and she took the one closest to the door, just in case. She sat on the edge of it and looked around his office, and was disappointed. There wasn't so much as a pencil on the desktop that she could use to defend herself.

"You've been asleep for twenty-one hours," Dr. Ashford said. "You were brought to sick bay at eighteen hundred hours last night. You woke up earlier than I expected."

Lily counted the hours in her head. So it was around three in the afternoon. "What happened?" she asked.

"You were brought in by Captain Marska and two of his crew," he said gently. "Do you remember?"

Lily remembered the blue eyes and inexplicable feeling of calm coming from him, as though he were an antidote to the numbing terror she felt when she woke up. She nodded. "A little."

"You were under the influence of a heavy sedative," he continued. He laid a small, flat instrument not unlike her cell phone—where the hell was her purse, anyway?— on the desktop. "I did a basic medical scan when you were brought in and it read the presence of tonismi in your bloodstream."

Aside from smoking pot in the woods with her friends a few times as a teenager, Lily had never used drugs. "I don't know what that is," she replied.

"It's utilized by the Nym, a race living outside the Fringes in its own quadrant."

Quadrant? Nym?

Sick bay?

That word had been tossed around when she was held by the man with the striking blue eyes. She pinched the skin on the back of her hand and if that was any indication, she was definitely awake.

Realization dawned on her.

"Oh, my God," she breathed. "This is real."

A wave of panic crested over her and she thought she might faint. Black spots appeared in her field of vision, and she put her head between her knees and forced herself to breathe. A few tears slowly coursed down her cheeks.

'There's more, Miss Stewart," Ashford said. Sadness tinged his voice.

Lily hazily remembered a big, burly, and very angry man, furiously telling her what year it was, as if she should know. She thought she'd known, and had been wrong. She sat up slowly and wiped her eyes.

"Oh, no," she said softly. "I'm not where I'm supposed to be, am I? What year is this?" She squeezed her eyes shut. "Please tell me I'm wrong."

"You're not," the doctor said. "It's 2867, according to the Earth solar calendar." He set a box of tissues on the desk. Lily took one and dabbed her eyes, but it was futile. She couldn't stop crying.

"You know," she said, "I almost believe this after what happened to me at work yesterday. It's one of two explanations, the other being that I'm hallucinating this." Either possibility was terrifying.

She sobbed in silence for a few moments, until the doctor quietly cleared his throat. "I have to notify the captain, Miss Stewart," he said.

"In a minute," she said. "He's the captain of what?"

"The *Defiant*, a patrol ship in the Commonwealth Space Fleet."

Space Fleet. Well, this was getting better and better. She nodded and sniffled into a handful of tissues.

"He'll need you to tell us everything you remember, when you're able to."

She nodded again.

Ashford tapped a small circular badge affixed to his shirt collar. "Ashford to the captain," he said.

"Marska here." The voice sounded through the disc, and it was familiar.

"Our guest has woken up and would like to speak to you."

Actually, Lily didn't, but she didn't think she had a choice in the matter.

The disembodied voice said, "I'll be there in five."

Ashford stood up, the device he called a mediscan in his hand. He held it out in front of her. "I'm going to give you a check-up, if you don't mind," he said.

"Here?" There wasn't an exam table or stethoscope in sight. And the walls were windows.

"Yes, you'll find it less invasive than at home." He flicked a switch on the mediscan and held it out in front of her for a few minutes. Lily watched him as he scanned her.

"Done," he said, and smiled.

"That's it? You're not going to take my blood pressure?"

"I did," he answered. "It looks fine, and the tonismi is out of your system. You've had some medical work done that's obsolete now, but otherwise you're very healthy." She must have looked at him with a question in her eyes, because he clarified. "You've had your appendix removed in a way that hasn't been performed in centuries, and today I picked up some dental work."

"My teeth are all mine," she protested.

"You've had a cavity that was filled in," he corrected her. "I can also see that your wisdom teeth were extracted fairly recently."

Lily's sniffled, but her curiosity was piqued. "Three years ago."

Any further analysis he could have offered was cut short by the arrival of the angry man from the night before. He stormed into the office, ignoring Ashford and focusing on Lily.

"You're awake," he said, his voice a feral growl.

Fear snaked down Lily's spine. "Yes," she squeaked.

"Not now, Lieutenant," said an exasperated voice from behind him. The big man stepped aside to let him through.

Lily immediately recognized his azure eyes, as striking now as they had been the previous night.

He was almost as tall as the angry one, but still lean and muscled where the other was starting to go to fat. His hair was so dark it was nearly black, and touched his collar as though he had forgotten to get a haircut, and a day's worth of beard graced his jaw. His uniform was impeccable in contrast, a dark blue ensemble with insignia pinned to it: four small silver stars. A small disc like Ashford's was clipped to the collar.

His blue gaze fixed on hers and stared at her with an intensity that made her fidget.

She had managed to force herself to stop crying, but at some point soon the tears would come again and not let up until her body decided it was ready. She pushed her overgrown bangs out of her eyes and straightened her shoulders, determined to show these spacemen that twenty-first century women were made of sterner stuff than she looked and felt.

Under the angry man's glare, she stood up. "Sirs," she said, glancing between them. "Lily Stewart."

The blue-eyed man held out his hand and Lily accepted it. So that little piece of etiquette hadn't changed in that last 850 years. "Rian Marska, acting captain of the *Defiant*," he said, in that same quiet, commanding tone she recalled from the night before. He had the firm grip she would have expected.

Releasing her fingers, he introduced his companion. "This is Lieutenant Grigha Steg, security chief." The man called Steg grunted an acknowledgment and kept his hands fisted at his sides.

Captain Marska and Lieutenant Steg took seats around the doctor's desk, a detail the security chief objected to. "It would be better to interrogate her on deck four," he protested.

Whatever deck four was, Lily didn't want to find out.

"No one's being interrogated yet," the captain said. "Sit down."

"But, sir…"

"Lieutenant, I appreciate your caution, but no." He turned to Lily. "I need you to be completely honest with me. We've never had an incident like this in Fleet, and my commanding officers and Steg here think you may be a spy. Are you?"

"No," said Lily automatically. Suspicion bloomed across the security chief's face and the captain raised an eyebrow. "I'm a receptionist and administrative assistant at Lazarus Cryonics. Or I was," she clarified.

"What else?" Steg demanded.

Lily thought about what else she was. Downtown apartment-dweller. Former director of operations at Stewart Tree Farms. Would-be high school history teacher, when she had the grief from her father's death purged from her system enough to return to school. "I have a bachelor's degree in history from Trent University," she said finally. "And before moving to Toronto and taking the job at the cryonics lab, I worked for my father's company."

"What kind of business?"

"Christmas tree farm." Catching Rian's questioning look in the corner of her eye, she explained, "A holiday. We grew trees to sell for it. Mostly balsam firs." She sighed. "I guess Christmas isn't observed anymore."

"Earth still has an annual winter festival," Ashford assured her. "Not with what you've just described, but I've heard of Christmas." She looked at him, surprised. "I grew up there," he added.

She brightened. "Where are you from?"

"Earth's demographics and geographic borders have changed a great deal," he said. "I'm from the Northlands, which was previously unpopulated. Most of Earth's population lives there now."

Lily tried to guess where the Northlands might be. "You're from the North Pole?" she guessed. She caught Steg's irritated look and tamped down her nervousness. The man looked like he could comfortably arm-wrestle a grizzly bear and have enough energy left over to rip a door off her car. He sighed in frustration, and the captain shot him a warning look.

"Earth has been home to shipyards for over four hundred years," Marska explained.

"No one actually wants to live there," Steg added.

"Another word out of you and you're going right back to security," the captain murmured. Steg shut up. Louder, the captain said, "Go on, Miss Stewart."

"Lily," she said automatically.

Their eyes locked. For another brief second, she felt something melt in her. Then it was gone, and his next words were all business. "Please continue."

But something else nagged at her, and she wanted it out in the open. "You're speaking English," she said to them.

The captain replied. "We're speaking one of the dialects of the original Republic colonies. There are fifteen official languages in Commons space and a number of dialects in each. This one is the most widely spoken in the Fleet, but most other officers are fluent in at least two or three. In fact, if you include the dialects as individual languages, there are more than sixty..." Ashford cleared his throat, and Marska quieted and looked at his hands.

"*Y a til quelque'un qui parle français*?" Lily asked experimentally. At their blank looks, she exhaled noisily. "I spent all that time failing French for nothing." She soldiered on, and continued her story. "I moved to Toronto in June. A lot of things in my life—" She fumbled for words. "Unraveled. I was hired by Lazarus Cryonics about six weeks later, to book appointments for consultations, answer the phone, reconcile their accounts. I did a lot of that at the tree farm." During her time at the lab, she ended up playing zombie games on the computer, the phone rarely rang, and she never had the chance to go over the books in her short time there. "There were two doctors at the lab, and me. That's it. Their names were Zadbac and Pitro."

At that pronouncement, Marska's and Ashford's eyes widened and Steg hissed, "Spy!"

"Final warning, Lieutenant," said Marska.

Lily ignored Steg and asked the captain, "You know them?"

"We know of Zadbac," Marska said. "Go on."

"I'd been working there about two weeks when a client named Andrew Claybourne made an appointment to look into having his head frozen," she continued. Ashford hid a smile. Marska tried to. Steg scowled.

"Cryonics was never successful," Ashford said. "One of the greatest scams ever perpetuated in history."

"Except me," Lily said.

"You were never dead."

Lily soldiered on, forcing herself to relive that final afternoon in horrifying detail. "I heard Mr. Claybourne yelling in the lab," she said. "In the doctor's office. I went in and he'd been attacked. It looked like someone had smashed his face in and bitten his hand. Dr. Pitro did it, I think, and he was...licking blood off his fingers." She shuddered. "Andrew Claybourne had a big needle sticking out the side of his neck." She gasped, remembering the news that morning. "There were two bodies that washed up in the river right before...they were found with syringes sticking out of their necks, too." Captain Marska nodded.

"I ran out of the lab to the street, but I tripped and Dr. Zadbac caught me." She took a deep breath and willed the tears away. "He did something to the air. I remember these orange stripes, bars, whatever they were, all around us, and he said no one could hear or see us. Then he sprayed me here." She pointed to the pulse point on the side of her neck. "The next thing I remember, I woke up in that room with that other guy pointing a ray gun at me."

She watched the looks being exchanged between the doctor and officers.

"Nym," growled Steg.

Marska cut him off. "Can you describe these doctors, Miss Stewart?"

She didn't question why, although they clearly knew about Zadbac already. "Creepy vampire-like psychotics" probably wouldn't cut it, but Lily was unsure how to describe them more succinctly. Her father had been the writer, not her. "Very tall," she said. "Thin, with heads that didn't really fit their bodies. They looked like bobbleheads." Ashford and Marska looked at her questioningly but she didn't explain. "Bulgy eyes. Zadbac's were all black and Pitro's lime-green. They both had really jagged teeth, too, but Zadbac's looked worse."

"So you've dealt with the Nym," Steg snapped.

"I'm not a spy!"

"She's not a spy," Ashford echoed. "Captain, remember what I told you last night?" Marska nodded.

Lieutenant Steg sputtered, "What? I have a right to know details about prisoners on this ship!"

"What details?" Lily asked, worried.

Addressing everyone, Ashford tapped the mediscan unit on the desk. "I took a quick reading last night when she was brought in," he began. "It showed the presence of tonismi and other details that corroborate her story of being from the twenty-first century.

"It detected antigens for diphtheria and pertussis. Diphtheria hasn't infected humans in hundreds of years and while some of the Fringes worlds have their own unique strains of disease, they're nowhere near as close to something like pertussis," he finished.

"I had a vaccine for them every ten years or so," Lily explained.

"You also had your appendix removed. The unit picked that up." He caught her glare and held up his hands in mock surrender. "I can't control what shows up in a general scan, Miss Stewart."

"What else?" she asked.

"You're a female humanoid, late twenties to early thirties, no chronic diseases, but it detected early-life respiratory issues. No one touched you, I promise."

Ordinarily, Lily would be pissed that someone had conducted a medical exam without her consent, while she was barely coherent, but these weren't ordinary circumstances. Besides, the scanner was pretty cool and she couldn't help but ask about it. "I had asthma when I was little and an emergency appendectomy when I was twenty-two," she said. "My appendix ruptured." She caught the collective wince of the men around her and added with a touch of pride, "Hurt like hell. How do you deal with them?"

"Laser surgery," Ashford said. "No sutures or pain, the wound healed with a tissue regenerator patch." More cringing from Marska and Steg. "The entire procedure would take about twenty minutes." Then he added, "And there are the dental extractions I told you I picked up."

"Yeah, my wisdom teeth. You probably don't even evolve with them anymore."

"Only humanoids with Milky Way ancestry do, but when they show up, they're removed as soon as they start forming," Ashford replied smoothly. "The gum tissue is regenerated in a matter of hours."

"I had holes in my gums for a few weeks. I spit out a lot of blood the first couple of days, too." Lily said this to gauge their reactions, and was pleased to see Steg blanch. If she had to have her health history recited in front of strangers, she may as well make them a little uncomfortable with it. "Oh, come on. It wasn't a big deal."

"You still have scar tissue. You've also had a couple of broken ribs," the doctor continued. "They healed naturally, but the breaks are still detectable."

Just how much could that thing tell them about her? She thought about the flower tattoo on her hip, a remnant from her university days.

"I fell out of a tree both times," she admitted. "I'm a bit of a slow learner."

Steg was still unconvinced. "That happens in the Fringes, too. Not everyone utilizes bone regenerators."

Even Ashford's patience with the security chief was at its limit. "I'm a doctor," he said evenly. "And it's my medical opinion that she is who she says she is. *You're* the soldiers. It's *your* job to figure out how the Nym made their way to the twenty-first century and kidnapped her."

"Gods," said Marska. He pinched the bridge of his nose between two fingers. "I've heard rumors like everyone else, but no one really thought this could happen." He shook his head and turned to Lily. "It would have been much easier if you had turned out to be a spy."

"Why? What did these Nym people do?"

Captain Marska looked away. Lily straightened in her chair and tried to sound authoritative. "Whatever they're doing, I think I have a right to know."

Marska exhaled. "Time travel."

The last day had been lifted straight from a sci-fi flick, so the idea of time travel didn't perturb Lily as much as it did the men in the room. "You sound surprised that it exists," she said acidly. "It's not like I'm sitting right here or anything."

Steg muttered something under his breath in an unfamiliar language. Marska shot him an irritated look before speaking.

"Time travel has been theoretically possible for decades now, but the Commons has outlawed any research in that area, and most of the Fringes follow that directive." He spoke calmly, but Lily could see the tension in his jaw. "Doctor, may she be discharged? I've arranged a cabin for her."

"Wait," said Lily. "If *they* can figure out a way to get me here, *you* can figure out a way to get me back. I want to go home."

"We can't," said Marska simply.

A new kind of fear streaked through her at the finality in his words. This Commons Space Fleet, the closest thing to an ally, refused to help her get home. She may be well and truly stuck in this strange time.

Marska reached over and touched her hand. The small contact sent a frisson of heat through her body. Maybe he sensed it, because he quickly pulled away. "We have accommodations and the means to care for you," he said. "You won't be left to fend for yourself."

As if she had even the faintest idea how to survive here. She still got nervous driving on the Don Valley Parkway during rush hour. She caught his eyes with her own and nodded, desperately hoping he was telling the truth.

CHAPTER 4

Rian argued briefly with Lieutenant Steg when it came time for Lily's discharge from the infirmary. She was engaged with the doctor, trying to secure the bag she had been brought in with but Ashford insisted it be kept in a decontamination unit for the time being. Steg wanted her cabin to be guarded at all times, and from his choice of words, Rian knew the security detail wouldn't be posted to protect her.

He had to remind Steg of who was in charge of the *Defiant* and repeatedly pointed out that she was incapable of being a threat. In the end, he brooked no argument and escorted her out of sick bay.

Crew quarters were located on decks fifteen through eighteen, although fifteen's weren't in use at the present due to intermittent gravity malfunctions. Rian sincerely hoped that when they reached Rubidge Station the *Defiant* would be put back together or even retired. And while he was hoping, he also wanted a permanent captaincy, preferably on a battleship with a crew consisting of members who weren't goof-offs fresh out of the academy or banished from other ships for being difficult, like Shraft and Steg.

They stepped in the lift and Rian ordered it to deck sixteen.

"So you guys don't do time travel," she said.

"No."

"Why not?"

"The theories out there are very risky, and we consider it immoral. Just because something is scientifically possible doesn't mean it should be explored. Potential incidents like this are why we never looked at that possibility."

"Like cryonics," Lily commented dryly.

"Like cryonics, yes."

"That was the argument opponents made when it became a thing on Earth. Some people were worried about reanimated bodies bringing back old diseases or now knowing who they were. Not to mention the moral issues."

"That never happened," Rian said. "Cryonically preserved remains didn't rise again, either."

"Just me."

"You were in stasis," he corrected. "That's very different. Dead is still dead, Miss Stewart."

The lift pinged and the door opened. She followed him down a long corridor. There were a few sad, wilting orange-leafed potted trees every few feet, bolted to a grimy blue carpet runner. She had to jog to keep up with him. "Lily," she said.

He stopped and faced her. "Beg your pardon?"

"You can call me Lily," she repeated. "Captain."

He thought about asking her to call him by his first name, but not in the corridor. There were crew members around, the shifts changing in engineering and communications, and many of them couldn't say "Captain Marska" without a few degrees of disrespect in their voices.

He stopped in front of a cabin and gestured to a pad next to the door. "Put your hand on it," he instructed. "We already programmed it to your DNA." She shrugged a little but obeyed. The door slid open. She jumped back a few inches, startled.

"Convenient," she said.

The one good thing about being on a rust bucket like the *Defiant* was that most of its crew quarters still had galleys with modest cooking space and water showers in the bathroom. Newer patrol ships boasted only processors and particle light stalls, something that would have thrown her world further into a tailspin. It looked almost like a regular apartment on any Commons planet, except for the sight offered through the viewports. It was the first thing Lily noticed.

"Wow," she said. She touched the viewport's plastiglas. "I never thought…well, space tourism was just picking up when I was kidnapped. Only billionaires could afford it." She looked at him, a small smile forming on her lips, the first she'd made since she woke up.

She had a lovely smile.

He looked away, feeling ashamed. He didn't have the right to notice things like that, nor could he afford to with his career on the line and a Nym threat to contend with. He had too much to lose. Instead he looked out at the starfield, at the asteroid belt beyond. "It's the most common means of transport," he finally said.

"You've been to a lot of places, then. Where are you from?"

He paused, unused to personal questions. "Repub-2," he replied. "A small planet just outside the galaxy where Earth is, and one of the oldest settlements." He turned away. "Let me show you how things work."

First, he demonstrated the galley panels and replicator. "You can cook, but the unit here dispenses only beverages and soup," he explained apologetically. "Most of the crew take their meals in the mess."

"Replicators? You can actually tell a machine what you

want and it'll make it for you? I can't believe they exist." Her eyes lit up as she took in the wall unit. A small set of dishes was strapped down in a cabinet next to the unit, and on the other side was the menu screen. She flicked her fingertips across it curiously, squinting at the choices.

"It's not quite that easy, but yes." If all he had to do to make her smile was tell her about the not-so-modern technology on the ship, he could comfortably talk to her for hours — maybe give her a tour of engineering. *As if she'll be this fascinated by navigation consoles and the finer points of transport units*, he thought. But he had been wrong before. Maybe she *would* want the details on life support systems. "I can increase the size of the text," he offered.

"It's not that. I'm trying to read it. You may *speak* something like English, but this looks like it's phonetic." She stepped back. "Oh, now I get it. This says 'coffee.'"

"It does."

"That *K* should be a *C*, and it's missing an *F*." She tabbed through the screen again, translating items, before going back to the viewport to gaze at the starfield beyond. "You know, the one decent thing Zadbac and Pitro did when they sent me out of 2017 was bring me to a time like this. I could be stuck in the Middle Ages."

The term was unfamiliar to him.

She must have picked up his confusion. "Medieval times," she tried to explain. "Dungeons and knights. You know. Ancient history."

"I don't."

"Not a good time to be alive," she summarized.

Rian thought about her healed ribs and ruptured appendix. Her time didn't sound like a good one to be alive in, either.

"We kind of consider your time a middle ages of sorts," he said.

"It wasn't. I have a degree in history. Believe me." She sighed. She froze for a moment, fear in her eyes again. "Wait," she said. "You guys aren't into dungeons and torture, are you? You don't slaughter what you think are undesirables or practice cannibalism?"

"No," he assured her, and her face relaxed. "The Commons Fleet doesn't even impose capital punishment."

"I'm not going to press the wrong button in here and end up sucked into space?"

Rian shook his head. She turned back to the viewport.

"What are you going to do with me?" she asked finally.

"We're not going to jettison you or leave you stranded, if that's what you're asking," he said. "I was up most of the night in conference with my superiors at Fleet. We're not changing course, and you're staying here for the time being. We don't know what the Nym know, and we want to find out what they're up to. You're being treated as top-secret." He led her to the bathroom and demonstrated how the shower unit worked. "Fresh water is a luxury in space," he warned. "The shower gets shut off automatically after seven minutes. Crew members can take longer ones if they want, but the water consumption is docked from their pay." He pointed to a button inset in the wall. "That's the dryer unit." He pointed to the vacuums built into the unit's walls that sucked off every last droplet of water from a body in a minute.

"No towels?"

"No need for them, but some crew members have their own." Leading her back to the lounge area, he showed her how to operate the computer.

She nodded perfunctorily as he demonstrated the unit. He could tell she wasn't thinking about her new home. "Tell me about the Nym," she finally said.

He tensed. Talking about Fleet's theories on their activity could be a security risk, but who could she talk to? "They're intergalactic scum," he said, and mentally kicked himself. *Very good, Rian, tell her right away how prejudiced you are.* But he was. Nothing good had ever come off that planet. "They're from a small planet of the same name, outside the Fringes."

He decided to sidestep Fleet's concerns and just give her their history. "They're terrorists," he said. "They invade other worlds and stations and take whatever they want and murder the inhabitants. They're a small race of people, praise the gods for that, but they're bloodthirsty and violent. Fleet and all of civilized space, including the Fringes, ostracize them." That was the one thing similar between the Commons and the Fringes. "We have trouble keeping up with them," he admitted. "Their technology is often much more advanced than ours, and it looks like that now includes time travel."

"What would they want with twenty-first century humans?" she demanded. She took her eyes off the starfield and faced him. "You don't know what it was like to see Andrew Claybourne with his face smashed in."

"No, but I *have* seen what the Nym can do," he countered. "And I'm not trying to trivialize your situation. But I've led rescue missions in the Fringes and seen what they inflict on a large scale. As far as we know, history hasn't been rewritten yet, so no damage has occurred to Earth."

"How would you know if history had been rewritten?"

The conversation was turning philosophical, something Rian had never excelled at. "Good point," he admitted.

"What happened to Earth, then? Besides these shipyards you keep talking about?"

He shrugged, but at least he knew this much about Commons history. "Individual colonies, the original republics, were slowly established independently of Earth and its governments, and they joined together and formed the Commonwealth in 2120. Earth's natural resources were depleted long before then, and synthetic resources were developed. The

Kurran Empire initiated contact a hundred years later, an alliance that still continues. Eventually, most civilians left for other stations and worlds, and Earth became a waystation of sorts. It doesn't have a large permanent population."

"So the sun didn't explode, climate change didn't fry people? No zombie plagues or atomic bombs?"

"No solar explosions, but the climate change has been significant, zombies have never been a problem there, and I don't know what an atomic bomb is," he replied. "Most of Earth is too humid to live comfortably. It's an acquired taste."

"At least a couple of horrible predictions didn't come to pass, then," she said, relief in her voice. She gestured to the galley and changed the subject. "How do I use those things again?"

He demonstrated how to activate the cooking panel and replicator. She generated some coffee, dispensing it in one of the cups from the cabinet. "Want some?" she asked, holding out the cup. He declined politely.

The look on her face as she inhaled the aroma was blissful. "At least some things haven't changed," she said. She tasted it. "It's really bitter, though. But coffee makes this whole ordeal a little more bearable."

Rian spoke honestly. "You're holding up really well."

She looked in her cup. "Well, ask me how I'm doing when I'm having a meltdown in a couple of hours. I've had a lot of upheaval in the last couple of years, and that's how I usually react to disasters. I'm fine at first, then it sinks in."

"What's happened?" Rian asked, surprising himself. He, like all good captains, stayed out of crew members' lives. But Lily wasn't one of the crew, he reminded himself.

"My father died just over a year ago," she began. "We were really close, and his heart attack came out of nowhere. One day he was there, the next day he wasn't." Sadness crossed her face, and in Rian's chest, a corresponding ache for her. "I tried running the family business by myself for a few months, but it was too much for me handle. I sold our property and moved to Toronto to start over." She looked around the cabin, but he knew that wasn't what she was really seeing. "I didn't think it would be here, instead. I'd been thinking about going into teaching, and I'm qualified to do something other than answer phones, but I needed something... easier to do, I guess. I had some money from selling our property and royalties from my dad's books—he was a sci-fi and horror novelist on the side—but I couldn't mope around my apartment forever. Being a receptionist was easy. All I had to do was tweak spreadsheets and play *Undead Uprising*."

"Simulator?" Rian guessed.

"Computer game, yeah." She sighed. "I'm sorry, Captain, I don't mean to unload on you like this. You probably have stuff to do."

Rian always did, but the *Defiant* wasn't much more than a glorified trawler at this point, hauling crap across the galaxy and patrolling a peaceful quadrant.

"I don't mind," he assured her. "Most of the things on my to-do list involve breaking up crew squabbles and hauling them out of poker games to do their work. I'm hoping for some crew changes when we get to Rubidge Station."

"What's at Rubidge Station?"

"The museum where you were supposed to go, the largest commercial presence in Commons space, and a Fleet military outpost where we'll be reporting everything we know of the Nym. And the *Defiant* will be receiving some much-needed repairs. It's the oldest ship in Fleet."

"It's not so defiant, is it?" she cracked.

He made a face. "If I had a credit for every time I heard that..."

"You could probably retire. Oh, come on, Captain, I'm teasing."

"Rian," he said automatically. She had given him permission to use her given name, he should offer likewise, shouldn't he? *Since when do you think like that?*

"Okay, *Rian*, I'm teasing," she said. She caught his raised eyebrow. "Oh, I get it. You're not Rian in public."

It wasn't that, although he nodded as if he agreed with her. He just liked the way she said his name.

———

Captain Rian Marska had left to do whatever it was spaceship captains did, and in the hours since he had left, she found herself bored. It was preferable to crying, although she had done her share of that, too.

She played around with her cabin's computer and after a few false starts found a small library available. Most of it was books about military theory and Fleet history, which she read a little of, but there was a modest fiction collection and she downloaded a few serial novels. Reading was a bit of a challenge at first; the English language had undergone some modifications over the last few centuries. All of the fiction was sci-fi, but she doubted it would be considered as such. Space battles really were waged now.

Rian had issued her a comm badge, which was clipped to her sweater's collar, but she was unsure how to use it. He hadn't given her any restrictions, and if she spent any more time prowling around the cabin, she would lose her mind. She damned her purse being stuck in a decontamination unit. She'd been halfway through a drugstore novel and wanted to finish it.

There had to be somewhere to get a proper meal, at least. Maybe Rian could show her where, but she didn't have a clue where to find him.

She left her cabin and went back in the same direction she

and Rian had taken from the elevator. Stepping into it, she recalled his verbal commands, but she didn't know which deck was what, so she looked around the walls for a directory of some kind. Nothing.

The doors closed and the elevator began a smooth ascent. Maybe someone would get on and help her.

It stopped and the doors whooshed open. A young officer in a rumpled navy blue uniform stepped in. He looked familiar.

"Mess," he commanded. He glanced at Lily and did a double take. "Holy shit!" he exclaimed.

Evidently the *Defiant* didn't see a lot of people dressed for the office. "Nice to meet you, too," Lily snapped.

"No, I just didn't think I'd see you again so soon," the officer explained. "Especially on the lift." He examined her face. "You don't remember me. I'm the guy you scared the crap out of in the cargo hold. I thought you were a zombie and tried to shoot you? Ring any bells?" He smiled expectantly, as though they were casual acquaintances who had bumped into one another at a movie theater.

Lily remembered now and glared at him.

"Ensign Taz Shraft." He stuck out his hand and grinned broadly. "Call me Taz."

He was younger than her by a few years, in his early twenties, and gangly, as though he were still growing. His dark blond hair stuck up like he had just tumbled out of bed and his eyes were an odd shade of lavender, a color Lily had never seen before.

Lily shook his hand. "Lily Stewart, but you already know that. As you can see, I'm not a zombie."

"I'm really sorry about that. It's just a little unsettling when someone you think is dead wakes up. Just so you know, I think dead bodies in museums are creepy and disrespectful. I was going to put you in the corner of the cargo hold where the gravity always works." He said this as though it somehow justi-fied pulling a gun on an unarmed woman.

The elevator doors opened. "Where are you headed to?" he asked.

"Somewhere I can get some food. My cabin has only soup and coffee."

"You're in luck," Taz said cheerily. Catching her dark look, he backtracked. "Well, not technically, but I can help you with dinner."

He led her through a set of doors into a large mess hall, half its tables occupied. He waved to a few people and Lily noticed some curious looks in her direction. At the replicators, he tabbed through the menus. "What do you feel like?" he asked.

"I don't know," she answered. She looked at one of options scrolling past. "I was looking for tomato soup in my cabin, but that doesn't seem to exist anymore."

"All you can get in the cabins is basic stuff," he explained. He flicked through the soup selections. "No tomato soup, whatever a tomato is."

"It's a vegetable."

"What about vegetable stew?" he suggested.

She would have to get used to this. "Okay."

He ordered a bowl of something fragrant and spicy for her and a huge tray of unfamiliar dishes for himself, helping himself from a pile of dishes stacked next to the replicator. He didn't look like he could eat all that, but maybe men had evolved with an extra stomach.

They took a table near a window, and Lily was again struck by the stars drifting past. She saw a large silver cone-shaped structure floating in the distance, and asked Taz about it.

"Old satellite beacon," he explained between mouthfuls. "From the early days of space travel. They were used for communication way back when. They're all over the Commons, but no one uses them anymore." He stirred a bowl of casserole on his tray, half of it already eaten. "So you're really from the twenty-first century?"

"I really am."

"You're the hot topic of the day on the *Defiant*," he added. "I should thank you, because before you woke up, it was me trying to wine and dine someone who turned out to be Lieutenant Steg's sister when we were at Golfell."

"You're welcome, I guess," said Lily. She had read a blurb about Golfell in her cabin. Military base and small commercial center

Footsteps behind her chair halted the conversation. Taz set down the remains of a piece of bread, stood up and saluted. "Captain," he acknowledged around a mouthful of food.

To her surprise, Lily's heart fluttered at the sound of his voice. She stood up and turned around to face him.

"At ease," Rian said smoothly. "Ensign, don't talk with your mouth full." Lily and Taz returned to their seats. He turned to Lily. "I see you've found the mess."

"Accidentally," she said. "I got stuck in the elevator."

"It's true," Taz confirmed.

Lily caught the look of surprise that peeked through Rian's professional demeanor at the sight of the two of them. "I remember him," she said. "He apologized. I can't blame him for reacting the way he did." She smiled. "Want to join us?"

Taz choked a little and coughed to cover it up.

"No, thank you," Rian replied. "I just stopped by for some tea. The replicator in my office isn't working again."

Lily had heard over and over about the state of disrepair on the ship, and it alarmed her. "You sound way too relaxed about broken things on board," she said. "We're in space, and you're *not* freaking about gravity malfunctions?"

Rian's mouth quirked up in the tiniest of smiles. "No, we have fail-safes."

"I once got stuck in a ditch off a highway with a flat tire," Lily said. "At night. It was snowing and my phone died. It scared the hell out of me, but at least I was still able to breathe outside."

"The *Defiant*'s life support is at optimum levels, Miss Stewart." The tiny smile disappeared under his professional captain mask. A shame, because a smile would have transformed his face.

"So there's no chance of one of the windows blowing out and everyone being sucked into space?"

"None."

"Good to know." She searched his face for any sign of the Rian who had spoken to her so reassuringly in her cabin and found none.

She'd heard him referred to as an *acting* captain. Maybe that had something to do with his shift in attitude. Or maybe he didn't like stupid questions, even when they came from an ignorant time traveler

Rian excused himself and Lily watched him get his coffee. "Did I insult him?" she asked Taz.

"No, he's been acting like there's a stick up his ass since he took command," Taz answered. "Although he was never the kind of guy who went out with the crew on shore leave. He's not the chattiest officer out there. That's probably why he's almost a captain already."

"So he's ambitious," she translated.

"To a fault. Everyone knows he wants a permanent captaincy."

"Is he married?" The question slipped out of Lily's mouth before she could stop herself.

"Hell no."

A thrill coursed through her at this information, and she immediately chastised herself for it.

"Hell no, he isn't married?" she echoed.

"He's thirty-four, thirty-five years old. You don't make commander, then first officer on the *Bradlaw*, and then acting captain at that age unless you have no social life," Taz explained. He raised an eyebrow at her. "What do you care if he's married?"

She ignored the question. "Dumb it down a shade. What's the *Bradlaw*?"

"One of the premier battleships in Fleet. It blasted a couple of Nym ships out of the star lanes when they were trespassing in Commons space."

"It was the Nym who kidnapped me," Lily said.

"Not surprising," Taz said. "It would be easier if we could just go into their space and blow up the whole planet, but that's not likely to happen."

Lily was going to ask him why, but he pointed to the remains of her stew. "Are you going to eat that?" he asked. The dishes on his tray were empty. She pushed the bowl across the table to him, wondering if people now had faster metabolisms than at home. Taz caught her pensive expression and set down his spoon.

"I know this is really terrible for you," he said. His voice had taken on an unusually serious tone. "But I think—I hope, anyway—you'll like living here."

Taz was shaping up to be a friend in all this, after all. "Thank you," she said.

CHAPTER 5

At 2200 hours, Rian finally went off duty at the insistence of the *Defiant*'s executive officer. Aside from a short nap in his office chair, he had gone without sleep for almost two days, and he felt every moment of wakefulness. Shortly before his summons to sick bay, he had taken a stim for the first time in years and unhappily discovered that they now gave him a splitting headache.

He had had meetings with his key staff a few times throughout the day in between conferring via vidlink with his commanding officers at Fleet. It had taken nearly an hour for Dr. Ashford to explain that Lily was who she claimed to be, transmitting his medical reports to them twice. It had taken careful manipulation on the parts of Rian and his first officer, Kostin, to convince the admirals that the best idea was to keep the *Defiant* on course.

Then they came across the hair-raising news that a tabloid on Rubidge Station had picked up a story about a time traveler in Fleet.

Rian swore before he could stop himself and was quickly reprimanded. "How could that happen?" he demanded.

"It's your ship," Admiral Kentz replied frostily. "Someone tipped off the media."

Rian took a deep, cleansing breath and saw that Commander Kostin was doing the same. Possibilities ran through his mind. The ship wasn't bugged or under surveillance; Rian knew that for a fact. "So you're telling me I may have a mole on board."

"It's a strong possibility." The admiral glowered at him through the vidscreen, as though it were Rian's fault. He hadn't had any say in his crew. If he had, the seven weeks that he had been leading the ship would have been very different.

Rian scrubbed his hands over his eyes. Why the hell couldn't that stim fully kick in?

He hated to ask his next question, one he had asked far too often since his posting to the *Defiant*. "How do I handle this?" Fleet hadn't prepared him for time travelers, crew feeding classified information to the media, or Taz Shraft, for that matter. Rian had a sinking suspicion the ensign was behind the office replicator's coffee turning green.

"Your ship will be checked for invasive communications devices," the admiral assured him, a smirk on his face. Rian prayed he hadn't accidentally turned in his captaincy. Admiral Kentz was looking for any excuse to slap him back down to commander. "We don't think it's likely, but we still have to consider it." He changed the subject. "We've already taken care of the cargo manifest for the museum. Your guest will be listed as 'irreparably damaged in transit.' For once, it's a good thing that your ship's gravity isn't working."

Rian ignored that last comment, knowing the admiral was trying to bait him. Rubidge Station's museum was opening in a few short days and the historical society was anxiously awaiting the shattered remains of their artifacts in the cargo hold. He said a silent prayer of thanks to the gods for the damaged artifacts. The faulty gravity would provide a good cover.

There wasn't any information to be had about the Nym's explorations in time travel, but they still theorized back and forth. Much to his frustration, the admirals wouldn't release any intelligence reports to Rian pertaining to that quadrant, only to say that they had been quieter than normal. The enemy faction hadn't tried to invade the Fringes in almost five years, and that was troublesome. "All we can tell you," Admiral Kentz said, "Is that from our observations, their planet's atmosphere and surface are beginning to break down. We were wondering if they had finally died off."

Rian schooled his features into what he hoped was a neutral expression. Admiral Kentz hadn't been aboard a patrol ship or battleship in over twenty years and had never engaged in war with the Nym. If he had, he would know that their dying off was a pipe dream.

When he finally returned to his cabin for the evening at the insistence of Commander Kostin, he thought about the solution he had proposed for Lily. Chances were low to impossible that she could return to her own time; the possibility of time travel notwithstanding, it was abhorred in civilized space. Cryonics for the purpose of resurrection, genetic engineering in conscientious beings, and slavery had been outlawed in the Commons since it was formed. He had dealt with the last two on several occasions in his sixteen years with Fleet, but there was nothing in their guidelines that could tell him what to do about Lily. He and Admiral Kentz had had a particularly aggravating discussion over that.

The admiral was initially keen on the idea of leaving her on Rubidge Station. "It would be perfect," the older man had proclaimed over their vidlink. "Rubidge is its own community and has a Fleet base to protect her. She could find work, friends, settle there. A patrol ship isn't an appropriate place for a time traveler. She'll get in the way."

Of what? Rian wanted to ask, but didn't. At this point the *Defiant* could hardly patrol anything with its antiquated weapons array, but he refrained from saying that. Kentz had assured him that the defenses would be overhauled at Rubidge, and then they could traverse closer to the sketchier areas of the Fringes. "With all respect, Admiral, she doesn't have any coping skills, and she isn't likely to learn them on station. It won't be as though she can explain herself to anyone there. It's been agreed that it's best we don't advertise her discovery for security purposes, which is why I've suggested that we carry on as scheduled. Miss Stewart has been completely cooperative during this whole ordeal," Rian said. "Another course of action to consider would be training her for a useful, non-visible position." He had been thinking of a pharmacy position, dispensing medication.

"Fleet doesn't look well on civilians aboard military ships," Kentz said.

"And I agree that regulation is in place for a reason. But these are special circumstances, and moving her around won't let her acclimate to Commons culture. She can study aboard the *Defiant* or anywhere else with Fleet's correspondence program. I also think we need to look towards the eventuality of the Nym finding her. She doesn't know how to protect herself."

"Why wouldn't they have found her already? They lost her over eight hundred years ago."

"Twenty-first-century cryonics could only preserve tissue up to a thousand years," Rian said. "That was the best-case scenario, and we know now that those preservations were never successful. My theory is that the Nym kidnapped her in her own time, brought her back, and somehow lost track of her. After a few centuries, they stopped caring and figured she was dead for good. If the media find out, the Nym may hear of it and put two and two together. That's simply too large of a risk to take."

She had told him what had gone wrong in her life before she was kidnapped; she didn't think her circumstances could get worse. Rian knew they could.

The admiral was quiet for a moment. "Noted, Commander," he finally said.

When Rian signed off, he had a bad feeling. *Commander*, not *Captain*.

Now, in the privacy of his cabin, his exhaustion melted away and he felt almost energized. *Hell of a time for the stim to finally kick in.* He had to report for duty on the bridge at 800 hours, and he should get some sleep, but he didn't want to. And he knew the reason why, and she was only a deck below him.

It wouldn't hurt to see what she was up to. She was still adjusting, and as the acting captain of the vessel she found herself on, it was his responsibility to see to her comfort. He tapped his comm badge. "Captain to cabin 16-4."

He didn't get a response. *Damnation.* He hadn't shown her how to use the comm badge he'd issued her. He had thought they were self-explanatory.

Then a soft, feminine voice sounded, "Hello, Captain."

Well, it wasn't *that* difficult, after all.

She waited for his reply. "Did I wake you?" he asked. Twenty-two hundred hours wasn't late on a patrol ship, but she could have been sleeping.

"No," she said. "Just reading."

"Would you like to get some tea?" he asked. Great, now he sounded desperate. He was aiming to be distantly supportive. He had to be.

"I would," she replied, surprised. "Mess?"

"I'll meet you there in five."

He thought about changing into civvies and decided not to. Best to be professional.

He arrived at the mess first and was relieved to see only a couple of off-duty engineering officers sharing a pitcher of beer at the bar. He picked a table in the corner, beside a viewport. An old satellite beacon hovered in the far distance, reminding him of times gone by.

She entered minutes later, saw him and smiled. His heart stopped for half a second, making him wonder if it was the stim's effect or seeing her. He stood up when she hurried to the table. He started to circle around the table to pull out her chair for her, but she made it there before he could.

"Hi," she said brightly. She looked better-rested than she had that afternoon. Her hair was damp and her clothes wrinkled. "This is a nice surprise. What are you having?"

"Tea," he replied. He led her to the replicator. No serving bots on the *Defiant*, of course.

Lily flipped the screen through the menu. "What's the tea like? Is there anything herbal?"

"All tea is herbal," Rian pointed out.

"I mean decaffeinated. If I have anything else right now, I'll never get to sleep."

"Oh." Rian understood, and selected a blend popular on his home world. They took their cups back to the table.

"This is probably really boring, but I figured out the shower." She giggled. "I really wasn't prepared for the blow dryer. I think the default setting is meant for a mastodon. I nearly got sucked in. But it made doing my laundry convenient." She gestured to her wrinkled dress and sweater.

"I'll have some towels delivered to your cabin," he offered. "And we'll be at Rubidge in three days, so you can buy new clothes."

"They take Visa?"

Rian stared at her blankly.

"I thought not. God, Rian, brighten up a little. I have a credit card that expired in 2021 and forty dollars and change somewhere being decontaminated. Does this station allow bartering?"

"We'll give you some credits," he promised. "Currency," he added.

"Got it. How long will we be there?"

"Two days, maybe longer." He sighed. "You know about the ship's problems." He remembered his conversation with Admiral Kentz. "I have to tell you something."

Fear flickered in her eyes.

"We may very well be walking into a media frenzy soon," he said. "Fleet is very worried about the Nym finding out about you. There was talk of leaving you on Rubidge to settle and start over, but with all due respect, you're..." He held out his hands.

"Completely helpless. You can say it."

"Exactly. You're staying here for the time being. You'll always have someone with you on station, and you will say as little as possible to anyone you don't know."

"That's limited to you and Taz."

Ensign Shraft was *Taz* now? He tamped down a small stab of jealousy. He was *Rian*, after all. He forged on. "We'll disguise you as medical personnel on station."

"Great idea, except you've forgotten I can't even use the shower without nearly killing myself."

"That's why you're going to act as a med-assistant. No one bothers them on shore leave, like officers."

"Do *you* get bothered on shore leave?" she asked.

"No," he said. "Not really." He tended to stay to himself or meet with another officer or two in a quiet, familiar pub, usually in civvies, when he left whatever ship he was assigned to. "I find most stations too noisy," he admitted. "I've spent my adult life in space. I prefer the quiet."

They sipped their tea in silence for a few moments, but he knew she wanted to ask him something. "What does 'acting captain' mean?" she finally queried.

"It means a temporary promotion," he explained. "They've handed me a shitbox and they want to see how I handle it." He paused. "Excuse my language."

"Excused. I've said worse."

"Officially, I'm still a commander. There will be two captaincies opening in the next few months, and I want one of them, on a battleship." For Rian, this was babbling. He shut up. "Apologies," he muttered. "I didn't mean to bore you. You have more important things to be thinking about." He curled his fingers around his cup.

"And those things scare the hell out of me," she replied.

Her eyes met his, and her hand slid across the table to touch his hand that was gripping his teacup. He almost jerked back out of surprise, but held still. At the touch of her skin against his, he felt a spark, a near-tangible sensation of under-standing and something else. *Want?*

What was she doing? She wasn't supposed to be offering him comfort. It was disconcerting to him, and he averted his eyes before she could see his reaction or he hers.

He pushed any thoughts not concerning her safety and well-being from his mind and let go of her hand. He had to. She was not a woman from the Commons or even the Fringes; she was itching to go home and couldn't. Any other kind of entanglement was the last thing either of them needed.

CHAPTER 6

Lily stayed close to Dr. Ashford and a young nurse around Lily's age named Mora Kharn when the *Defiant* docked at Rubidge Station. As Rian feared, there was a group of journalists waiting for their arrival, having already harassed another docked Fleet ship and not getting the story they were looking for. They were clustered in a public corridor outside the airlock access way.

"Just ignore them," Mora whispered to her. Lily nodded and walked faster to keep up with the taller woman's long stride. She clutched a Fleet-issue overnight bag holding a change of clothes borrowed from Mora, who had promised to take her shopping. "It's just in case," the nurse said. "None of my stuff will fit you anyway."

The *Defiant* was being taken out of service during its repairs at the station, which meant everyone had to stay off ship. Lily alternated between the thrill of being on a real space station and the terror of being caught unaware by an unknown predator. She wished she at least had the option of returning to her cabin, the only sanctuary she had.

You wanted to start over, she told herself.

The media shitstorm began that morning. Rian had called her in at a crew meeting in one of the ship's conference rooms and explained that somehow the tabloids had learned of a time traveler, and every action was being taken to find out who had blabbed. He talked about ship-wide invasive scans and comm audits, and Lily tried and failed to keep up with the terminology. It didn't look like the *Defiant* had been mentioned by name in the media, but Rian was still furious. He was calm, but she recognized the ticking in his jaw and his fists clenching and unclenching.

Fleet had had no choice but to confirm that time travel had been made possible by an enemy faction, but gave no other details. Mora had downloaded one of the tabloids to what looked like her old e-reader and had shown it to her before they were cleared to leave the ship. "They all have exclusive stories with insiders at Fleet, and one says that the time traveler is only from a couple of years in the future and another says five hundred. I think you're safe."

The crew had to walk through a series of security checkpoints to the inner area of the Fleet outpost after leaving the public corridor. They passed through a huge circular doorway and everyone was subject to palm and retinal scans, and then through something that reminded Lily of an airport security scanner. Her curiosity was piqued when one of the men in uniform whistled. She turned her head, ready to tell him what he could do with his whistle, but Mora rolled her eyes.

"Go to hell," Mora shot back.

Taz forced his way through the scanner, and the grunt said hello to him. "You're holding up the line," he said, and caught the look between Mora and the security officer. Mora glared at his amused face. "Let's go," Taz said, and pushed them both.

"What was that?" Lily whispered.

"Too much *sala* a couple of years ago," Mora said, and left it at that.

She was issued a station badge and assigned to a room in the Fleet barracks. She looked around for Rian, but Taz said he was probably in a meeting. "You're a popular topic of conversation," he said. "You'll probably have to go, too."

As if on cue, her new badge trilled and she jumped. She tapped it. "Hello," she said sunnily, as though she were answering the phone. She couldn't help it; it was an old habit. Mora and Taz snickered. Lily didn't see what was so funny. She didn't have a rank or title like they did, and it felt weird referring to herself as Stewart.

Rian's voice—purely professional—requested her presence in conference room four at her earliest convenience. "I can go now," she answered. It wasn't like she had anywhere pressing to be, unless she counted Mora promising to take her shopping. She didn't have a clue where the conference rooms were, but Taz was already leading the way. Lily barely got out a "See you soon" to Mora before she had to take off.

"Lucky you," he said. "You get to meet Admiral Kentz. He runs Fleet in this quadrant."

Lily almost had to run to match Taz's longer strides. "I don't like the way you said 'lucky.'"

He slowed down and shrugged. "I'm not good with authority."

"I never would have guessed."

"It's why I'm still an ensign on a garbage scow after six years in Fleet," he continued. They walked through a maze of hallways and security points before turning down another corridor lined with glass-walled rooms. They headed to the end of it, and Taz said this was where the bigwigs at Fleet met for high-security issues.

The door opened before either could press their hands into the palm lock, although Lily doubted it would have worked for either of them. A tall, dignified man in his sixties with short white hair stood in the doorway, his Fleet uniform decorated with gold braids and medals. Rian stood at his side, looking far less pompous with his simple insignia. "Ensign Shraft, thank you for escorting Miss Stewart," Rian said. "Dismissed."

Taz saluted and turned back down the corridor, and Lily was sorry to see him go. His presence would have made dealing with the suits a little less intimidating.

The windowless conference room was overtaken by a huge table running down its center, with small inset computer screens at each chair. The walls were decorated with pictures of stations in deep space and officers in varying styles of uniform. More than a few had features that weren't quite human—elongated eyes there, light blue hair here, an occasional greenish cast to scaly skin. There was a replicator along the back wall, and a few people inside had cups in front of them.

"Sit down, Miss Stewart," said the white-haired officer. She met Rian's eyes, and he looked at a pair of empty seats near the head of the table. The older officer took his place at the head and Lily followed Rian, sitting next to him.

She didn't know what to say, and all eyes were on her. There was an assortment of men and women in uniforms as decorated as the one at the head of the table, and despite their polished military stances, they regarded her curiously. "Hi," she said self-consciously. Their eyes never left her. Did any of them have a friendly bone in their bodies, or was it programmed out of them in boot camp? A few of them shifted in their seats, but no one returned her greeting.

The white-haired man finally spoke. "Good afternoon," he said. "I'm Admiral Donn Kentz." He quickly introduced the others around the table, a mix of admirals and senior captains from nearby zones and stations, many with names Lily would have trouble pronouncing later.

Well, they probably thought *Lily Stewart* was a weird name, too.

He then emphasized that everything said in the conference room was top secret and had to remain that way, with a pointed glance at Lily. When all was said, Admiral Kentz steepled his fingers and tried to smile. She quickly figured out it was a gesture the admiral was unused to. "How are you faring, Miss Stewart?" he asked in an artificially bright voice.

Lily sighed. "About as well as anyone would expect, considering I've been vaulted ahead more than eight hundred years," she said. She hadn't meant to sound sarcastic, but it was a stupid question she was tired of hearing. "I'm fine," she clarified. "Wonderful." She caught Rian's startled expression in the corner of her eye. "Actually, Captain Marska and the *Defiant*'s crew have been very supportive." She deliberately placed emphasis on *Captain*.

The fake smile didn't leave the admiral's face. "Commander Marska has told you about your chances of returning to Earth?"

Jerk. "Slim to none," Lily replied.

"Correct. We'd like to hear your version of the events, Miss Stewart."

Lily suppressed a sigh and told the admirals about her last day at Lazarus Cryonics, her creepy employers, and the kidnapping. Waking up drugged and disoriented in the cargo bay, and finding out she had been sent to the year 2867. She left out her conversations with Rian.

"How do you know these Nym people haven't done this to others?" she finally asked. "I could be one of hundreds." It was something she had mulled over when the *Defiant* was docking at the airlock.

The officials around the table glanced at one another. "Unlikely," a woman said. Lily tried to place her. Admiral Brynn, Brynon, something like that. "We would know about it. The Kurran Empire and the Commons have always been on friendly terms, and we would have told one another."

"Who says any time travelers got stuck in only your jurisdictions?" Lily asked, and then regretted it. Rods up their asses or not, these people had to know what they were doing, and she was hardly an expert in intergalactic diplomatic relations. For all she knew, civilized space was limited to just this Commonwealth, Kurran Empire, and the planets they called the Fringes.

Rian elbowed her slightly, and she shut up.

"Our surveillance in Nym space shows no actual indication of time travel," Admiral Kentz pointed out. "They have been more active outside the Fringes, though, and this is probably related to it."

"Exactly. That's why I think I may not be the only time traveler."

"You are," the admiral told her. "You don't yet understand your new home. Believe me, we would know if this had happened before."

"I'm sorry," she said. She couldn't keep the frustration from coloring her words. "I'm a little stressed out about this whole situation. I think anyone would be if they found out they were a traveling exhibit for 850 years after waking up drugged in a strange place."

"You haven't been an exhibit that long," Kentz said, as though that made everything okay. "The artifacts being unloaded from the *Defiant* right now before she goes into the repair bay are being thoroughly investigated and documented. The original manifest has been scrutinized and so far the artifacts' whereabouts have been confirmed. You were added to the exhibit only three years ago, which corresponds to the Nym's activity close to our territory."

"So I've only been stared at for three years instead of eight hundred," Lily snapped. "Fabulous." Beside her, Rian let out a very strange cough behind his hand.

"Miss Stewart, I assure you that you were always treated with dignity," Kentz protested, his voice dripping with condescension. "The Commonwealth Space Historical Society was very excited to discover such a well-preserved specimen for its traveling collection, and you were going to stay in the new museum here permanently."

"I'm not a specimen," Lily shot back. She was really starting to resent being treated like an idiot.

"Lily," Rian hissed through his teeth.

"Commander?" Kentz raised an eyebrow at him. Rian looked down at the table.

Curiosity got the better of Lily. "Where was I all that time, anyway?"

"On Darcan-2, a small planet close to Earth, mostly used as a mass crypt for cryonic remains," another admiral replied. He looked at Kentz, and the older man nodded consent for him to speak. "Earth began storing them there in 2150. It was forgotten about when cryonics was finally abandoned due to its failure rate, and the planet was finally cleaned out a few years ago by an archaeological team. You were there."

"Why were all those bodies left on Darcan-2?"

"Earth was well into an environmental crisis at the time," Kentz interrupted. "Its non-renewable resources had been depleted and it was badly overpopulated. Earthers were looking into other habitable planets. Darcan-2 was one of the planets considered for colonization by the Interplanetary Relocation Committee and they decided to test its habitability factors using the remains. That was the experiment that finally killed any lingering faith in cryonics. None of the bodies reanimated, of course, but it was discovered that the crude preservation techniques were toxic when exposed to air. So the IRC decided to turn Darcan-2 into a cemetery and it was, as Admiral Betner said, pretty much forgotten.

"A few years ago, a group of Earth-based researchers decided to test out a synthetic fuel based on petroleum," he continued. "It was one of the resources depleted hundreds of years ago."

"Wars were fought over it in my time," Lily replied.

"A compound similar to petroleum that could be created in a lab was found on Darcan-2," Admiral Betner interjected. "Teams were sent out to clean up the remains and harvest the compound. What they came up with was an unusable fuel that was expensive, difficult to produce in large quantities and potentially unsafe for space travel. But they also found you, perfectly preserved and uncontaminated, which we know now happened because you weren't interred with Earth techniques."

"I also wasn't dead."

"That, too. Your coffin was donated to the historical society, and you were set up as a twenty-first-century Earther exhibit."

"If I've been an exhibit for three years, wouldn't people remember me?" she asked. "Someone's going to put two and two together."

"We've looked at that possibility," a woman piped up. "The artifacts were loaned out in rotation. You were actually displayed only four times, for a week each time. The historical society was concerned about toxicity if you were moved incorrectly. If anyone looks into it, the official answer is your remains decomposed." Lily made a face.

"As to who left you on Darcan-2, we're working on that," Kentz said. "Earth still has documentation, albeit limited, on the identities of those interred there. There isn't a record of a Lily Stewart." Catching the incredulous look on Lily's face, he quickly added, "There aren't a lot of records, anyway.

You've got to understand, this was almost a thousand years ago."

"I know," Lily agreed. "I'm surprised that anything exists, actually. It was like that at home, whenever a parking lot was dug up and they found a medieval king buried underneath." She sighed at the blank faces. "King Richard III? Never mind. I know it's a long shot, but did you find out what happened to Lazarus Cryonics?"

Kentz shook his head.

"We're working on the theory that you weren't on Darcan-2 for long in the traditional sense," he continued. "If the Nym are using time travel, they may have dropped you off there three years ago. As we've said, we're unsure about this new technology."

It sounded like a plausible theory, but Lily really wanted to know what had happened to the lab. Any media coverage on a small cryonics facility on the outskirts of Toronto was long gone. So was Toronto, for that matter. Lily's research into Earth revealed that the only populated area was what had once been the North Pole for its more habitable climate, which was downright tropical in the summer.

Kentz interrupted her musings. "In light of the Nym activity, we would prefer to keep you in Fleet custody," he said.

Lily nodded. "Captain Marska told me as much. But what do you mean by 'prefer'?"

"It means you're a free citizen of Commons space," Rian explained. "Technically, you can't be forced into doing anything. You're not a criminal. You were in the wrong place at the wrong time. You're free to travel through the galaxy when Fleet establishes an identity for you." He caught her questioning look.

"Commander Marska," snapped Kentz. He turned to Lily. "We can provide identification for you. While the Nym is our biggest concern, the media is a close second. We've done everything in our power to prevent them from knowing about you, but the story got out. We're still conducting an investigation." Almost simultaneously, every face around the table looked disgruntled at this betrayal. "Fleet is going to operate on schedule as though nothing has happened to deflect this incident as long as possible, and that means the *Defiant* is leaving when her repairs and upgrades are completed. Ordinarily we don't permit civilians on patrol ships, but Commander Marska has pointed out that you're getting settled there, and we're offering you the choice between staying on board the *Defiant* for the time being, where it will set a course for Kevnar Station over the coming weeks and you will be settled there, or immediate custody at the base here. The *Defiant* will be transporting a science team en route to Kevnar."

"What's waiting for me at Kevnar Station?"

"We feel it prudent to keep you under Fleet protection indefinitely if you're amenable to it, and think it best if you were trained for a career," Kentz said.

"What will I do here?"

"Work and re-establish yourself. There's a very large non-military community here."

"I hate to break it to you, but there's not a lot I can do," Lily said. "I have a history degree that's even more useless here than it was at home, and I doubt my work experience is relevant."

"What did you do?" He sat back in his chair and tented his fingertips again.

Was it just Lily, or did the guy actually seem interested? "I was the business manager at my family's tree farm when I finished school," she said. "I ran it until my father died. Then I worked as a receptionist at Lazarus, which I already told you about. I was planning on going into teaching."

"Unfortunately, teaching isn't an option," the admiral said.

"I gathered that already. What about something in research?"

"We were thinking along the lines of an assistant position," Kentz continued. "We have a list of Fleet-oriented careers that you can pick up and study for at your own time and pace, and you can be placed on a station. Commander Marska has suggested pharmacy and library assistant positions, although the library assistant would require quite a bit more study, a degree at the academy and more practical training given your lack of familiarity with current technology."

"What about the pharmacy job?"

"Most pharm-techs study via correspondence. Many go on to a career as a pharmacist or nurse, but that's getting ahead of ourselves."

And probably impossible for Lily, but a pharmacy assistant job was within her capabilities. "That doesn't sound too bad. What would I do?"

"Pharmacy dispensation and basic first aid."

It was better than leeching off Fleet, stuck on a station and reading serial novels for the rest of her life. "Okay," said Lily. "How do I sign up?"

"Commander Marska will direct someone to help you with that," the admiral said. He stood up. Everyone around the table followed suit, and Lily quickly rose to her feet. "Dismissed."

Rian led her out of the conference room. "What now?" she whispered.

"I'm sure we'll be called back eventually," he said. "I definitely will be." The admirals and senior captains filed past. "They'll want to know your plans shortly."

"What plans? I told them I'll be a pharmacy clerk and I'd rather stay—" She caught herself before she could say "with you." "—on the *Defiant*," she finished.

Was that a hint of a smile on his face? "That's definitely safer," he said.

"No kidding. Admiral Kentz looks like he'd be pissed off if I asked him how use a replicator." They left the corridor and stood at a bank of elevators. "Now where?"

"Barracks have been assigned to the *Defiant* on deck D-4."

"Wherever that is. I got called into the meeting before Taz and Mora could show me. Lead the way."

It was a quick trip to the barracks, and Rian showed her to the simple room she had been assigned. His was down the corridor. A few crew members milled around, some in civvies, waiting for others to begin their brief liberty.

There was nothing in Lily's room to keep her occupied, not even a TV—*vidscreen*, she corrected herself—and she had no idea where to find her new friends. Rian had disappeared into his room, telling her he had some reports to read and would find her later. She let herself bask in that knowledge for a few minutes. He seemed like a good person; she just wished he'd loosen up a little. He didn't have to be a captain *all* the time. In all this, she had found a few bright spots, and he was one of them.

She didn't have to ask his permission to prowl around the station. She was a Commons citizen now. What she was looking for was—what? Hunkering down in a booth at a pub with him, discovering what made the acting captain tick?

Yes, and more, she realized, and she wasn't likely to get it.

How lost could she possibly get on a station, anyway? She fingered the credit card in her pocket, issued to her on the ship a few hours ago. It didn't look like any credit card she had seen before, a little black square thing with a digital face like a clock's and an inset pad that read her thumbprint. It was made of something metallic and lacked a name or signature strip. The credit card of the future. She didn't know what a thousand credits could buy and, she thought ruefully, had no idea of its value to dollars.

There was only one way to find out. She left her room and found herself face-to-face with Mora, who had changed out of her uniform into something sparkly and low-cut, and Taz, who wore his Fleet-issue pants and had changed his shirt for a black pullover. "Hey!" he said. "We were looking for you. The admirals let you go already?"

"Yeah." Lily rolled her eyes.

"That's what I thought," Mora said. "Ready to hit Rubidge?"

Rian strode out of his room and saw them. Lily waved. "Forget something?" she asked.

"I just got called to the repair bay," he said. "The engineers want to tell me what's wrong with the aft shields."

"They want your input on the shitbox?" Taz said. Mora winced before Rian could scowl.

"Watch your language, Ensign."

"Sir, are we finally moving to better things, *sir*? Is the *Defiant* finally going to the scrap heap?"

"No, she's being repaired, Ensign." He nodded at Mora and Lily. "Nurse, Miss Stewart." He headed off down the corridor.

"See you later, Captain," Lily called.

CHAPTER 7

Yes, Lily could definitely get lost on Rubidge Station. Its commercial sector was a shopping mall crossed with Pearson Airport on Christmas Eve. She was glad she hadn't ventured out on her own; it would have taken a Fleet search party to find her.

Taz and Mora traded barbs back and forth as Lily looked around in awe. The lack of overhead lighting made it feel like nighttime on a carnival midway. Light spilled from the shops' doorways and tiny lights strung around poles and tables at restaurant patios—could they be called patios when they weren't actually outside?—and flashing advertisements and neon signs. Music blared from every other storefront and pub, and they passed by a large aquarium built into the floor that housed what looked like a small shark, except it was glowing and purple. Barkers enticed the passersby to try their hand at what appeared to be ring toss, but the rings were bright electric loops that shimmered and disappeared when Lily saw a kid playing, and there were stands loaded with food, perfume, scarves, vids... she was getting dizzy.

She didn't know she had stopped and was looking in all directions until Mora took her arm. "Come on," she said.

"Just a minute."

Mora and Taz waited while Lily tried to digest everything around her. "Wow," she squeaked. "I don't even know where to start."

"Drinking!" Taz said automatically.

"Gods," Mora sighed, exasperated. "Later. We're going shopping."

Lily didn't have the faintest idea where to start. "Okay," she said. A vendor gestured to her and pointed to stacks of shimmering blankets. Lily smiled and mouthed *No, thank you*. The vendor discreetly flipped her off. Some things *had* stayed alive over the ages.

"I'll be at the Flare when you're done," Taz told them.

Lily thought he would be waiting awhile. Shopping for clothes wasn't her favorite thing to do under the best of circumstances. She tended to it in big bursts when she was down to three pairs of socks without holes. "Lead the way," she told Mora.

The nurse grinned. "How did you shop at home?"

"Oh, go somewhere, try on a bunch of stuff, force yourself not to cry when you see how you look in the dressing room mirror," Lily said. "That *is* what we're doing, right?"

Mora laughed and led her into a well-lit boutique. It was quieter in there, although no less crowded. "Not quite," she said. "What do you mean by trying on clothes anyway?" She stopped at a row of headless mannequins and fingered the fabric on a short skirt Lily never would have dared to wear.

Lily half-listened to the question as she took in the store. There were no clothes racks or shelves of folded sweaters, just mannequins attired in the wares and holograms suspended from tablet computers that customers turned around. Every so often someone would change the image, and another blouse or dress would appear. "You pick out something in your size," she explained. "Then go to a dressing room and try it on."

Mora let go of the skirt long enough to gape at her. "Then what did you do with the clothes?"

"Well, if they didn't make you look like a manatee, you bought them. And if they did, you gave them back to a clerk and they went back on the rack."

Disbelief crossed Mora's features. "So you could be wearing pants that a total stranger wore. No wonder you got so many vaccines."

"Despite what you seem to think about our hygiene, we weren't crawling with mutant strains of ass fungus."

"That's disgusting."

Lily laughed. "No one ever died from trying on khakis at an Old Navy. Do you even *know* what whooping cough is?"

"It sounds like slang for a venereal disease."

Lily laughed again. It felt so good. She was enjoying herself for the first time since waking up in the cargo hold, and chatting with a girlfriend for the first time since her own best friend poached her boyfriend two years ago. Although Katy had never made suggestions the way Mora was now, who was trying to convince her to spend her credits on something low-cut, short, and, as she described it, fun to wear on a night out.

"Mora, I just need some clothes for everyday for now," Lily protested. "All I have is this uniform and the dress I woke up in."

They flipped through the holograms on a table, and Mora grumbled about her unwillingness to experiment but pulled up the store's offerings of more conservative clothing. Lily breathed a sigh of relief. Blouses and T-shirts were still available.

"So how does this work?" Lily asked.

"We'll find a clerk with a datacorder and she'll take your

measurements," Mora said. "Then you pick the stuff you want and it's replicated according to them."

"This is ingenious," Lily breathed.

"Exactly. Everything fits the way it's supposed to, which is why I really think you should consider that." Mora pointed to a mannequin wearing a filmy black lace number that almost resembled a nightgown. "I think I might order it, but in blue."

"Mora, I can't wear that."

"Why not?" She looked at Lily patiently for an explanation.

She fumbled for one. "It's not really me. It wouldn't fit right."

"Yes, it would. Datacorder, Lily." She pointed to a clerk with a handheld scanner, remotely measuring a customer.

"It's just... not me. It's too feminine. It's what you wear when you want someone to hit on you."

Mora stared at her. "Well, yeah, that's kind of the point."

"It would fit you better." The nurse was tall and slim.

This earned an eye roll from Mora. "Why?"

"You're tall. Athletic," Lily finally said.

"'Athletic' is the kind term for not having boobs or an ass," Mora said. "I don't worry about it anymore. Much. You actually have a figure. You've been blessed."

Mora's compliments made Lily smile. Petite and curvy like the mother she knew only from photos, she had always felt a compulsion to lose ten pounds or at least grow a few inches, especially after Cameron left her. Katy had been tall and auburn-haired, with perfect skin. No matter how diligently Lily had applied sunscreen growing up, spending all that time outside on the tree farm had left freckles on her arms and across her nose. She swallowed those old insecurities and regarded the black dress again. *Why not?* It was guaranteed to fit. "Okay," she said. Mora gave her a devilish grin. "But that's it for any sexy stuff. I need practical clothes."

Mora keyed in the order, and a sales clerk with tawny skin and blue hair that Lily suspected was natural immediately sped over with a datacorder at the ready. At the sight of it, Lily's gut clenched and she remembered her appendectomy. Mora saw her apprehension, and leaned down to whisper, "Don't worry. It isn't medical."

She relaxed and let the clerk scan her while cheerily filling her in on the boutique's sales. She recognized Mora. "Are we indulging today?" she asked brightly.

"Definitely. Fleet's posted me to their worst ship but at least they gave me a transfer bonus. I deserve a treat." She pointed to the black lace dress. "Can I get that in red and blue?"

The blue-haired clerk tittered and keyed in the order. "Is it true you have a time traveler? That's all anyone's talking about."

With shaking fingers, Lily spun around the suspended hologram and tapped the touchscreen to bring up the shop's pants and skirts. "They're keeping us in the dark, too," Mora replied smoothly. "I read about it in today's *Rubidge Rumor*, but they're always talking out their asses."

The clerk agreed, and left them to their shopping. Lily settled on a few shirts and pairs of pants that would have been acceptable back home. "I need shoes and underwear, too," she told Mora.

"We'll go somewhere else for underwear," Mora promised and brought up another hologram. She picked out a sensible pair of boots that everyone wore on the *Defiant*, and flats that would suffice as something more formal after Lily talked her out of sky-high heels that would have left her with a broken ankle.

The clerk tallied up their orders and clicked on their credit cards with the datacorder. They left the shop empty-handed, and Mora explained that their purchases would be sent for pickup at the barracks. "How convenient," Lily said. "I like shopping now."

Mora laughed, and escorted her to her favorite lingerie place, where Lily ignored most of her suggestions and picked out underwear. "This is the best part," Lily exclaimed over the holograms. "No more looking sickly and jaundiced in a fitting room, struggling with bra straps."

Mora's reaction was both comical and a relief to Lily. "Okay, so you actually tried on *underwear*? That's of one of the most revolting things I've ever heard. Shopping in your time just sounds worse and worse."

"Look at this from my perspective, at least. I'm just glad bras still exist."

"They do indeed, and they can do miraculous things for women like me." Mora pulled a small digital watch from her pocket and checked the time. "We should go to the Flare and see if they've kicked out Taz yet." They summoned a clerk and made their purchases.

They went back into the darkened foyer, strings of tiny lights wrapped around support posts that twinkled like stars. "He's that bad?" Lily asked.

"Horrible. He gets drunk and then makes an idiot out of himself." Mora shook her head. "Although he tends to do the last part without alcohol anyway."

They ended up in a dim, noisy pub called the Solar Flare, already populated with half the *Defiant*'s crew. Mora ordered a couple of beers at the bar from a human server, but the floor was packed with robots. Serving bots, Mora explained. Lily looked around for Rian but didn't see him. True to Mora's prediction, Taz was seated at the bar, a half-full glass of something red in hand and talking animatedly with a heavily tattooed blonde woman.

Mora and Lily took seats at a table inside with a few other infirmary staff, including Dr. Ashford. He introduced the middle-aged woman at his side as Pelly, a curator at the new museum. Lily politely listened to Pelly's chatter about the exhibits and noted that she didn't say a word about the missing Earther. The curator was more excited about the huge crate of a prehistoric animal's bones from some faraway planet, and lamented how long it would take to assemble them. Lily nodded and let her mind wander to Rian and when she could see him again.

———

RIAN WAS FINALLY DISMISSED from an unending series of meetings at 2100 hours, with the unfortunate promise of more to come in the morning. Things were not boding well for the advancement of his career.

Fleet was only marginally impressed with his leadership of the *Defiant*, to put it generously. Since he took over as acting captain, there had been an assortment of complaints from the crew and the higher-ups at Fleet, ranging from criticism of his handling the ship's near-tragic encounter with a star unexpectedly going nova to simple human resources issues. Rian tried to argue that it wasn't his place to mediate petty squabbles over alleged ownership of tables in the mess, but his points fell on deaf ears. As to the dying star, he pointed out that if he had followed Fleet regulations—engage the hyperspace engines and get the hell out—the *Defiant* wouldn't be anything more than space junk now. Those engines simply weren't up the task. There had been no warning of the star's death. He'd had no choice but to cut the power to the engines and use the reserved fuel to bolster the shields and ride out the explosion. It had been risky and under normal circumstances downright stupid, but he'd had no other option. What was embarrassing was having to be towed to the nearest station by *Bishop's Pride*, helmed by the fearsome Captain Ursuline Jena, for refueling and repair.

The bots that Ensign Shraft had reprogrammed to dance had been damaged, some beyond repair. Admiral Kentz claimed that he had received dozens of complaints from the crew who now had to do a lot more manual labor. Due to the *Defiant*'s advanced age, there wouldn't be as many replacements as Rian had hoped for, because the newer bots weren't compatible with the ship's antiquated computer systems. He didn't know which was worse: the lack of bots or Shraft not being transferred.

Then the museum curators had a litany of complaints about the condition of the artifacts on arrival at Rubidge. Rian wouldn't worry about the altered cargo manifest, and it didn't look like anyone noticed the missing Earther exhibit. No, the staff on Rubidge was upset about damaged pieces, damage that wouldn't have occurred in the first place if the *Defiant* hadn't been forced to transport their crap when Fleet knew about the problems in the cargo hold. Two priceless statues had chunks broken off, and the hot temperature had altered the chemical elements of some artwork, causing paint to change hue.

There was that mocking transmit from a known fuel smuggler in the *Defiant*'s assigned territory, who saw the aging ship lumbering through space on patrol. The message consisted of the smuggler laughing for five minutes. The *Defiant* hadn't responded to it. What was the point? Rian wasn't sure why that message that was his problem, and Fleet didn't offer any solutions, but it was still blamed on him.

Finally, there was his handling of Lily Stewart's discovery in the cargo hold. For once, Ensign Taz Shraft wasn't the cause of a disaster on the *Defiant*, and Rian resented the pain in the ass even more for it. The complainant wasn't named, but Rian would have bet a week's salary it had been Lieutenant Steg.

Lily should have been treated as a spy or a terror suspect from the beginning, Admiral Kentz lectured. Hindsight is always 20/20, but someone in his position should never rely on the possibility of living to see it. She should have been transported to the brig immediately and treated by the doctor with a security detail, not carried through a vulnerable ship by the acting captain. Kentz, once again, stressed *acting*. Then he should have interrogated her properly, not asking her questions and escorting her to a cabin like a godsdamned concierge.

Rian's hands clenched under the table at the thought of Lily being kept in the brig like a criminal. Its cells were made up of charged force fields, and they offered a hell of a shock, sometimes fatally to smaller prisoners. He saw her being shocked and burned, and closed his eyes briefly to block out the images.

"Something wrong, Marska?" Kentz demanded.

"No, sir." Rian had been right to treat Lily the way he had.

On top of the litany of complaints about his job performance, he was still stuck on the *Defiant* indefinitely, and when they left Rubidge Station, he had to haul a science team halfway across the galaxy to some godsforsaken uninhabited planet. The only bright side to it all was that Lily could stay for the time being; in addition to the reasons addressed when she was present, the media had no idea the *Defiant* existed and wouldn't think to bother a dilapidated patrol ship. Thank gods its cargo manifest was private and encrypted.

At least the old girl was being repaired on station. Deck fifteen and the cargo hold would have fully functioning gravity, and her weaponry was being upgraded.

Best of all, he could keep Lily around a little while longer. When he left the conference room, he wondered how her excursion in the commercial sector had gone. There was only one way to find out.

Rian rarely ventured out of military bases when he was on a station, and a quick look around the barracks deck meant he was going to. He knew that the Solar Flare and the Constellation were popular nightspots for Fleet officers, so he took the lift up to the commercial sector. Immediately after stepping off, he was hit with the noise and smells and crowds of Rubidge Station. There was the usual assortment of station residents, tourists and military personnel, and he took his time looking for the tall, blond ensign and redheaded nurse he knew Lily was likely in the company of.

He followed a group from another Fleet ship and stepped around throngs of people staring in rapt fascination at a game of three-star monte being dealt by a man wearing a ridiculous top hat. He ducked into the Constellation, a quieter pub with a higher-priced menu that deterred junior officers, spotted a couple of the admirals who had eviscerated him in conference, and left before anyone saw him. The Solar Flare was a level down and his next guess.

There he found what looked like half the *Defiant*'s crew, mingling with one another in various states of inebriation. A lieutenant from navigation yelled a hello from the patio and held up an empty beer glass. It was the warmest greeting he'd received since taking command.

He worked his way around a few tourists and potted palm trees until he was inside, and he scanned the interior for Lily. His eyes adjusted to the dim light, and he narrowly avoided being run over by a serving bot loaded down with drinks. Ensign Shraft was at the bar, getting lectured by a woman covered with tattoos, and he was nodding clumsily over his glass.

He saw Lily at a table by the window, looking out at the corridor at an aggressive perfume hawker. She didn't notice him until he rested his hands on the chair across from her, and she jumped a little. A smile bloomed across her face. "Hi," she said. "Sit down. Do you have time for a drink?"

He was grateful for the invitation; it saved him the trouble of having to ask her if the seat was taken without sounding like a fool. "Yeah," he said. "Finally." A server made a beeline for their table to take his order. Coffee was at the tip of his tongue, but he was in a pub, and he had had a trying day. "Kashaff whiskey, please."

"How did everything go?" Lily asked when the server left.

"So-so," he admitted. *Horrible*, he thought. He had a feeling if he told her how the meetings had gone she would listen, but he didn't want to bore her. "Long and short of it is, I'm still the acting captain, and the ship is getting some repairs and upgrades while we're here."

She nodded. "What kind of upgrades?"

"She'll be able to handle the newer torpedoes available, and the cannons will be refurbished," he replied, thankful for a topic he knew something about. "We had adequate weaponry before, but this is what's used on newer ships."

The server returned with his drink and asked Lily if she wanted a refill. She declined and took a sip from her half-empty beer glass. Rian gave the server a couple of credit pieces.

"Is that what you're used to back home?" he asked.

"Beer? Yeah, we have that," she said. "This is just a lot stronger than what I used to drink. I won't be able to finish a glass. Mora ordered it for me."

"Where did she take off to?"

Lily shrugged. "I think she has a thing going with one of the guys here." She pointed to the bar, and he saw the nurse's short cap of red hair. She grinned. "She took me shopping. It was quite the experience. Better than back home."

Rian raised an eyebrow. "How so?"

Lily told him about racks and described changing rooms and Mora's reaction to how things were done in her time, and

Rian's reaction was much the same. It was horrifically unsanitary.

"I have enough stuff to tide me over until I find my own place," she finished after giggling at the look on his face. "It's nice to have something to wear besides my work clothes. Dresses were never my thing."

"No?"

"I grew up on a farm, Rian. I spent my life in the dirt until I met my ex, then returned to it until I moved to Toronto."

An ex. Interesting. He had never got around to asking if she had a partner back home who would miss her, and he was guessing now that she hadn't. For some reason he was dying to know about the ex, but forced himself not to pry. "The dirt? How so?"

A faraway look crossed her face, and he wondered what she was remembering. "I was an only child, and my dad was a single parent. We played ball hockey in the driveway and climbed trees. Not the ones we sold for the holidays—they were too small—but there were trees all around our property that had been there for decades. So my clothes were always bound to end up stained or torn."

"What about your mother?" It was a more polite, professional question to ask instead of one about an ex.

"She died when I was a baby—a car accident. Um, land vehicle. Dad remarried when I was four, and he and Sandy stayed together until I was in high school. She was my mom, really, but she remarried before my dad died and we didn't stay in touch besides the occasional e-mail." She looked at him curiously. "You know, every time we talk, we discuss me. What about you?"

"I'm pretty boring, Lily."

"I want to know, anyway," she said. Warmth spread through him at her interest. "What about your family and where you come from?"

"Career Fleet," he said. "Most Fleet kids grow up in boarding schools and I'm no exception. Born on Repub-2, I went into the academy at eighteen, and I've been on a ship ever since. Sixteen years."

She leaned forward, resting her chin on her hand. "Brothers or sisters?"

"One sister," he said. "Nalia. She's my twin."

"That's so cool! She's an officer, too, I take it?"

Nalia was as spontaneous and carefree as Rian was quiet and disciplined. Their parents had actually been relieved when the academy balked even at the mention of her applying. "No, she's a teacher at a primary school on our home planet. She's married, with a two-year-old." He missed her.

He also envied her for her relationship with her husband, a ship mechanic. They had an easygoing, loving relationship, the kind their parents didn't appear to have and Rian wished for in his weaker moments.

"So you're an uncle and a spaceship captain. What else do you do?"

"Being a commanding officer takes up a lot of time."

"You must have hobbies and interests," she insisted. "I used to read a lot. It's harder here, but I'm getting used to it." She caught his raised eyebrow. "The language has changed. 'Y' and 'C' aren't used as much, unless they're talking about the Commons. My ID spells my name as L-I-L-I, for instance. So tell me, what do you do?"

"I read, too, but mostly military theory and history." He thought of one of his pastimes that he missed. "Climbing. And horror vids."

"Movies?" she translated.

"I don't know what they are," he admitted.

"Shows," she explained. "You watch them on a screen."

"Then movies, yes."

"Me, too," Lily said.

There were cinemas on station, although none showing any decent vids, otherwise he would have invited her to see one. Strictly to show her Commons culture, of course.

There was a small commotion at the bar as the blonde woman slid out of her seat next to Shraft and left. He gave the noisy, dramatic sigh of the moderately drunk and ordered another drink from a serving bot. Rian shook his head. "What's wrong?" Lily asked.

"I'm not used to this kind of atmosphere," he admitted.

"You're not a bar-hopper, then? Want to go somewhere?"

Rian tore his gaze from the bar to look at Lily, slightly stunned. "Sure," he said. He thought quickly. "The station has an aviary, botanical gardens, a zoo. Where do you want to go?"

"Wherever you like," she said, rising from her seat. "This is all new to me."

———

ANY IDEAS in Lily's mind about whether Rian was naturally quiet or if that was his professional appearance evaporated. He was quiet, giving him a mysterious air that she liked. She had asked an amused Mora back at the pub before his arrival if he had any girlfriends, and Mora had giggled in reply. Like everyone in Fleet, the nurse said, he had had a couple of discreet flings along the way but nothing serious. "Do you have a thing for him?" she yelled over the roar of the crowd.

Well, yes, Lily did, but she wasn't going to proclaim it in a noisy pub.

He was intelligent, thoughtful, and, she was learning, irritating Fleet with his unorthodox ways of leadership. He hadn't spoken to her about it directly, but she had sensed as much when she asked him how his conferences went, and guessed that when the boss wanted to deal with him privately, it wasn't to play golf and talk shop. Still, he had made enough of an impact to be first officer on a battleship by the time he was twenty-six, a feat even the most vocal detractors on the *Defiant* admired.

And he was good to look at. Lily wasn't about to discount that, or that she was a sucker for the tall, dark, and handsome type. Deep blue eyes that had kept her focused and almost lucid when she came out of stasis, and ink-black hair that he appeared to have forgotten to have trimmed lately, but Lily liked it. It made him more human and less the intimidating, distant captain. He was the polar opposite of Cameron, who could draw a roomful of people around him just by walking in, and made friends wherever he went. It was all an act, as Lily later found out when he told her that he was really in love with her best friend.

She was starting over. She wouldn't think of that now. Cameron's desertion had occurred long before her move to Toronto and she had already put it behind her.

Rubidge Station's commercial sector was still busy even at this late hour, but the attractions he brought her to were quieter. There was a large group of tourists oohing and aahing over the aviary, a cavernous, sweet-smelling room full of small colorful birds that resembled parrots. They flew through the room freely, accepting pieces of fruit from onlookers' hands. They were loud, too. Their high-pitched screeches bounced off the walls as they dive-bombed heads. One bounced off Rian and poked its beak at his neck, and he asked if they could go.

"Where to next?" she asked. He rubbed his neck.

"We could go to the botanical gardens," he replied. "Or the library. As long as a bird doesn't try to kill me."

"Let me see." She pushed his hand away and peered at his neck. There would be a small bruise, but no lasting damage. "They're not venomous?"

"Not that species."

She touched a fingertip to it to assess the damage and quickly drew away before Rian could, remembering his reaction the other night in the mess. Rian turned his head to look at her, one eyebrow raised in an expression that she was sure he had a patent on. "The gardens," she said.

Was that disappointment on his face?

The botanical gardens were two decks up from the aviary, and Lily had to remind herself she was on a space station. There were more familiar plants here than she expected, and a wave of homesickness washed over her, as strong as the artificial sunlight pouring over the gardens.

"Rian," she breathed. "This is beautiful." They wandered through a dirt pathway lined with shrubs and flowers, plaques in front of them explaining their species and origins. She pointed to a copse of trees in the distance, a few hundred feet away. "Those are similar to what we grew at home." She pointed to another, closer group of trees. "Those are oak trees! But they're small." She wandered over the grass to the oaks, full-grown but standing a scant nine or ten feet up.

"Growth hormones," Rian explained, following her. "They do that to make room for more species."

Lily was already reading a small plaque nailed into the tree trunk. It wasn't identified as an oak tree, but it originated from Repub-1, and before that, Earth. She looked up at its branches and was pleased to see that they looked like they could hold her weight. She'd certainly climbed higher trees, and this one had some good footholds. "Will I end up in jail if I climb this?" she asked.

"No. They frown on picking flowers, though."

"Good to know." She wrapped her arms around the trunk and hoisted herself up.

"Lily, haven't you fallen out of trees before?" Rian asked patiently.

"I've fallen out only twice. I've lost count of how many times I've climbed them."

"As an adult?"

"Especially as an adult." She had spent many hours nestled in the branches of a tree after her breakup with Cameron, and more after her father had died.

It was a quick climb, and she settled on a sturdy lower branch and triumphantly grinned down at Rian. She brushed some tree bark off her clothes. "Come on up," she said.

"I don't think..."

"Captain, I absolutely promise you I will never tell a soul that you climbed a tree. And you told me you climb in your spare time, so I know you know how."

"I climb mountains in simulator chambers," he protested, but he smiled sheepishly and followed her example, using the same footholds. He hauled himself up and Lily scooted over on the branches to make room for him. Their feet dangled over the branch, their thighs touching. "Now what?" he asked.

"We could keep climbing."

"No way. *I'll* probably be the one with a broken rib in sick bay, and it'll give Admiral Kentz one more thing to ride my ass about."

Lily laughed. Rian was coming alive. "It's just good to know you're not always so starched and proper all the time,.."

"No, I'm not."

They sat in comfortable silence for a few moments. Across the garden Lily heard a short conversation in a language she didn't recognize, followed by giggling.

"Thank you for bringing me here," she said quietly. "This is perfect. It reminds me of home."

He swung his feet a little, and she thought he might be feeling foolish at being stuck in an oak tree. "Tell me about your home," he said.

Dozens of comparisons between her new and old lives ran

through her head. "I miss the weather," she began. "I never thought about it, but I always thought wind and sunlight would always be there." She hadn't thought about that until they walked into the bright gardens. "I'm still getting used to seeing stars when I look out the windows. You know what it's like to look up at them when you're on a planet, but still knowing you're firmly on the ground." He nodded. "I don't miss my car, but I wonder what happened to it." She caught his quizzical glance. "Mode of transport, also strictly on the ground. Mine wasn't that great, and I was thinking about selling it and sticking to the subway, but my job was so far away from my apartment. Subways are —*were* —underground commuter trains." He nodded again.

"I don't miss Toronto," she admitted. "I miss my old life, before my dad passed away. That's something even all this—" she gestured to the immaculately kept lawns and trees, "—can't bring back. I was still grieving that before this happened."

"Do you like it here?"

The question didn't surprise her, but his tone did. He sounded worried about her, and on a less-than-professional level. "Rubidge is a nice place to visit, but I wouldn't want to live here," she replied.

"I mean this time and deep space."

She looked at a bright blue flowering shrub. "It'll take a while to get used to," she said finally. "And I did want to start over somewhere new. This just wasn't what I had imagined. But yeah, I think I like it so far."

It was the truth. There were aspects she would probably never get used to—starfields, for one, and the idea that there was life outside Earth—but she wasn't in a bad place.

His hand crept over hers and loosely grasped her fingers. The touch sent a shock through her.

"You don't touch people often, do you?" she asked, and

stole a look at him.

"No." He had a half-smile on his face, and his blue gaze flickered over her mouth. She knew what he was thinking, what he wanted to do. She knew he wouldn't do it anytime soon; he would have to analyze the situation for any variables. One was potentially falling out of a tree again but she had survived worse, and he likely had as well.

She closed the gap between them and kissed him. Immediately his fingers tightened around her hand and his other arm snaked around her waist. She leaned into him, deepening their kiss, and he responded eagerly, pulling her closer to him and surprising her. He disentangled their hands and clasped her hip, and ran her hands up his arms to rest on his shoulders and neck.

He broke their kiss and let her go reluctantly. He opened his mouth to speak, but Lily shushed him with a finger to his lips. "Don't apologize," she said. "I won't kiss you again if you do."

That was a lie. She was going to kiss him again the first opportunity she had. The smile across his face told her he knew that, too.

But he didn't reply. Instead, he took her face in his hands and kissed her again, more possessively this time. His tongue probed her mouth when she gasped in surprise. Just as quickly, he released her and scooted over to the tree trunk. Lily watched him descend with an unexpected grace and then followed.

"Why would I apologize?" he said. "You started it."

He had a wide grin across his face, an expression she had never seen him wear before and wanted to see again. He took her hand, loosely twining his fingers through hers. She knew it would only be temporary; as soon as they left the botanical gardens or saw someone in a Fleet uniform he would let go. But for now, she would enjoy it.

CHAPTER 8

He had lost his mind, and was well on his way to not giving a damn about it if he wasn't careful. But Acting Captain Rian Marska still managed to put his best professional face forward as Rubidge engineers gave him a tour of the *Defiant*'s improved maintenance access ways the following afternoon, following a morning spent in a meeting discussing new patrol territories. The ship's weaponry was receiving the promised upgrades even as he crawled on his hands and knees through the tunnels, and he was pleased to hear that the port side lift that tended to get stuck between decks had been repaired. The artificial gravity was going to be fully operational throughout the ship in the coming day, and the office replicators reprogrammed. It would save Rian trips to the mess for coffee, at least.

It wasn't a permanent captaincy on a battleship—a goal that Rian saw slip from his grasp every day—or even a post on a ship built in the last thirty years, but at least the *Defiant* wasn't a total laughingstock anymore.

He ignored the engineer's subtle insults about the superficial hull damage that had been sustained when the ship crossed paths with the dying star. As far as Rian knew, the man had never set foot on a ship when it was in the space lanes, nor was he military, so his opinion was moot. He also tuned out Lieutenant Steg's murmurs of approval at the mention of the new weapons locker security was receiving. He snapped back to full attention when he and the crew who had looked over the *Defiant* were escorted off ship, and he thanked the engineers for their work. It was a vast improvement.

The engineer explained some of the patches that had been installed in the power grid: "Easy enough to do when you've got the manpower and money. In less than a day you have an old clunker like the *Defiant* almost as fast as a ship just off the yards." He and Rian backed out of an access tube, and Steg asked about the new capabilities of the hyperspace engines. The engineer rattled off some statistics, comparing the *Defiant*'s specs to newer ships, and Rian tuned out the chatter around him as he listened. Steg elbowed him.

"Lieutenant?"

"Is this personal?" he demanded in a hoarse whisper.

"I beg your pardon?"

"I saw you around the aviary last night with our guest." He spat out the last word.

"Excuse me?" Rian whispered back. "Are you insinuating something?" Steg's narrowed eyes told him all Rian needed to know. It unnerved him how close the burly ex-prizefighter was to the truth, but it really wasn't the security chief's concern anymore. "Do I have to remind you of your place?"

Steg had the sense to look startled. "No, sir," he muttered. "Apologies." Without another word, the security chief followed Rian off the ship. The airlock hissed shut behind them.

Figures in EVA suits slowly descended from a waiting station shuttle to begin work on the ship's hull and exterior weaponry. The sight of the suited mechanics caused a ripple of apprehension to run down Rian's spine. He had had the requisite extra-vehicular activity training in the academy and forced himself into taking annual elective courses in outside repair, but he was still nervous about being in space with only a suit for protection. The fact that Fleet hadn't had a fatal accident in over a century was of little comfort.

He dismissed the crew in the foyer for the evening, eliciting genuine smiles from them. Maybe this was a sign of things to come.

He hadn't seen Lily since that morning, when he spotted her and her friend from sick bay heading out to breakfast. He knew the nurse was due to spend a few hours with her father, one of the admirals who *wasn't* out for his blood, and he wondered what Lily had got up to.

He was acting like a schoolboy, mooning over her and trying to figure out ways to see her again. They could go out to dinner, he thought. The station was certainly large enough so they could find an out-of-the-way place where they could talk. That idea made him more apprehensive than it should. What if she only responded to him because of stress? That happened sometimes. Senior Captain Ursuline Jena, renowned and feared officer currently aboard *Bishop's Pride*, had fallen madly in love with and married a man she rescued from a shuttle accident. The union had lasted less than two years, although Rian was liable to chalk up the marriage's failure to the man turning out to be a gray market arms dealer in his spare time.

He was overthinking this, as usual. A kiss was just that. So was dinner.

The crew dispersed, and he went off in search of Lily.

———

RIAN WAS nervous as he approached the barracks, the likeliest place Lily would be. After what had happened the night before, an uncomfortable awkwardness had descended on them when they left the gardens. He attributed it to not being able to touch her in public when he wanted to. She was quickly growing on him, and the memory of her shimmying up a tree and encouraging him to do the same had been in the back of his mind all day. It was out of character for him, and it had felt good. He wished it could have continued, that he could kiss her again and see where things went from there, but that wasn't going to happen anytime soon.

He pressed his hand into the palm lock next to the door. He heard a muffled "Come in—oops!" from inside, then, "Enter."

She was wearing a pair of slim black pants and green sweater that matched her eyes. She was surrounded by packages from her shopping excursion the night before. She had a blouse in one hand when she entered the room and he saw clothes spread across the unmade bed. "This is great!" she exclaimed. "Everything fits perfectly. This is so much better than getting into a catfight at a Boxing Day sale." She began folding the new clothes. He picked up something black and lacy that was draped across the nightstand. A dress made of thin fabric, with a complicated set of straps. She took it from him and her cheeks flushed pink. "It's a dress," she explained.

"I can see that."

"Mora talked me into it. I'm sure I'll find somewhere to wear it eventually." She carefully folded the delicate lace and stowed it in her duffel.

Rian could think of a few places, but didn't make any suggestions.

"I didn't think I'd see you tonight," she said. "Taz said you and a few other of your higher-ups were looking at the new and improved *Defiant*."

"I was. It's the next best thing to getting a new ship. I gave everyone the evening off. They deserved a break, and we're departing early tomorrow."

"Seven-thirty, right?" He nodded.

She held up a small datatab. "I bought this today," she said. "Taz helped me pick it out. I told him about the pharmacy job and he said I'd need something to read my textbooks on. I'm still learning how to use it."

"You'll need one for writing notes, too. Some people prefer handwriting with a stylus over typing."

"I'm one of them." She opened a smaller package and took out some toiletries. She uncapped a bottle of shampoo and sniffed. "I don't know what this is supposed to smell like, but it's good. You said some ships don't have water showers?"

"No, but the stations do. You'll still get to take showers if you live on one."

"Good. Some things you just don't want to give up." She smiled and tucked her purchases into the duffel.

"Have you had dinner yet?" he asked casually.

"No."

"There's a place on 18-F that I've been to a few times," he began, but she was already dropping her credit chip in her pocket and slipping on her shoes knowingly. They didn't speak again until they were in the lift, heading to Deck F, on the outer edges of the commercial sector.

"Have you read anything interesting on your new datatab?" he asked.

She looked at him blankly for a few seconds. "Oh, right, my e-reader. Taz transferred some his files to it and I've been reading up on space history. If I'm going to be passed off as a local, I should act like one." She paused. "Datatab," she repeated.

"Short for datatablet."

She asked for some clarification on other terms, and he was pleased to answer them. His ego was wounded at the notion that her reaction to him could be stress-based. But it wasn't as though she had launched herself at him and torn his clothes off last night, although his body tensed at the thought. Thank the gods for *that*, because his self-discipline would have been severely tested. He would have rejected her, but it would have been difficult. Acting Captain Rian Marska was a lot of things, but he wasn't someone who took advantage of vulnerable women.

Except for kissing her the second time. *Damn.*

Was taking her out to dinner considered taking advantage? The unpleasant idea popped into his mind like a skib sting. No, he decided. He would keep it strictly professional and put any other notions aside, even though he was loathe to.

The restaurant he picked was small, a little-known gem favored by station locals and staffed with people instead of serving bots. It was the place he and his friends preferred when they had been in the academy, and it was far less rushed and crowded than the pubs on the lower decks. They took seats at the back and ordered tea to start. Then he watched her flip through the table-mounted menu screen with a critical eye before sighing in frustration.

"Pick something for me," she urged. "I don't know what any of this is."

"What foods do you hate?"

"Pickles and anchovies, if they still exist."

"They do, although anchovies are an Earth delicacy."

"Seriously? Ugh. Pick something with at least one vegetable." There was a challenging note to her voice. He tabbed in the orders through the menu.

"That's it?"

"A server will be along shortly, but yes."

"Oh." She leaned forward and looked at him expectantly. He wasn't sure how to respond.

"Where would I find information about Earth?" she asked.

"From my time. News clips and the like."

"We can go to the library here and download some history files," he said. "I don't know how much will be relevant to your case, but they have billions of files."

She shrugged. "I want to know if anyone was looking for me when I was kidnapped," she said quietly. "I didn't have a lot of friends in my life at the time, and my stepmother was out in Vancouver, but I'd like to know. Self-centered, I know."

"No, it isn't. I think you mentioned you had a husband for a while?" Rian kept the question casual.

"God, no," she replied. "The last serious relationship I was in ended a couple of years ago. I thought I was going to marry him at one point, and we lived together in the basement apartment on the farm, but he took one look at my best friend and decided she was the one for him. I felt like an idiot when I found out. When I was finalizing the sale of the tree farm, I heard from a couple of mutual acquaintances that they were expecting a baby." She paused. "I don't know why I'm telling you this."

Rian absorbed this information, an unexpected swell of rage flaring when he thought about the bastard who had broken her heart in the worst possible way. What would possess anyone to give her up?

Professional, he reminded himself. He would have to give her up shortly, and he'd never really had her to begin with.

———

THEY STOPPED at the library after dinner. She was surprised by it, a fact that she whispered to him as she took in the consoles lined up in rows around the office-like space.

"Why are you whispering?" he asked.

"Because we're in a library. It's the polite thing to do."

"I see." Rian had no rejoinder to that.

"People read in libraries," she patiently explained. "They come in for peace and quiet."

"Interesting times you come from," he said. He showed her how to buy a datakey at the automatic info kiosk and download files to it from one of the consoles. She did searches on names and places foreign to him, and sighed when nothing came up. Then she did searches focusing solely on Toronto, Canada, twenty-first century, and cryonics. There was more than he expected, but he had never been one for ancient history. She downloaded news clips from the excavation to Darcan-2, everything she could pull up on the Nym, and at his suggestion, one of the texts he'd read in the academy about Earth's history from first contact with the Kurrans to the present. She also picked out a couple of novels and a text on Fleet pharmacy procedures.

"I was hoping there would at least be some newspapers archived here," she said.

"What's a newspaper?"

"They're like your news clips and vids," she explained. "Only they're printed, and you bought them from a news box or a corner store with change."

"And how often were they printed?"

"Daily."

Daily printed news matter. "Your homes must have been full of them."

"No," she said. "You put it in the recycling when you were finished with it."

Rian was incredulous. "Let me get this straight. *Every day*, you would print an entire book you'd throw away after reading it?" Lily nodded. "What a waste of resources. No wonder Earthers left."

"Now you can see why I was surprised to find out that Earth didn't accidentally blow itself up." She kept her eyes on the console as she pulled some more information, but she was smiling. "I think that's it." He showed her how to disconnect the datakey, and they left the library.

————

THEY WERE the only ones in the lift back to the barracks deck—unsurprising, since most of the *Defiant*'s crew was probably living it up on station while they still had the chance. Lily was quiet, likely contemplating her assumed fate on Earth.

He stole a glance at her. She was looking at the floor. Involuntarily, he reached for her hand. *Strictly as a gesture of support*, he told himself. She curled her fingers in his and stepped closed, raising her face to meet his level.

All thoughts, all pretences of being professional around her were sucked out the airlock when she looked at him like that. He kissed her hard, backing her up against the lift's wall. He felt a murmur of surprise against his mouth and realized he'd caught her off-guard. Her hands found his shoulders and pulled him closer, and her lips parted. Her tongue met his eagerly and he groaned, pressing against her. The lift's pinging between decks registered as loudly as red alert sirens, and his hand blindly groped the wall for the emergency brake. The lift squeaked as it halted, giving them a bare few minutes alone before he had to restart it or risk being caught by a maintenance crew.

Rian kissed her like a man starved, unable to suppress his gasp when she pulled his shirt from his waistband and let hands explore the contours of his back. Her touch was electrifying, but jolted him back to reality. Quickly he sprang away, breathing heavily. He pressed a button and the lift whirred back to life. "Apologies," he said.

"What for?" She had a dazed look on her face, a look he had caused. Despite everything, he couldn't help feeling a little masculine pride at the sight. Desire roared back to life once more.

"That was inappropriate on my part," he admitted, tucking his shirt back in.

"What about mine?"

She had him there.

The lift doors opened. He stood at near-perfect military stance, fully expecting to see Admiral Kentz or Lieutenant Steg, or, gods forbid, Ensign Shraft waiting to step on, but no one was there. Rian silently offered a prayer of thanks to the gods and presumed he was at the end of this week's quota of luck.

He walked her through the corridor to her door as though he were in the academy, escorting his date back home after a night of beer and horror vids. She leaned up and kissed the skin below his ear, and his pulse quickened. "You could come in," she murmured into his ear. He slid his arms around her waist and pulled her to him.

That thought had entered his mind, too, and he nearly accepted. He *wanted* to, but he couldn't, especially not here. "That's not a good idea," he whispered regretfully. It wasn't just what Lily was; it was the station itself. He caught her hurt look and dropped a kiss on her lips. "Please believe me. I want to."

"So then come in. Just so you know, I was going to make you some tea."

He smiled at that. "We both know neither of us wants tea. It's just that here and now—it's not a good idea. Our locations are traceable, and neither of us needs more hassle from Fleet."

She muttered something derogatory about Fleet.

He kissed her in reply, and let her go at the sound of voices coming off the lift. "Good night," he whispered. The voices came closer. "Departure at 0730 tomorrow," he said.

She mock-saluted him. "See you tomorrow, Captain."

CHAPTER 9

The *Defiant* stayed in orbit around Rubidge Station for another day after her crew returned, and Lily watched it through the viewports sometimes. It was the size of a small planet, rust-colored, with constant traffic and ships leaching off its lower decks.

She tried to make her cabin a little homier. She had some clothes to put away and was pleasantly surprised to find a stack of towels waiting for her when the crew was permitted to board the *Defiant*. She also found a new tablet computer with a matching stylus and a datakey that contained her texts for the pharm tech training, the history of Fleet and some star charts, information she was now downloading to her datatab. Everything she would need to know to fit in Commons space. She had a good idea of who left everything, and it warmed her heart.

She felt like an idiot over what happened on their last night on Rubidge. Not over what happened in the elevator, but what happened next. She hadn't seen Rian except in corridors since they returned to the ship a couple of days prior and hadn't had a chance to explain that propositioning men wasn't a habit of hers. Not for lack of wanting to, but definitely due to lack of skill in that area. But as she had learned in the last couple of weeks, life was nothing but a series of firsts. She had hoped he would take her up on her invitation and had been sorely disappointed when he turned back into the distant captain. Or worse, he thought her reaction to him was rooted in psychological trauma and he was needlessly playing the overprotective hero.

Except he wasn't—not really. His kiss in the elevator had told her as much.

Only Lily Stewart could travel 850 years into the future, meet someone like him, and have him reject her because he didn't think she was really attracted to him.

The files finished unpacking into her datatab. She scrolled through them with a fingertip and touched the heading *Commonwealth Galactic Academy Pharmaceutical Technician Program: Introduction* and brought up a note that Rian had obviously attached to the file. After some careful reading, she was able to translate it:

Just so you know, I wanted that cup of tea. R.

She sighed like a high school girl receiving her first love letter, and wondered where he was. Probably learning how the new things on the *Defiant* worked; half the crew had spent the last two days crawling around tunnels and playing with new programs. Especially Taz, who was immediately caught trying to transport one body part at a time into another part of the ship.

She opened a file and began reading about Earth's history since her kidnapping. There had been a world war in what would have been her lifetime, and two more before an uneasy truce was declared across most of Earth shortly before mass interplanetary immigration began. Still, no one had acciden-tally detonated a nuclear weapon or unleashed a zombie virus on mankind. She was relieved to discover than the human race hadn't turned out to be as stupid as she had anticipated. In 2092, for instance, Earth's depletion of fresh water had dwindled enough so a new water sterilization procedure had been implemented in what had once been India. The technology was cheap, portable, and could purify just about anything. It had been essential for what eventually turned into an intergalactic space travel alliance across Asia, who initially terraformed three small uninhabited planets a galaxy away from Earth twenty-five years later.

The Earth-bound population had been reduced to less than three billion by the time the new colonies formed the Commonwealth in 2220, and that number had been halved when the Kurrans made contact in 2280. The Commonwealth had been keeping an eye on the Kurran corner of the galaxy for several years. They had debated whether or not to extend an olive branch, unsure if they were friendly or not. Most of the colonies were unprepared for a war. She bookmarked articles on them to read later.

She closed the history file and opened the first text of for her pharmacy training. It looked straightforward enough, something she could complete on her own in a few weeks, with a few exams she would have to write before beginning practical training in a pharmacy. She would have to ask someone about a couple of machines mentioned in the outline. Someone in the infirmary could probably help if they weren't too busy. The whole ship had been in a flurry of activity since leaving Rubidge, poking around the new machinery and fine-tuning it to their specifications.

The intercom beside the cabin door pinged, and Rian's voice said, "All available crew, conference hall in ten minutes."

Was she supposed to go, too? She tapped her comm badge hesitantly, still wary of it. "Captain Marska?" Nothing happened, so she tried again. "Stewart to Captain Marska? Can you hear me?"

That did the trick. "Marska here. I'm expecting you in the conference hall, too," he said quietly.

"I'll be there." She slipped the Fleet-issued med-assistant smock over her black blouse and pants and left her cabin.

She figured out how to get to the conference hall and paused in its doorway, looking for some kind of order. She saw a sea of uniforms mingling with one another, taking seats at random places, so she looked for a familiar face. She spotted Taz waving at her and looking like hell. There was an odd odor in here, coming off more than a few crew members who also looked like they had been out carousing with Taz.

"Are you okay?" she asked, looking up at his bloodshot eyes. She discreetly breathed through her mouth.

"I will be once I get a decent night's sleep. I've been on the go since the last night on station, and I haven't had a chance to recover from the hangover. Where were you, anyway?"

"Reading in my cabin," she lied.

"I was looking for you," he said. "We went to the White Dwarf. You should've been there. Kostin destroyed himself and got on the stage with one of the dancers. It was spectacular. We got it on vid before the club manager kicked us out. His girlfriend is *so* pissed off."

"I don't know Kostin, his girlfriend, or what the White Dwarf is."

"First officer, navigation second-in-command, and a strip joint."

"While seeing green alien space tits sounds interesting in theory, strip clubs aren't really my cup of tea."

"You don't get green alien space tits on Rubidge," Taz insisted. "Commons space is mostly humanoid. Besides, the White Dwarf has guys, too."

"Taz, while I support everyone doing what makes them happy, do I seem like someone goes to strip clubs? Really, tell me." She crossed her arms and arched one eyebrow at him dramatically.

"You said you wanted to try new things!"

"I was thinking along the lines of replicators and space shuttles and things I didn't have at home."

Whatever rejoinder Taz could have offered was cut off by Admiral Kentz calling the room to order. Rian stood beside him. What was Kentz doing here?

The admiral offered an insincere welcome to the science team aboard and detailed the *Defiant*'s repairs and upgrades. It was officially on par with other patrol ships, eliciting snickers among the crew and a tight-lipped smile from the captain. A lab had been set up to allow the science team to set up shop temporarily before their mission, where they could grow crystals of some kind, Lily deduced, in peace. Some kind of secretive weaponry in the making. Her mind drifted back to her datatab. She should have brought it with her.

"Our other security issue is the custody of our time traveler," Kentz said, and her ears perked up.

"You all know by now that an unnamed Fleet ship ended up with a Nym kidnapping victim from ancient times," he continued, as though there could possibly be anyone aboard who didn't know Lily by now. "Battleships are attempting to infiltrate Nym space and investigate, and we've managed to keep the details of the victim out of the media."

Several dozen pairs of eyes swiveled in Lily's direction. She shifted in her seat but met them. "Howdy," she said. A ripple of laughter spread through the conference hall. Kentz glowered in her direction.

"You all know she's here, and Fleet is pleased to see that everyone has remembered our policies on intel containment and confidentiality. None of the other ships are aware of her presence." Lily wondered what he meant by their policies. She had skimmed over that part in the Fleet history module in her texts. He continued. "She'll remain here for the time being and will eventually settle in a Fleet-controlled environment."

"As a pharm tech," Lily piped up.

"Yes, Captain Marska suggested that occupation." He turned to the rest of the crew. "Obviously, her returning to the twenty-first century is out of the question due to the Commons' long-standing positions on time travel and the possibility of altering history."

Lily shivered. She had never thought her return in those terms before. But how could she alter the course of history? She had been a receptionist. Administrative support staff didn't have that kind of power.

She looked at the faces trained on her and caught Rian's gaze. His azure eyes were full of want, the same look he had outside her barracks door on station. Heat coursed through her, and she forced herself to look away, hoping no one noticed.

Kentz cleared his throat, bringing the attention back to him. "Miss Stewart is cooperating fully with Fleet," he said. "And we're going to find out exactly what the Nym are up to. No other time travelers have shown up, but if the Nym have been going back and forth between centuries, they must be stopped. The time continuum as it has already occurred must not be changed."

Lily got the message. A receptionist probably couldn't do much damage on her own, but a receptionist with evil alien scientists and a space army on her tail could. The ramifications boggled her mind.

Kentz re-emphasized the importance of security and secrecy, and urged the crew not to pester her. They hadn't in the first place—the questions she had received had been curious and respectful, with more than a few awed looks when she described cars and airplanes—but Kentz's instruction made her feel a little lonelier. Taz and Mora still had jobs to do, after all, and she wasn't sure where she stood with Rian.

When they were finally dismissed, Lily kept her head down and headed for her cabin. She toyed with the idea of going to the mess, but she wasn't hungry. She resigned herself to a quiet evening tackling the first module of the pharmacy program and watching a couple of episodes of *Lightning's Luck*, a TV show Mora recommended.

Taz caught up to her, reeking of that alcoholic odor she had noticed earlier. She must have made a face because he asked, "What is it?"

"Nothing."

Realization dawned on his face. "Oh, you're noticing the smell. We were drinking tambith whiskey at the White Dwarf. I took a shower this morning, just so you know." He raised his arm and sniffed. "Damn. No wonder communications smells like death. You have to sweat it out. At least I'm not the only one who stinks."

"I noticed."

He changed the subject. "So, where are you going?" he asked.

"My cabin, where else?"

"I'm off shift at 1900 hours today. I was thinking I could teach you to shoot. I'm as good at handling a laser weapon as I am at coding and hacking."

"Taz, the idea of you handling a gun scares the hell out of me." They stepped in a line waiting for the lift.

"I didn't shoot you when you woke up in the cargo hold, remember?" he pressed. "And you were making sudden movements."

Lily rolled her eyes. "What sudden movements? I was drugged and could barely move."

"A dead body crawling out of a coffin, no matter how slowly, qualifies as a huge fucking sudden movement."

The surrounding crew was listening to their exchange and responded with a wave of laughter. A throat cleared behind Lily and Taz, who whirled around to face Rian and Admiral Kentz. The admiral peered at Taz's insignia.

"Watch your language, Ensign..." He paused.

"Shraft," Rian finished. But he was looking at Lily, his face set in rigid, professional lines but his eyes sending her a look of naked need that made her blush.

"Apologies, sir," said Taz. The lift doors opened, and he followed a bunch of communications officers into it. "So, Lily, 1900 hours? Meet me in security."

RIAN BREATHED a sigh of relief when Admiral Kentz's shuttle left the *Defiant*. The admiral would return to Rubidge Station before transferring to a ship that would take him to Fleet headquarters on Commons Prime, far away from where he could waste the time of Rian and his crew.

He returned to his office off the bridge and was pleased that the replicator produced a cup of tea instead of something sludgy and green. He brought up all the classified files Kentz had transferred to his office computer and took a moment to stew before delving into them. There really had been no need for the admiral to gather half the crew to tell them something they already knew and remind them of policies that had been drilled into them on their first day of basic training. Idly he wondered how someone like Kentz had ended up in his position. During his walk-through of the ship, he had taken control of a navigation console from Lieutenant Asmo and nearly changed the ship's course. Rian and Asmo had readjusted the direction under Kentz's irritated look.

He turned to the classified files, detailing Fleet intel on Nym activity over the last decade. Aside from a few skirmishes between battleships and Nym battle cruisers and Lily Stewart's appearance, there wasn't anything that explained their ability to time travel. They rarely even left their corner of the galaxy since the Fleet's adoption of a "Shoot first, ask questions later" policy when it came to their cruisers in Commons or Fringes space.

Obviously, that didn't mean anything. Everyone knew the rumors of the Nym's technological capabilities, but there wasn't much in the way of hard evidence. They would have to develop better transporter and ship cloaking mechanisms for time travel to work based on the accepted theories outlined in Rian's files.

One popular theory involved the use of a vortex. Essentially, find the right kind of vortex, engage the hyperspace engines to a specific rate of distance, then abort the hyperdrive and allow the vortex to carry the ship into another time. It was unproven; the reality of space travel was that if a ship found herself in a vortex, she was coming out in pieces. That was what happened a couple centuries back to a few science ships dumb enough to test out that theory before the ban on time travel took effect. There really was no such thing as the "right" kind of vortex in space. Besides, even if that were possible, there hadn't been a recorded vortex anywhere near the Nym world in years.

Another, more plausible but untested theory hypothesized the use of wormhole-like energy currents that could transport matter through a space-time rift, treating the energy waves like doors into different eras. Wormholes occurred naturally and far more often than vortexes, but a ship was likely to meet her demise in the same manner. Assuming the Nym had manipulated space rifts naturally, this theory was likeliest.

But what if they had actually developed a device that could propel them back and forth through time? Rian made a fist at the idea.

His computer shrilled to signal an incoming message, interrupting his train of thought. He checked the sender's ID: N. Marska. His sister. He considered dismissing it, but knew she would keep calling until he authorized her message. He tabbed the "receive" icon on the screen, and his twin's face appeared, blue eyes sparkling. She had changed her hair again, and bright red streaks ran through her shoulder-length black curls.

"Hi, little brother," she said.

She was ten minutes older than him and never let him forget it. They were closing in on their mid-thirties now. It was well past time to let it go. He forced himself to smile. "Hi, Nalia."

She propped her elbows on her desk and rested her head on her hands. "You know damn well why I'm calling and why I'm calling you in your office instead of your apartment."

"Cabin," he corrected.

"Whatever. I just put Anya in front of the vidscreen and Jonn's at his poker game. I called Dad and he said you were docked at Rubidge for a couple of days." She grinned. "You know what I want to know."

He really wished she would stop reading the tabloids. "There's nothing to tell, Nalia," he said. Fleet's ability to monitor every message was never far from his mind.

"Oh, come on. Even Dad told me that everything in the press is lies and there really was a frozen body found on a patrol ship with crappy life support."

"Nalia! Shut up!" He could tell her what life support actually was later.

"You happen to be commanding a shit-hauler with a notorious reputation and you're one of three ships that docked at a Fleet base since the story broke. One of the others was a newer patrol ship, the other a battleship. Am I right?"

"Damn it, Nalia." He really wished he could cut off visual

on messages and use the kind of telephone technology Lily had told him about. He pinched the bridge of his nose and tried to remember how often Fleet monitored messages sent from captains' offices. Never, as far as he knew. And if their father had been talking... "How did you figure it out?" he asked quietly.

"I didn't. I was messing with you. You just told me." She sounded positively gleeful.

Aggravation clenched his gut. "Are you trying to get me court-martialed? That could happen, you know."

"Military channel," she said automatically. "I think you're safe." She rolled her eyes, and Rian uttered a silent prayer to the gods that she would finally grow up soon.

"*Sabi eabht ermabt releabvart a eabh ro ealish*?" Nalia asked devilishly.

For the gods' sake. It was the secret language she and Rian had created as children. *Is the time traveler a he or a she?* "You're acting like a child. I can't talk about that now." But he knew Nalia and her persistence. Her refusal to stay out of anyone's business was one of her qualities that made a Fleet career impossible. He had to distract her somehow. "I met someone," he said suddenly.

Nalia raised an eyebrow. "Seriously? You never tell me about your girlfriends."

"She isn't my girlfriend."

"Now who's acting like a child?"

She had a point there, but he was doing it out of necessity. "This is very new and I don't know if it'll go anywhere yet," Rian continued. That much was the truth. "I feel very... differently about her than anyone else." Also the truth. Manhandling women in lifts wasn't something he usually did.

"What's she like?"

"She's a pharm tech," he lied. Half-lied. She would be one

soon. "Very smart and outgoing. She has a great sense of humor."

All true. Lily didn't hide herself at all. He liked that very much. No pretensions about her.

"Is she pretty?"

She was more than that. "Yes," he finally said. "She's beautiful." That word still didn't convey her smile or the curve of her hips.

"Is she on board the *Defiant*?"

Rian didn't answer immediately. Nalia's jaw dropped, and he got a bad feeling that she had just put two and two together. "Oh, my gods!" she gasped. "What happened to Mr. Captains-Don't-Get-Involved-With-Subordinates?"

He breathed a sigh of relief. She hadn't come up with four. "I didn't know she was going to be joining the crew," he protested.

"A patrol ship has a pharmacy now?" she asked suspiciously.

Damn. He thought quickly. "She works in the infirmary dispensary," he said. "And we've only been out to dinner a couple of times."

"I never thought I'd see the day my by-the-books little brother broke his own rules." She snickered. "What's her name?"

Rian hesitated.

"If you don't tell me, I'll know you're making her up," she warned.

Lily was an uncommon name in the Commons, but not unheard of. He could tell Nalia the truth, and he did.

She leaned back in her chair and gave him a sly smile. Rian tensed. He knew that look. They were kids again, and he had been caught passing around a bottle of sala with his friends at their boarding school. He was about to be blackmailed.

"Don't you dare," he hissed.

"Mom and Dad will be thrilled."

"Nalia, don't. If and when I decide Mom and Dad need to know, I'll be the one to tell them."

"But you never tell them anything," she wheedled.

"There's nothing to tell."

"You have no idea how pissed off Dad was when he heard about your promotion through military channels."

Actually, Rian did. He had received an angry message from the retired Captain Marska two days after he took over the *Defiant*. "He only did it to make a fuss and remind me he's my father. This technically isn't a promotion, and he knows it," he pointed out. "I'm still officially a commander."

Nalia dismissed that comment with a wave of her hand. But then, she wasn't military. She didn't get it.

"Just tell them," she said, an uncharacteristic softness in her eyes. "They worry about you."

Rian snorted softly. Their parents were Fleet through and through. They had gone months at a time without seeing them when they were kids, only remembering they were parents when school administrators notified them about achievements and punishments. Nalia couldn't even offer a token excuse like the expectation of grandchildren—she had that covered with her toddler, whom they had barely seen in her two years. Nalia's husband's parents, owners of a freighter company, doted on the little girl instead.

But Rian knew if Nalia told their parents about Lily, there would be calls just to be difficult, an investigation into her background, and then all hell would break loose.

"If this goes anywhere, I'll tell them," he promised. He paused. "I'd like to be in a position where I have to."

"I know you," Nalia said. "Remember our deep, mystical twin connection. You really like her."

"I have other concerns, too," he began.

She cut him off. "Rian, you told me you met someone.

You even described her in terms broader than 'she's female.' You never do that."

Rian's hand hovered over the "disconnect" icon on the screen before she could wrestle more information from him. "Nalia, I have security issues with a known alien terrorist faction to worry about. I have to go now."

"Good night," she said. "Call me when you get the chance, or I'll tell on you."

———

LILY SURPRISED TAZ in their weapons training.

"It's a laser rifle," she pointed out. "It's easier to aim with a charge instead of bullets." Her father had taught her to shoot with pellet guns and a hunting rifle, putting bullets in rows of Diet Coke cans balanced on a fence.

The *Defiant* had a target shooting simulator on board, and Taz had set up a program that projected moving human-sized targets across a screen along its back wall. He had prepped a few weapons for her and she had hit a few targets on his command, making the projections explode into pieces before a new one took shape.

"This is easier than the laser pistol," she said. "I learned to shoot on something similar." One of the targets shattered as the charge, set to stun, hit its mark.

"Remind me never to piss you off," Taz remarked. "Let's try two." He adjusted the projection from a console and a pair of black outlines raced across the screen. Lily felled one immediately, but the other was being difficult. Its form shrank as it ran towards nothingness and dashed side to side. She fired three more charges before it finally exploded. The status light on the top of the rifle changed from green to yellow.

Taz noticed it. "This'll have to be charged soon," he said. "And I have to clean up before a few security officers come in to try out some new toys they picked up on station. They'll be here in a half-hour or so." He took the rifle from her and clipped a charger to its stock before stashing it in the weapons locker.

"They're training at eleven?" She remembered military time. "Twenty-three hundred hours," she corrected herself.

"Patrol ships never sleep."

"What are you patrolling, exactly?" Whenever Lily looked out a window, all she could see were endless stars and, in the distance, the occasional abandoned satellite or rare ship.

"Nothing while we're orbiting around the station," Taz replied. From the control console he turned off the projection. "We're heading to the Fringes, the area where people don't start firing at Commons ships, to drop off that science team and keep watch for smugglers. If we find any, we call in a larger patrol ship, like *Bishop's Pride*, or a battleship to take care of the rest."

"Everyone keeps talking about the Fringes. What are they?"

"Independent republics. The further away from the Commons they are, the more they hate civilized space."

"And you don't arrest anyone yourselves?"

"Not often. Depends on the pirate and his ship. A ship like the *Defiant* mostly just points to the bad guys and lets others take the credit, and in between does the crappy jobs no one else wants to do, like hauling museum artifacts." He double-checked the weapons locker to make sure it was secured. "Lights!" he barked harshly, and the room's illumination decreased. "I could teach you some hand-to-hand combat," he offered.

Lily regarded him for a moment. He wasn't quite as tall as Rian, and almost skinny. If she didn't know he was a soldier, she wouldn't have considered him threatening at all. "I don't know," she said. "Most of you in Fleet are twice my size. You also have a desk job. Is there even a point?"

Taz looked offended. "I'll have you know I graduated from the academy with a concentration in engineering *and* an award for hand-to-hand combat. I'm only stuck in communications until I've decided to stop enjoying myself at my job. And I'm sure what you meant to ask about is if there are there effective self-defense methods besides kicking someone in the balls. There are. That's the first place we anticipate being attacked by a woman. You have to catch them off-guard."

"You sound like you speak from experience." Knowing Taz and his attempts at womanizing, he likely was.

They left the room, and he palm-locked the door behind them. He was quiet; his expression darkened. She had hit a nerve.

"Yeah," he said. "My ex-wife's mother."

They waited for the elevator, and Lily tried to process this new information. "Wife?" she squeaked out. *Ex-wife?* He wasn't even twenty-five.

He shook his head. "You won't believe me, but I'll tell you. Alcohol is required." A few guys bearing security insignia and carrying gun cases stepped out. Taz ordered the elevator to the mess. He was quiet until they sat at the bar, beer in front of him and a glass of blue wine for Lily.

"I got married when I was seventeen," he finally said. "Arranged marriage. They're common where I come from. Vu'saar," he explained, seeing the question on her face. "It's a small planet in the Hefronn Galaxy. If the *Defiant* was heading there at top speed, it would take about four months, to give you an idea of how far away it is. It's beyond the outer Fringes, minds its own business, and hates technology."

"Vu'saar, then. Aren't you human?" she asked.

"Humanoid," he corrected. "Same as you, with a few subtle differences. Most Vu'saarns have telepathic or empathic talents. My empathic talents are very weak, and my ex-wife has none. Our parents were elders there, and probably still are. It's a position you're born into, similar to royalty."

"So you're a prince." The idea of Taz being royalty would have made Lily giggle if he weren't so unusually serious.

"I *was*," he said. "I was the oldest child in the family and entitled to take a place as an elder, except I'm not a telepath. They don't look kindly on non-telepaths in the ruling class. Another elder family had the same problem with their oldest daughter, so they decided we should marry and live as commoners. I was fine with that, and so was Maranda." He took a long drink from his beer, and Lily followed suit with her wine.

"We got along fine. We didn't love each other," he stressed. "We had an arrangement, if you get my drift. She was seeing someone else."

Lily nodded, pretending to understand.

"It was a political alliance, Lily. Our parents were mortified that they made children who had to speak to be heard, and they wanted us out of sight. Anyway, one night Maranda went out with her boyfriend and I was out with my brother. I came home first, and at dawn Maranda was dragged home by her mother, who was enraged that she was having an affair and I didn't care. We never..." Taz had the decency to color. "Um, you know. Knew each other that way. We were just friends sharing a house. My mother-in-law beat the shit out of both of us, and we were disowned by our families. Me, Maranda, and her boyfriend got on a freighter to a planet on the Fringes-Commons border. They joined the freighter crew, I joined Fleet. I haven't been back to Vu'saar since."

"What happened to Maranda?"

"Arranged marriages aren't recognized in the Commons, so there wasn't an annulment to worry about. We stay in touch. She's doing well, has a couple of daughters now."

"And so during that beating you—" Lily gestured with her hand.

"They took a couple of hits. Hurt like a son of a bitch."

Taz spoke the last part with his usual affable style, but it was forced. There was a palpable negative energy around him that Lily had never seen before. What a terrible thing to experience, especially so young.

He polished off the last of his beer with more gusto than necessary. "Please don't tell anyone," he said.

"I won't."

"A lot of people in the Commons don't like Vu'saarns," he continued. "They think I read their minds when they're not looking, and I can't do that."

Lily sort of understood, and sympathized with him.

He tried to lighten the mood. "Besides, if I could read minds, I might actually have better luck in the bars, right?"

CHAPTER 10

Lily was hunched over a table in the mess, datatabs and a coffee cup spread out in front of her. She scribbled notes on one of the datatab's screens with a stylus in between scrolling through information on the other. She was wearing what Rian was starting to think of as her uniform: slim black pants and a nondescript blouse, blue this time, another simple outfit from her excursion on Rubidge Station. Her dark hair was tied back in a ponytail, and she kept scraping her bangs out of her face. Aside from handwriting her notes instead of keying them on a portable comp, she looked completely at home.

Rian knew she was studying the Fleet pharmacy program and had an exam in two days' time. He had tried to keep his distance the last few days in a vain attempt to regain his professional demeanor, the call from his sister notwithstanding.

He admitted this morning that it wasn't working. Lily Stewart was under his skin, invading his thoughts at inconvenient times. He couldn't read intel reports about Nym infiltration without thinking of her being kidnapped, nor order a coffee at his office replicator without remembering her marvel at the devices. When he signed off on security logs, he thought about her friendship with Ensign Shraft, which, if he was honest with himself, he envied. The man was an idiot by choice. The gods knew he was bright enough to manipulate long strings of code to make a bunch of bots dance for his amusement but had shown little interest in taking his talent with computers in a positive direction. When Rian thought about it, he *was* friendly with most of the crew, and now he wished he was the one who had thought to teach Lily something about self-defense. It would have been a perfect excuse to be with her for a little while without raising too many suspicions. Only a few, anyway. Captains usually didn't teach people to shoot with a laser rifle. And hand-to-hand combat—forget it. As soon as he touched her, he wouldn't be able to stop, and not in a way that involved a sleeper hold.

Rian couldn't believe he was jealous of Ensign Shraft, a junior officer whose reputation for goofing off and causing mayhem was already legendary throughout the entire Fleet. It was a new feeling, and he didn't like it.

He needed to see her and talk to her beyond a perfunctory "hello" in the lift or corridor. Just to get her out of his system. That idea was what had compelled him to look up her location and make his way to the mess.

She was deeply engrossed in her datatab and had tucked the stylus behind her ear. When Rian quietly cleared his throat, she jumped a little in her seat, and the stylus clattered to the tabletop.

"Captain!" she said. "Good God, you scared a year off my life." She set the datatab aside.

He took the seat across from her. "How are you?"

"Almost through with Sanitation and Handling Protocols," she replied. "I finished Dispensation Procedures a couple days ago, and I've been reading through Fleet history when I get bored with technical stuff."

"It's required for all programs," Rian said. "So is a module on Commons history."

"Which is fascinating," Lily immediately replied.

He stared at her skeptically. "I didn't get where I am by believing everything I hear," he said, but he let a hint of a smile quirk at his mouth. "If you're reading the same text I had to, it's one of the most boring trials you'll ever go through."

She sighed. "You got me. But at least I'm picking up the language differences, too," she said, triumph in her words. "I'm changing the *Y*'s to *I*'s and switching *C* and *K*. It isn't as hard as I thought it would be. I was always worried everyone would start writing like they do in texts."

Rian raised an eyebrow, silently asking for an explanation.

"Text-speak," she clarified. "Short written messages through our phones. A lot of nonsense short words and symbols, like using the number 2 instead of writing 'to.' Lots of emojis."

"Wouldn't that create confusion?"

"It's like any other form of written communication. You just have to get used to it." She leaned back in her chair and sipped at her coffee. "So, what brings you here? Lunch isn't for another hour and a half." She glanced at the large clock inset in the mess wall.

"I'm not needed on the bridge right now."

Lily cocked her head, as though she was remembering something. "When *are* you ever on the bridge, anyway? Don't captains actually fly ships?"

He was amused at her naiveté. "It takes more than one person to do that," he explained. "I do work the consoles like the other higher-ranking officers on the ship, but I oversee everything that happens on board."

"So you're really a manager, and everyone else does the work."

"No," he protested. He would have been insulted if it had

been anyone other than her saying it, and the smirk on her face told him she was trying to yank his chain. "I'm usually on the bridge or in my office, which is off the bridge. I know what the crew is up to." He tossed her question back to her. "Why are *you* here?"

"My cabin has too many distractions," she admitted. "Taz and Mora got me into a TV—vidshow," she corrected herself. "*Lightning's Luck*." Rian was familiar with the vidserial, a fluffy drama whose characters spent their time on the titular starship, frequently encountering black holes and engaging in adultery.

"They have me addicted to it, and all I've done in my cabin the last two days is watch archived episodes," she continued. "Mora is having everyone over at her place when the new season starts next month, and I want to be caught up in time."

He was pleased to hear that she was making friends besides Ensign Shraft and finding acceptance among the crew. But then, she was the kind of person people gravitated towards. She was, as he told Nalia, bright and warm with a sense of humor. It was hard not to like her.

Which he did. Very much so.

"Actually, I was worried you might be mad at me," Lily said. "You've been avoiding me since we left the station."

"I haven't been avoiding you," he countered. That would mean he didn't want to see her. He did, he just wasn't sure about doing so.

Rian Marska, acting captain of the *Defiant*, who had graduated at the top of his class and steered a shuttle out of the maw of a vortex as a mere lieutenant, who had become the second youngest executive officer in Fleet's history, was flummoxed in dealing with Lily, pharmacy student and time traveler.

"Lily, I want to see you," he began. She smiled in return.

"But…" Her smile faded. *Damn!* "This is a very unusual situation we're in."

"No shit. Especially my part of it."

"I know." He groped for an explanation. "Which is why I haven't been more… aggressive when it comes to you."

"Rian, what are you saying?" She kept her voice low.

"I like you," he faltered. "A lot." Gods, answering to the admirals over his treatment of her was easier than this.

"I like you, too, so what's the problem?"

His heart flip-flopped. He tried to form an answer that wouldn't give her the wrong idea, but she wasn't finished.

"I know you're worried about me having psychological trauma and a bunch of other issues," she said. "And you would be right. I'm in a new place in a new time and I'm going to be adjusting to that for a while yet." Her voice dropped to a throaty purr—consciously or not, Rian couldn't tell, but it affected him. "But that has nothing to do with the fact that I like you. A lot," she added, echoing his earlier declaration. "And while I'm still learning how this society works, I don't appreciate anyone presuming how I feel or explaining away my feelings with psychobabble." She leaned forward, challenging him.

His mouth went dry, and he cursed his having to go back to the bridge. It took every ounce of his self-control to not take her by the hand and run to his cabin. He tried to form a sentence, ask her what she wanted, but she broke the silence first.

"So where do we go from here?" she asked. "And don't ask me to dinner. The mess doesn't have the same ambiance as that place on Rubidge."

Rian found his voice again. "There's not much else to do on the *Defiant*. We're nowhere near a spaceport or station." If they were, he would have asked her to go climbing. It was an activity he missed.

"What about a vidshow?"

"This ship isn't like newer vessels. We don't have much in the way of entertainment on board. We don't even have a big vid or holoscreen for the mess. The crew would be much more amiable if they could see a zero-g fight occasionally."

"What about your cabin?" she suggested brightly. He felt his eyes widen in amazement, even though he knew he shouldn't be surprised. He knew already that she didn't hesitate to speak her mind, and he liked that about her. "It's homier than mine, otherwise I'd invite you over. I would even cook, but I can't here." She held out her hands innocently. "I'll have to get my hands on a cookbook and learn what people eat these days. I can't believe tomatoes don't exist anymore."

"They probably do, and if not, there's a way to replicate them," Rian explained. He tried to steer their conversation back to the issue at hand. "I'd like to invite you over," he continued carefully. "I'd prefer to do more than that." She tilted her head to the side expectantly, and he caught himself. "Not—well, I'd—oh, damn."

"Please continue," she said smoothly.

"What I mean is, I'd rather do things properly," he said hastily. "I'm a little more traditional that way."

"Usually I am, too, but we're on a spaceship. There's not a lot in the way of date venues."

Rian wasn't very good at relationships, but he desperately wanted to start something with Lily. He also wanted to keep his job, and he knew that Fleet would give him a hard time about that balancing act. "There isn't," he conceded. "But you know the positions we're both in." His voice dropped to just above a whisper, and she leaned closer. She nodded, and he saw the disappointment in her eyes. He wanted to kick himself. His eyes darted around the mess, looking for any eavesdroppers. A few of the crew had noticed he was sitting with her but didn't appear to care. "But we could still see each other here. I know it's not much, but..." He trailed off and held out his hands helplessly. He hated feeling helpless. It frustrated him that he had finally met a woman who fascinated him like no one else had, and she turned out to be from another era and assigned to him for protection. It was just his luck.

"I know, and I know you're not saying any of these things to spare my feelings. It's not like you're trying to let me down gently." She stared at him. "Is it?"

"Gods, no."

"So until everything settles down, we'll keep meeting like this," she confirmed. She sighed again. "This is just like high school all over again. Sitting in the cafeteria studying for an exam and getting distracted by a boy I like."

He felt his eyes widen at the cavalier way she spoke, and an unfamiliar warmth spread through his chest. "You have your first examination soon, don't you?"

"You've been checking up on me," she teased. "It's the day after tomorrow, 1400 hours. Dr. Ashford's proctoring it and transmitting it to Fleet. And tomorrow I have a check-up. Apparently, I need vaccinations."

He nodded. Commons citizens were required to be vaccinated against Coll particles—invisible motes that gave off artificial life support systems and caused a perpetual flu. There was also an immune system booster than encouraged better absorption of nutrients, and a Fleet-mandated immunization against venereal disease. There was also an optional contraceptive implant, and he wondered if she had come across that little piece of information in her studies yet.

The new vaccinations would be helpful should she ever find herself the subject of a mediscan reading. They could make her original immunizations less visible, although he had no idea how Dr. Ashford could disguise her healed ribs and missing appendix. But he wasn't the one with the medical training.

"Vaccinations are a lot less uncomfortable than when you were a kid," he said.

She tapped a datatab. "I've been reading about them. No more syringes. Mostly transdermal delivery now."

At the mention of syringes, Rian felt a faint shudder course through him. She noticed it and shook her head. He glanced at the clock. "I have to get back to the bridge," he said reluctantly.

"No time for a coffee?"

"I just wanted to see you," he replied honestly.

"How did you know where to find me?" He gestured to the comm badge clipped to her collar. "Oh, right."

Rian got up from his seat, and she raised her hand to her temple in a mock salute, a knowing grin across her face. "See you soon, Captain."

———

MORA AND LILY were quickly becoming each other's confidantes. It was nice to have a female ally on a patrol ship whose crew was largely male, and she wasn't much older than Lily, having celebrated her thirtieth birthday a few weeks before they met. She had also started off her Fleet career in the pharmacy after finishing what she described as a useless degree in obscure planetary cultures. She had a broken engagement behind her as well. They had a lot in common.

Mora was administering her vaccinations today. She showed Lily the transdermal sprays, slim tubes that reminded her of her old asthma inhaler, and how the doses were calibrated according to genetic information supplied on the mediscan. "If you're in a hospital, you'll be doing this. Mixing meds is beneath us nurses." She grinned, showing off a perfect white smile. Lily knew it probably put countless patients at ease, especially male ones.

"What are you doing, exactly?"

Mora tried to simplify her explanation, but Lily got lost in the terminology. She caught familiar terms like "body mass" and "estrogen," and nodded.

"Don't worry," Mora assured her. "That shows up later on in your coursework. All you have to do is follow the mediscan's readouts." She held up the first spray and glanced back and forth between it and the mediscan. "Are you almost caught up with *Lightning's Luck*?"

"I watched two episodes last night when I finished studying for my exam. The ship was stuck in a wormhole and Captain Trid was trapped in engineering with the doors sealed."

"Oh, good. You're almost through with the first series, then. Captain Trid's hot, isn't he?"

Lily recalled the blond, muscled captain with telekinetic powers that always failed him at the worst times. "Yeah."

"I wouldn't object to a posting on that ship." She held the spray against Lily's upper arm and depressed its plunger. Lily felt a tiny whoosh of air and her skin cooled as the med solution spread. "Although Captain Marska isn't hard to look at either, even if does act like he has a rod up his ass."

Lily stiffened slightly. A rush of something harsh hit her senses, and it had nothing to do with the immune system booster she had just received. It was... jealousy?

Mora caught it. Mirth danced in her eyes. "Not my type, though," she said smoothly. "He's way too serious. I like men who don't always play by the rules." She tossed the spray into a bin designated Med-Waste. She was watching Lily to gauge her reaction.

She let out a breath she didn't know she was holding. Mora prepped another transdermal spray for the second part of her vaccination. Without looking up, Mora said, "He's yours, though."

What the hell. Lily trusted Mora. "He's not mine," she said carefully, but added, "He's smart and thoughtful."

Mora was ready with the new spray. "I know we haven't known each other long, but I think we're becoming friends, and there's something you need to know. Two things, actually." She positioned the spray in the crook of her left arm, over her pulse point. "First, this one's hot." She activated it and Lily squealed in surprise. It felt like she had held her arm over the steam issuing from a teakettle. "Sorry." Mora had a sheepish look on her face as she dropped the spray in the waste receptacle. "And second," she continued, "I know how to keep a secret, which is good because I'm a nurse and incurably nosy." Her expression grew serious. "What is going on with Captain Marska?"

"Have you been talking to Taz?"

"Occasionally, but everyone talks to Taz. Medical professionals are bound to a confidentiality agreement. I also saw you two at a restaurant on Rubidge. So, tell."

"Rian and I are friends," Lily replied simply.

"*Rian?*" The look on her face was priceless.

"I swear to all the gods everyone here believes in," Lily began, but she was laughing. "Okay, I'm telling you this as your patient. I want it to turn into something more. I'm *hoping* it'll turn out to be something more." She caught Mora's bemused expression. "Please don't tell me there's no chance things could work out. I really like him."

Mora was poking around a cabinet. "Good. He needs to get laid."

"Mora!"

"I'm saying that as a medical professional. Everyone needs to." Her expression darkened for a moment. "Especially me."

"Am I bound to the same confidentiality clause as you?"

"No, but we're friends, and discretion is implied." She removed more small vials and tubes from the cabinet and read the labels, frowning at them.

"Anyway, it's not like that," Lily told her. "We really don't have much choice but to take it slowly."

"You know we're stuck in deep space, right? No one can work every hour of the day and night. Well, except the captain. I guess you have your work cut out for you after all." She turned back to the cabinet and rummaged through it again. "Damn it, I try to keep this organized." To Lily, she said, "Now, I'm giving you the VDI. It's mandatory if you want to work anywhere controlled by Fleet, and most of the Commons planets require it, too. Aha!" She removed a pair of tiny packets and a laser scalpel. "It keeps your bits from turning green and falling off if you pick up the wrong one-night stand."

Lily giggled at her explanation.

"Thanks to dumb soldiers who can't tell the difference between their rifles and guns, we all have to have these." Mora held up a small, flat box studded with tiny holes. "This will administer a local anaesthetic. I'm going to insert the implant under the skin on the back of your hip, and you won't feel a thing. Lay on your side, please."

Lily obediently lay back on the exam table and slid down the waistband of her pants a few inches. "Hey!" said Mora, admiring the tattoo that graced her hipbone. It was three inches wide, a design of green leaves and vines, with delicate pink and blue flowers throughout. "I like that."

"I rebelled during university."

Mora placed the locan just over her hipbone, numbing the skin. Lily deliberately kept her eyes on the exam room's closed door. True to the nurse's word, she didn't feel anything. "It's pretty," Mora said of the tattoo. "A lot nicer than the ones you can get here. The colors are brighter."

"Let me guess—lasers? We use needles where I come from."

"I'd do that if I could get a locan first," Mora said. "That tattoo is worth it. Do you want the contraceptive implant?" She raised her eyebrows in mock-suggestion.

Lily had already read about the common implants and medications in her text and had been amazed at the contraceptive and VD implants, both so much better than what she was used to. They beat condoms for sure. If this was to be her new home... She nodded.

Mora prepped another locan and tiny implant and painlessly inserted it under the skin in her right shoulder. "It has to be changed every four years," she cautioned. "It'll show up on medscans, and a doctor or nurse can tell you when it's time." She picked up her mediscan and flicked it on, hovering it over the length of her body. "Everything looks good," she reported, tapping at the screen. "In a regular check-up, no one will be able to pick up your old vaccines unless they were looking for them. Your appendix and broken ribs are still showing up, but if you find yourself under the care of a doctor who isn't Fleet, just tell them you grew up in the Outer Fringes. Their medicine is pretty primitive compared to what we have in the Commons." She turned off the mediscan. "All set. The new series of *Lightning's Luck* is only a month away. Are you sure you'll be able to get through the next two series by then?"

"Definitely."

"And think about what I said." She winked.

"I am already."

Mora offered her a saucy wink as a goodbye, and Lily smiled.

CHAPTER 11

Lily bit her lip as she surveyed the mess of clothes blanketing her bed. There wasn't much to choose from. She had played it safe in the shops on Rubidge Station, selecting clothes that were the most familiar to her and could blend in anywhere. Half a dozen pairs of unadorned black pants, simple shirts in plain colors, and a few sweaters did not make for an exciting wardrobe. She missed her worn-in jeans and T-shirts from home.

There *was* that black dress Mora had picked out for her, hanging out of an open dresser drawer. Lily had discovered by accident that none of her clothes wrinkled, and had tried to guess what the fabric was before giving up. She had scrunched up a few blouses and stepped on them, left her pants twisted up on the bathroom floor, and hadn't seen as much as a crease. So there was another unexpected perk to living in the future. Her blue linen dress was still crumpled in a ball in the corner of the room. She'd get around to cleaning and pressing it another time, although God knew where she could wear it. Wearing it here would be like wearing overalls to a corporate board meeting. Everyone would know she didn't belong.

She picked up the black dress and held it up, critically eyeing herself in the mirror bolted to the bedroom wall. There was no question that it fit better than anything she had owned, but it wasn't something she could wear around the ship. She didn't even own a bra that would work with such a dress. It was held up with a profusion of thin straps and was cut low in the back. It had taken her almost ten minutes just to try it on and figure out where everything was supposed to go. She sighed and tossed it back in the open drawer.

She fiddled with her hair, making a note to find out where to get it cut as she scrubbed her bangs out of her eyes. She had been planning on getting a haircut in the next day or two when she was still on Earth, and had spent some time on her computer at Lazarus Cryonics looking for a decent stylist in her area. If she could find a pair of scissors on the *Defiant*, she would just trim her bangs herself.

Lily touched up her makeup a little—850 years ahead of her time, and at least she could still get mascara in a tube—and again surveyed herself in the mirror. Aside from the weird seals on her shirt and pants in lieu of buttons and zippers, she looked the same as always.

She couldn't believe how irritated she was at her wardrobe. It should be the least of her concerns after waking up in a spaceship's cargo hold centuries out of her own time, only to find herself a top-secret military project and forced into going back to school, to boot. If anything, the exam she had written that afternoon should be on the forefront of her mind, and it wasn't. Even though she had scored 91% on an exam whose subject matter was dry as chalk, and she hadn't earned an A-plus in anything since her first year of university. The Napoleonic Wars, she recalled wryly. Her knowledge of that era was even less relevant now than it was at home.

Lily had never been very fussy about her appearance; as she had told Rian back on Rubidge Station, she had grown up in the dirt. She put effort into looking presentable, but she hadn't gone through a phase where she had to look like a model leaving the house. She had never dressed to attract male attention specifically, so why was she sighing over a bunch of clothes now? She was especially aggravated with herself because the one man she wanted to notice her already did, and he never seemed to care what she was wearing. All of this worry was for nothing. Still, it would be nice if she could look special for once.

She knew Rian would be off-duty this evening; he had told her during an afternoon coffee break. Lily had asked if she could see the bridge. She wanted to know if it looked like the ones on TV, and then she had to explain again what TV and *Star Trek* were. It turned out that that the modern equivalent involved 3D and holograms in the middle of a living room floor. There were 3D movies, too, but Rian said he preferred the old-fashioned ones on a screen. It was reassuring to know that not everything had changed.

Rian had promised to show her the bridge when it was quiet and he was on duty with a couple of officers he trusted not to go tattling to the higher-ups. "Why would they get upset?" she had asked.

"You don't work on the bridge," he explained. "The admirals tend to get bent out of shape when someone who doesn't work there goes poking around."

"I wouldn't do that," she protested.

"I know you wouldn't, but Fleet doesn't see it that way. I *will* take you, I promise." He'd looked at her over the rim of his coffee cup, the hint of something more than a bridge tour in his eyes.

She wanted to talk to him without the time restriction of a coffee break or curious glances from other crew members. Her comm badge was lying on the nightstand, and she tapped it lightly. "Stewart to Captain Marska."

His voice was crisp and professional. "Captain here. Is everything all right?"

What if she had caught him at a bad time? "Everything's okay," she replied. "I just—are you busy right now?"

"No, I'm in my cabin."

"Oh." She felt a little awkward and berated herself for it. Where else would he be? He had said the *Defiant* didn't have much in the way of entertainment. "Could I see you?" she asked bluntly.

There was a pause. "Of course," he finally said, surprise edging into his voice. "Do you know where the captain's cabin is?"

Oh, dear God, he was inviting her to his apartment. *Cabin*, she corrected herself. "No," she admitted.

"Deck seventeen, cabin one. I'll see you in a few minutes, then?"

She nodded, then remembered he couldn't see her. "I'll be right there."

There was a staircase beside the elevators at the end of the corridor, and she took them, grateful that there wasn't a total reliance on technology these days. Cabin one was directly beside the elevator, and she pressed the small doorbell set into the wall beside the palm pad. The doors slid open and she stepped inside.

Rian was waiting, a look of mild shock on his face. The door closed behind her as she stepped forward. "Hi," she said, damning the breathiness in her voice. This was the first time she hadn't seen him in a Fleet uniform. He wore a dark blue shirt and what looked like this century's version of jeans, well-worn and faded at the knees. Behind him, in the living area, a TV played a news broadcast on low volume.

"Hi," he echoed.

She smelled food in the air, something unfamiliar but good. "I'm sorry," she said. "I didn't know you were having dinner." It was around eight in the evening, she remembered. Not a good time to just drop in. "I should go."

"No," he immediately protested. "I want you to stay." Finally he moved and crossed the room to the small kitchenette. He stirred a pot of something. "There's enough for two, if you want some."

Lily found herself nodding. "Okay," she said. "Can I help with anything?"

He shook his head. "No, you arrived right on time." He gave her a small, conspiratorial smile, and she felt her heart turn over. He set out plates on the table and dug around the fridge. "I think I have a bottle of wine in here," he said. "Do you want a glass?"

"Yes, please."

He produced a pair of glasses and a clear bottle of the same pale blue wine she had had in the mess with Taz. "Sit down," he suggested and pulled out a chair. She obeyed and watched as he spooned a thick stew of meat, vegetables, and rice on the plates. He took the seat across from her and poured the wine.

"You don't use your replicator?" Lily asked.

"Not much," he admitted. "I don't have a big repertoire of recipes, but I can cook a few things."

"I'm a good cook," she told him. "I'll figure out how to when I move." Something flashed in his eyes at the mention of her leaving, but it was gone when he blinked.

He held out his glass in a toast, and she raised hers. "What's this to?" she asked.

He touched the lip of his glass to hers. "To not feeling awkward," he said. "You keep looking around like something's going to spring out and bite you."

She laughed and felt some of the tension ebb away. "It's just different seeing you out of your element," she explained. "In your home."

"It's not what you were expecting?"

"I didn't know what to expect." She looked around the space, not much larger than her own cabin. It was lived-in but tidy. A few framed pictures graced the wall opposite the viewport, and there was a makeshift workspace set up beside the TV stand. A computer screen jutted out from the desktop, like the one in Dr. Ashford's office. A few feet from the TV, there was a couch flanked by end tables bolted to the grey-carpeted floor. An open doorway off the living area led to what Lily guessed was his bedroom. She felt herself flush thinking about it. "I like it," she said finally. "It's a lot homier than mine."

They finished their meal, and she asked him a few questions about him and his career in Fleet. He was thirty-four and had known he wanted to command his own battleship since he could walk. Until Lukas Kostin had been assigned to the *Defiant*, he had held the record for being the youngest executive officer in Fleet history. He and his twin sister were very close, and he laughingly described how she always knew exactly where to find him whenever he was in deep space.

Lily told him about her upbringing and described the Christmas tree farm. She hadn't attended church in years but told him the religious origins of the holiday and what she had gleaned from Dr. Ashford and her datatab's files in how it was now observed on Earth. "It doesn't seem as commercial as it used to be," she explained. "It's more about the family and food, like it should be."

When they finished, Rian stacked their plates in a wall-mounted dishwasher. He explained the complicated process of their cleaning and sterilization with particle light, and she tried to understand. It still beat washing dishes by hand, and she told him so.

Rian hovered by the TV. "Do you want to see a vidshow?" he asked. "I downloaded a few, and I haven't made any time to see them."

"Sure. You like scary ones, right?"

"I do." He pressed a few buttons on the console, and they took seats on the couch. He was hardly two fingers' width away from her, and she was very aware of his presence. This was the first time they had truly been alone. The attraction she felt between them had grown into an electric current, keeping her pulse high and catching her breath in her throat. She chanced a glance at him as he brought the half-full wine glass to his lips. He was *gorgeous*. She swallowed. He caught her looking at him and smiled, setting the glass on the nearest end table. He leaned back on the couch and slid an arm around her, drawing her closer to him.

Lily sank against him. Her senses were on high alert, and she felt every intake of breath, smelled the soap he used, and underneath it, *him*. His hand rested on the curve of her hip; his breath lightly ruffled her hair. Immediately her body responded, and her body tightened in anticipation. She wanted his hands everywhere.

As if he could read her mind, Rian's fingers edged under the hem of her blouse until they rested on her skin. She gasped audibly. It was maddening—who would think that a light touch could have such an effect? His hand crept across her hip to caress her abdomen, and she bit back a moan. He had made no other advances to her, and she had to fight herself from climbing into his lap.

Shouldn't she?

She turned her attention back to the TV. A science team was excavating an uninhabited planet that was supposed to be cursed and had uncovered a gigantic scaly alien, motionless in green sand. One of the scientists leaned over it, exactly the way someone shouldn't do in a movie, and the alien opened yellow eyes and snapped its jaws at the scientist, latching its fangs into his skull.

Lily started a little; Rian's arm tightened around her and

he laughed softly in her ear, sending a shiver through her that had nothing to with aliens playing possum.

"Now you see why I picked this vid," he murmured, and she felt his lips graze the skin below her ear.

Now they were getting somewhere. That small kiss set off something in her that she didn't know existed, and she turned to face him. He looked caged, like he was ready to jump at her if given half a chance. Lily wanted him to.

"You really don't know the effect you have on me," he said softly.

Her breath caught. He reached for her again, pulling him to her until she was almost in his lap. "Tell me," she whispered.

He held her head in his hands and brought her face down in a slow kiss. "You're all I can think about," he murmured against her mouth. "I don't care about what the crew complains about; I don't think about how much I want to get off this ship." He kissed a slow line across her throat. "All I can think about is your smile, and how we can talk about anything." His fingers slid down her back and dipped into the waistband of her pants. She gasped. She wanted him to touch her without the restriction of clothing.

"So you've found a new friend," she tried to tease. She adjusted herself until she was straddling him. She could feel his erection through their clothes, and it sent a primal thrill through her.

"I don't think about doing things in my office with my friends that would get me demoted," he corrected.

A surge of heat shot through her at that admission. "You think about that?" she breathed.

"I think about a lot of things where you're concerned." His hands found the fastening on her blouse and he slowly unsealed it, revealing the plain black bra beneath. He pressed his lips against her collarbone. "I don't think about..." He trailed off, as though he were about to let something slip that he shouldn't. Instead his hands crept lazily up her torso to softly cup her breasts, her nipples beading into his palms through the fabric of her bra. She arched into his hands, wanting more, but he slid them back down her body and over her hips, slightly pushing down the waistband of her pants. He noticed the flower tattoo on her hip and ran his fingers over it. "I like this," he said. "It's sexy." His blue eyes caught hers, full of uncharacteristic mischief.

Lily had regretted getting inked within a year, but Rian's reaction made her glad she hadn't had it removed. Her hands slid over his chest and shoulders, feeling the expanse of slim muscles beneath the fabric of his shirt. She slipped her hands under the hem, and his breath constricted as her fingers touched his skin.

He kissed her fiercely, a harsh, possessive clash of lips and tongues, and she impatiently shrugged out of her blouse. She tried to pull up his shirt, but his hands lightly clasped her wrists, stilling her.

An exaggerated, high-pitched roar blared from the TV. Lily couldn't help but giggle.

"And that just reinforces it," Rian muttered. He released her wrists and his arms circled her waist. "I hadn't planned on doing this on my couch," he confessed.

"No, you were thinking about your office," she pointed out, a wicked grin spreading across her face. He lightly nipped her earlobe, and she squealed in response.

"It would be difficult to get there without anyone notic-ing," he admitted. He slowly kissed a trail down her neck to her throat. "My bedroom's a lot closer."

Their lips met again, but Lily pulled away and stood up. "Race you," she teased, and bolted.

The open door beckoned to her, and its dim illumination was as bright to her as the proverbial light at the end of a tunnel. She barely made it through to the doorway before he hauled her against him, her backside pressed against his front. His breath tickled her ear. "I think I won," he said, and his fingers brushed against her abdomen. She unsuccessfully bit back a giggle.

"I'm ticklish!" she protested.

His touch immediately shifted to a light caress. "It would kill the mood if I had you in hysterics, wouldn't it?" he asked. His hands moved to tease her nipples through her bra.

"Anyway, I call a tie," she gasped.

His teeth grazed the back of her neck. "Are we really going to argue about this?" Before she could answer, he turned her around so she faced him, and looped his arms around her waist. His mouth descended on hers, and he reached for the seal on her bra.

"Wait," she chastised him.

His hands stilled, and he looked at her like she had lost her mind.

She felt like a dolt for having to ask this, completely ignorant of the protocol. "Um, I have my VD and birth control implants," she said.

"Uh-huh," Rian said, and reached for her bra's seal again. Catching the look on her face, his hands froze at her back and he asked, "Is that a problem?"

"I just wanted to let you know. So you don't have to...worry about anything."

"If you didn't, I do." His fingers found the seal again.

"One more thing." The frustrated look on his face would have been priceless if Lily wasn't feeling the same herself. "It's not fair that I'm already half-naked and you're not," she complained.

"You're not half-naked," he protested. "But you would be if I took this off." He slid a bra strap down her shoulder.

She took a handful of his shirt and lifted it. He helped her and stripped it off, shucking it to the floor. He stood before her, lean-muscled, his blue eyes boring into her. There was a small round scar on his left shoulder that had to have been a deep gash at one point. She touched it gingerly. "How did you get that?"

"Civil war on Naa'natcha when I was an ensign," he replied. "Fleet stepped in. Enemy laser rifle was set to stun."

She stood up on her toes and kissed it. He reached around her back and with a muffled curse against her hair finally unsealed her bra, tossing it to the floor. She grinned against his shoulder, let her hands creep down his abdomen, and unsealed his pants. Her fingers slid into them and grazed his erection, and a low moan sounded from his throat. He tilted up her face and his mouth crushed hers, tongues tangling as he guided her towards the bed.

She lay down as Rian kneeled over her, his lips moving over her throat and collarbone before finding one taut nipple. He eagerly took it in his mouth, and Lily's breath caught as he caressed it and then the other. She felt his hands unfasten her pants, and she lifted her hips slightly as he slid them down her legs. He raised his head, and his eyes looked over her now-naked body. Any self-consciousness she felt at being so exposed evaporated when she took in his appreciative gaze.

His head dipped further south, and his tongue found the aching spot between her legs. Her hands fisted in his hair as he explored her, setting off tiny electric sparks through her body. She felt the first wave of climax and her breath came in irregular pants. His tongue delved further into her and she moaned. He raised his head. "I don't want you to stop!" she insisted.

"I'm not," he said.

"Rian, this is *not* the time to let your sense of humor show," she muttered. He slid a finger into her, then two, stretching her. "I'll take that as an—" She gasped harshly. "An apology."

She groaned in disappointment when he withdrew his fingers from her, then watched as he pushed off his pants. He positioned his body atop hers, propping himself up on his elbows. His knee nudged her thighs further apart; his kisses became more urgent. The head of his cock nudged against her, and she gripped his shoulders in anticipation before he thrust into her. The feeling of connection and completion was so gratifying that she cried out.

He stroked her hair, concern across his features. "Are you okay?" he whispered.

She kissed him in reply. "Better than okay."

One hand slipped beneath her hips, lifting her up as he began to move with an agonizing slowness that left her on edge. Before she could plead with him, he increased his pace, thrusting into her more forcefully. She wrapped her legs around him as he stroked deeper into her, bringing her closer again. She felt the tension in his body as he fought for his own control.

She lost hers first, crying out as her orgasm finally racked her body. His rhythm sped up, intensifying and prolonging her climax even as his body went rigid with its own. He sagged against her, burying his face in her neck and tightening his arms around her. For a moment they breathed in sync, then he rolled over and took her with him. His thumb gently pressed against her lips before he kissed her. Wordlessly, their gazes caught each other's. There was an unexpected tenderness in his eyes, a look that warmed her heart.

———

RIAN HAD PULLED the blanket over them, and he lay with Lily snuggled against his chest. Her eyes were closed, but his years in the military told him she wasn't really asleep. He had had to catch more catnaps than he could remember for him to recognize the signs of deep sleep. She stirred a little, and his arms curled around her instinctively.

He was in deep shit. Not just professionally, although the Fleet higher-ups would roll over if they knew what he had done. No, this was personal. Fleet he could handle; despite their presumption that Lily was some kind of helpless, backwards idiot and victim, he couldn't be court-martialed for having a relationship with someone under his command. If that was the case, two-thirds of Fleet's captains and all of the admirals would have been tossed out on their asses. A life in the Commons Fleet meant near-total devotion to it. Officers usually gravitated towards partners who understood those obligations.

When this got out, and he was almost certain it would no matter how discreet they were, he and Lily would never stop being the objects of scrutiny. He knew there had been whispers going around the ship since they started sharing meals and coffee breaks. The *Defiant* was a patrol ship often in sleepy parts of space, and there was lots of time to gossip.

He had already broken his own rule about not getting involved with someone on his ship. But she wouldn't be here for long, he remembered sadly. She was going to finish her pharmacy course shortly, then leave for practical training at Kevnar Station before being assigned to a clinic. And she would be gone.

That thought discomfited him more than breaking his own rules. That was why he was in deep shit. He didn't want to let her go. Lily—on some station or, Gods forbid, a well-equipped battleship—in *danger*, having to pretend to be someone she wasn't, stuck in yet another unfamiliar place with more daunting technology. He didn't want that to happen. He wanted to keep her with him for as long as he could.

He lightly stroked her hair, loose and spread over her shoulders. Her eyes blinked open and she leaned, away into the pillow, and propped herself up on her side. She had a satisfied smile on her face, and she stretched. The sheet slipped down, and Rian's heart sped up a little at the sight of her. He reached for her and ran his hands over the curve of her breasts, her neck, to cup her face. Her hands moved to caress his back and she kissed him, and *gods*, could the woman kiss.

He could never get enough of her. He knew that now, and that scared the hell out of him more than anything.

———

His alarm trilled at 0600 hours and the bedroom illumination eased on. He kissed Lily's shoulder and neck until she stirred. She rolled over to face him, a smile spreading across her face. He knew there was one on his, too.

He had to start his rounds in an hour fifteen, but that thought slipped from his mind as his hands took on a mind of their own and pulled her to him. It was Lily who remembered and reluctantly pulled away. "I could go for another repeat," she murmured.

So could he, and he told her so. Their second time had occurred a bare five hours earlier, when they had woken up in the middle of the night unable to get back to sleep.

"But you have to be at work soon," she lamented. "And I have to read up on Fleet medical ethics. I scheduled another test three days from now."

"I'd rather stay in bed with you," he said, but he reluctantly got out and reached for his bathrobe, draped over the bedpost. He left Lily in bed as he headed for the shower, turning back in the doorway to look back at her. The sight of her—come-hither look on her face, hair tousled, one bare leg peeking out from the sheet—nearly did him in. A frisson of need shot through his body, but he didn't have time to indulge it properly.

"If you look at me like that, I'll never make it to the bridge."

She sighed dramatically. "I'll replicate some breakfast, then." She tossed off the blankets and stood up. She caught his wide-eyed stare and pulled a sheet off the bed and wrapped it around herself. "Go shower. I'll have coffee ready when you get out."

He grabbed her around the waist and led her to the bathroom. "I'll have coffee in my office."

CHAPTER 12

Lily didn't just have a very boring module on ethics to study back in her cabin. She could tackle that in a few hours. She had also been combing through the volumes of data she and Rian had downloaded at the Rubidge Station library, and she had stumbled across a tiny file buried in with some other historical texts on Earth. These ones were standard in what must be the modern equivalent of master's programs in Milky Way ancient history, a subject no one in Fleet ever studied. She dug into the file's subdirectories and came across some short video clips from the twenty-first and twenty-second centuries.

Wonder of wonders, there was an eight-minute segment from Toronto's local news, detailing the explosion of a cryonics lab in northwest Toronto and the disappearances of its two doctors and receptionist. It added to another layer of mystery surrounding the pair of decomposed bodies found in the Humber River a few weeks before, which had just been identified as James Richards and Graham Kent, identified using DNA from relatives. The syringes that had been stabbed into their necks had held an unidentified toxic substance that corroded the police department's forensic unit's equipment, and the homicide unit was baffled. Richards and Kent had been the lease holders of the lab, and Lily now saw how Zadbac and Pitro had taken hold of the property.

The inferno had occurred moments after Lily was abducted. It had leveled the industrial park, a bus shelter in front of the building, and damaged a condo development that was under construction. Not a trace of human DNA had been found in the vicinity of the industrial park. It was mentioned that the daughter of "noted" science fiction and horror author Daniel Stewart was the lab's receptionist and hadn't been accounted for, with police doubtful that she survived the blast. Local music entrepreneur Andrew Claybourne had had an appointment scheduled that afternoon and was likewise unaccounted for. The cause of the explosion was unknown.

The clip was used as an educational tool to illustrate the limitations of Earth's science in investigation and the sensationalism used in journalism; it was included in a text by a current researcher on Earth's ancient culture. Lily felt her chest constrict watching the clip a second time and seeing Wilson Avenue choked with black smoke and flames. *They probably never found out the cause of the explosion*, she thought sadly. Zadbac and Pitro must have used something from their time. It was the sole piece of information she had found detailing her disappearance, and instead of relief, she felt sick.

She dug further into the datatab's files. Surely an explosion of that magnitude had made international headlines. There had to be something from the CBC or the *New York Times*. But there wasn't. It was just that little news clip from a Toronto TV station.

She sighed and set the datatab aside. Her mind wandered to Rian and last night, and with that, a twinge of guilt when her spirits picked up. In the morning, she thought Rian might have gone back into his professional captain mode and dismissed the night together as a mistake, but he hadn't had an attack of misplaced conscience in the morning. She wanted to see that side of Rian again, and had no doubt she would. Even though she was unsure what to call their relationship now. It was a very bright spot in this upheaval.

She picked up the datatab again. She had more research to do. She and Rian weren't going anywhere away from this ship.

She opened a file on the Nym. A highly intelligent alien race of sociopaths, one of many in space but the only ones close to the Commons and the Kurran Empire. Many had low-level empathic talents, making her think of Taz's story. The Nym's devotion to science and technology and their pursuit of power was legendary and far surpassed any other culture in space. They were a fairly small group, usually keeping to themselves on their home planet outside the Fringes between trying to invade one world or another every few years. They had tried to annex several quadrants over the centuries with varying levels of success, defeated only because they were outnumbered. They were rumored to keep their population at less than twenty-five thousand, killing infants deemed imperfect and adults when they reached old age. One document claimed that they had auto-destruct chips implanted into their bodies. Another said they simply took a lethal overdose at the appropriate age. But since none of them had ever been successfully captured and interrogated by a Commons or Kurran authority, no one knew for sure.

Their world was protected by a treacherous asteroid belt, reinforced with a Nym-designed force field that could incinerate even the most intrepid of battleships. Outside intelligence was conducted safely out of the Nym atmosphere, and random pieces of data collected. The Nym had been strangely quiet for several years now, which Lily knew worried some of Fleet. They weren't a people known for simply minding their own business, like most of the worlds in the Fringes. If they weren't regularly monitored, one might assume that they had simply died off. That happened in the Fringes sometimes; planets could destabilize and stop supporting life. It was a downside that made living in Commons space more attractive.

Unstable planets... that was something. Lily's fingers scrolled through her datatab and came up with a short list of planets known for instability, whether it was changing air quality or rotation or a whole list of five-dollar words she couldn't make out. Vu'saar, Taz's home planet, was on the list. Irregular changes to the atmosphere caused mutations in its inhabitants, often resulting in telepathy. She remembered his story in the mess. Vu'saarns considered non-telepathic offspring to be second-class citizens, even when they were born into their nobility, like he and his ex-wife were. His home planet and his lack of telepathy were clearly a touchy subject for Taz, so she wouldn't ask him about it. Rian would probably know more about the planets in the Fringes, anyway.

Rian. She had stayed behind in his cabin in the morning, waiting for the shift change to take place before she darted back to her own room without anyone seeing her. Rian had been apologetic, but Lily had understood. Right now wouldn't be a good time to make their relationship public, if that's what they had. Thank God she had forgotten her comm badge in her cabin. The crew would never let Rian live that down if someone looked up their locations.

She closed the files on the datatab and reviewed her notes for her upcoming test, again to be proctored by Dr. Ashford, but she couldn't concentrate. She finally set aside her datatabs and turned on the TV. She had two episodes of *Lightning's Luck* to get through before the new season started. She had taken a coffee break with Mora and a couple of her counterparts in engineering late in the morning, who told her about the speculations and hype surrounding the season premiere.

The show was a nice diversion from her current situation,

despite Mora's friends, who scoffed at the impossible story-lines and technology. "You mean warp drive doesn't exist?" Lily had asked.

One of them had gone into a long, detailed technical speech detailing the need to get a ship into hyperspace to achieve the level of speed the show's namesake reached. Lily took his word for it and joined Mora in mocking them for watching it, too.

Ten minutes into the episode, as the shirtless captain of *Lightning's Luck* fought what looked like a giant Gila monster using a couple of twigs, her comm badge beeped from its spot on the coffee table. "Captain to Stewart."

She paused the TV and picked it up. "Stewart here." He sounded crisp and professional, so she tried to as well. Still, her heart leapt a little at the sound of voice. "What can I do for you, Captain?"

He gave a low, throaty laugh that made her shiver. "I can think of a few things," he murmured. "But coffee right now would be good. I have to talk to you."

She had come back from a break with Mora not two hours ago, but this was Rian. She was going to take seeing him wherever she could. "Five minutes," she said, breathiness creeping into her voice.

"I'll see you there."

She turned off the TV and clipped her comm badge to the collar of her blouse. She checked her hair in the mirror and gathered her datatabs before leaving her cabin.

He was waiting for her, sitting at their usual table. There were a couple of crew members milling about, and they raised eyebrows at the sight of them together again. Lily ignored them and took her seat. Rian kept his hands firmly around his coffee cup, and Lily's gaze flicked between him and the starfield out the window.

"It's good to see you," he said softly. He looked up, and

the look on his face made Lily's breath catch. "But I have some bad news. Unrelated to *that*," he added quickly.

"What is it?" Lily asked, alarmed.

"We received word of Nym activity just outside the Commons borders. One of their ships was spotted, and a patrol ship followed it."

"And?" Lily leaned forward.

"It disappeared."

"Maybe it's just faster than the patrol ships. Everyone says that Nym technology is eons ahead of yours."

"No, *Bishop's Pride* caught up to it, and it just evaporated," he said tersely. "The captain and her crew saw it happen, and then their sensors confirmed it. It shimmered, she said, and then it was gone. There are no hypergates there, or vortex activity. It's just empty space, not even any habitable planets."

"I don't know what a hypergate is."

"Nature's way of letting a ship into hyperspace," he clarified. "Energy currents. We can force our way into it on a patrol ship with hyperspace engines, but smaller crafts, like freighters and passenger transports, use them if they don't have that kind of equipment. It lets a vessel move faster through space."

Lily nodded. "Could the Nym ship have imploded? Or maybe a hull breach?" She had read up on the dangers of space travel and couldn't help but notice the lack of oxygen masks available in an emergency. Not that they would do much good in the event of a hull breach.

Rian's upraised eyebrow told her he noticed her research, then he shook his head. "Ships don't simply implode without warning. The *Pride*'s sensors would have picked that up. A ship blown to pieces would leave debris behind, anyway."

"Cloaking device? Even the *Defiant* has one of those..."

"The *Defiant*'s cloaking device is rudimentary at best, and I'll be first to admit that. This isn't a battleship. The *Pride* fired on the exact coordinates of the Nym ship. A cloaked one could still be fired upon. But the torpedo just sailed through the space where it was."

Lily racked her brain, trying to recall her father's books and what she understood about modern space travel.

"Fleet intel can't explain it," Rian said finally. "The Nym know something that we don't, and we can't figure it out."

Fear sliced through Lily. "Could they actually be in the Commons and you don't know about it?"

The look on Rian's face made her hands shake around her cup. "That's a possibility," he said. "Fleet wanted to take you into protective custody. I've spent the last hour and a half in vidconference with a few admirals, including Kentz. Half want you in custody, half want you here. The Nym activity aside, we don't know if they know you've even been found. They're very reclusive." He held up a finger, halting her next question. "We have excellent safeguards in place, Lily, I promise. If we didn't, they would have invaded and annexed the Commons years ago. Our security is as good as theirs. They've never broken into our classified information, which includes you, nor have they invaded a station."

"But everyone on this ship knows who I am!"

"And only this ship. That was inevitable. But everyone in Fleet is held to high degrees of confidentiality. When someone is posted to a ship or station, they aren't at liberty to discuss secrets about their previous missions. That rule is strictly enforced."

"You sound so sure no one breaks them," she argued. "Taz told me about killing zombies once." *Damn.* She hadn't intended to let that slip out.

Rian shrugged. "Lethal autoimmune toxin on Corlon. It's common knowledge. I was there, too. Half of Fleet was. But I guarantee no one on this ship has ever talked about classified missions, to you or with each other. Fleet has a mind-wipe protocol in place to discourage that."

"What?" Lily dropped her cup. It smacked against the tabletop, and a few drops of coffee sloshed out the sides.

"You haven't gotten that far in your course, then. It's well-known. That kind of insubordination results in a mind-wipe. Memories of whatever shouldn't be talked about are erased," he explained patiently.

"That's barbaric!"

"Possibly, but it's an effective deterrent, one that hasn't needed to be utilized in years. People respect the Fleet, Lily. And it's the most drastic punishment we have. Commonwealth space doesn't sanction the death penalty."

"Then how did the media know I was on the *Defiant*?" she countered.

"Well, technically, they didn't, although that mystery's been mostly solved. All the media could make out was a rumor that someone on an unnamed ship was found buried alive in a pile of museum artifacts. That bit of information made it to Rubidge Station and was spread—we're still unsure as to who let it leak. The newshounds picked it up and embellished on it. Unfortunately, they got it right. None of the legitimate news sources ran that story. We checked the tabloid vids, and Fleet's been keeping an eye on the stories. One of Rubidge's broadcasters made up an interview with the time traveler that was an obvious fake, and it died down."

Lily sighed. "You have an answer for everything."

"Not the Nym dilemma yet." He gave her a small smile that was probably meant to be reassuring, but it seemed strained and forced.

Lily was still thinking about what the media knew. "But the newsvids guessed things a little too accurately for it to be just a coincidence," she pressed. "Are you sure no onboard has blabbed?" Catching Rian's sharp intake of breath, she added, "Don't lie to me."

He closed his eyes briefly. "You're right. We *have* noticed that the original story is a little too close to the truth. But you don't know the tabloids and what they come up with."

"You didn't invent tabloids. Ours were making up stories about Bat Boy and Elvis sightings in truck stops long before I woke up in a coffin." Rian raised an eyebrow in confusion, and she sighed again. "Never mind. The point is, newspapers have been making stuff up to sell more copies for thousands of years. Someone snitched, Rian."

"It's a possibility."

"And it wasn't Taz," Lily added.

"Ensign Shraft didn't do it. Neither did your friend Mora Kharn. We checked their transmits and comp activity already. They were the first suspects, and neither of them fit the profile of a traitor to begin with. Shraft has the Fleet, and only the Fleet, in his life."

Lily nodded. Taz had too much to lose.

"Nurse Kharn's father is an admiral," he continued. "A mind-wipe would be the least of her worries if she betrayed us."

"What about Ashford?" she asked. Her gut recoiled at the thought, and she instantly regretted the suggestion. The doctor was one of the kindest people she had ever met, and fiercely loyal to Fleet.

"He has too much to lose, too. This is his last posting before he retires on a full pension, and he doesn't fit the psych profile, either."

"Steg?" The security chief was not a fan of Lily or Rian.

Rian shook his head. "Grigha Steg has seen everything in his career, and you're one more unusual occurrence." He leaned back in his chair. "Believe me, Fleet has looked at the profiles of everyone on this ship and examined every piece of communication, including mine. Nothing fits with the Nym."

"You're missing something," Lily said sharply. "Who's to say that someone here doesn't have, I don't know, a two-way radio that acts independently from your ship? One that links directly to the Nym?"

"We already considered that."

"Of course you have." Lily knew she sounded petulant, but she *knew* she was right. They were missing something. She stewed in silence for a couple of minutes, sipping at lukewarm coffee.

"We did a check of energy emissions," he explained. "All devices leave a detectable trail, I guess you would call it, after they've been used. If you use a computer to send a transmit to a friend on Rubidge Station, for instance, and you turn off the computer, its use can be verified by an emissions detector. Devices emit them, like an odor."

Like a wi-fi hotspot at home. Lily nodded. "And nothing out of the ordinary has been detected."

"No." Frustration crossed his face as he ran a hand through his hair. "The odds aren't great, but right now the only reliable hypothesis is the media guessed too closely."

"Fleet's questioned reporters?"

"Of course not. This thing is finally dying down. That ridiculous vid serial is starting a new series soon, and they're all over that."

Lily was grateful for the change in topic, a subject that kept going in circles. "You mean *Lightning's Luck*? You watch it then?" She tried to keep her tone light.

"Don't tell me the crew has you drooling over that excuse for a captain, too," he muttered. "In real life, getting stuck in hyperspace can kill you."

"I only drool over one captain," she said. At his bemused expression, she added, "Well, not drool. But you get the point."

"Noted and appreciated."

"Wait a minute," Lily said. "You mentioned the episode where Captain Trid and the ship got stuck in hyperspace. It was when the engines failed and he ended up having end-of-the-world sex with the navigator in his office."

Was Rian *blushing*? "You watch it, too!" she crowed.

"I've watched a few episodes when I felt like turning off my brain for a half-hour."

"I bet you watch it for the same reason all the other guys do."

"To criticize its inaccuracy?"

"No, for First Officer Kila Devo," Lily teased. The half-Kurran actress was tall, with light greenish-blonde hair, and her uniform highlighted her best assets, which weren't her acting abilities.

"She wouldn't make it past basic training. She can't even hold a laser rife properly. She'd put a charge through her foot in real life."

His comm badge pinged, interrupting him, and a disembodied voice said, "Rikk to Marska."

Rian tapped it. "Captain here."

"The transmit sensor modifications have been completed, if you want to check them out."

"Be there in five." He tapped the off the badge and stood. "I'd like to kiss you goodbye, but..." He gestured around the mess.

"I know," said Lily. "What time are you off-duty? You could kiss me then." She rose to her feet, too.

"Twenty-one hundred hours."

"Your place or mine?"

The teasing tone evaporated from his voice. "Mine. I have to have my comm badge with me all the time, and if I'm in yours—well, you know." He looked at her apologetically.

"I do." She touched her fingertip to his sleeve. "See you tonight."

CHAPTER 13

R ian left the bridge promptly at 2100 hours, to the surprise of his crew. He returned to his cabin and had changed into his civvies when his computer screen blinked an incoming message. He checked the transmit address: Nalia. *Of course.* His sister swore up and down that she could sense his whereabouts, and she was right more often than not. He also knew she would keep transmitting until he answered.

He pressed the accept tab, and Nalia's face filled the screen. "Make it quick," he said by way of greeting. "I have company coming."

"Hello to you, too. Who's the company?"

"A friend."

"Oh, the ladyfriend. Well, well, well." She grinned triumphantly.

"Don't you have a husband to pester?"

"I do, and he's watching the fight in the lounge with his brother."

Rian knew there was some kind of zero-g boxing match happening. He'd heard a few crew members arranging a viewing in someone's cabin. "Uh-huh," he said. He left the transmitter and went to his kitchen, where he found last night's half-full bottle of wine.

"Where did you go?" He heard the irritation in Nalia's voice.

He returned to the screen. "Getting supplies for my company."

"What's her name again? Just tell me truth, and promise you'll sit down for a proper talk in the next couple of days."

"Lily, and yes, she's coming over. And I have a lot of work to do and some other issues have cropped up, as they tend to in the military. But I *promise* we'll get caught up very soon."

"So you're still seeing her?"

Gods help him. Rian could have told his sister that the Nym's lasers were slicing through the *Defiant*'s hull right now and his personal life would still be at the forefront of her mind. "Yes, and I hope to continue to," he said finally. Knowing that answer wouldn't placate Nalia, he told her the truth. She'd guess, anyway. "I can see this being serious," he admitted. He hoped it would be.

But he wanted it to continue. Lily was smart, inquisitive, and cared about him and Fleet. She was understanding of their situation, but didn't mind—at least thus far. An image popped into his mind: stepping down to commander and settling on a station as an executive officer to an admiral or senior captain. He had been offered that before accepting acting captaincy on the *Defiant*. He could have Lily with him, and she could work in the station's clinic. No one would know exactly who she was, and they could share an apartment and take furlough together and be a real couple. He had never thought of anyone in those terms before.

Nalia was staring at him. "You just completely zoned out there for a few minutes. You've got it *bad*."

"Just thinking," he said. "And probably getting ahead of myself." Definitely getting ahead of himself.

There was a chime at the door. "She's here," Rian said. His fingers hovered over the disconnect tab. "I have to go."

"Can I meet her?"

"Another time."

She pouted with childish gusto but waved. "Have fun."

Rian groaned and ended the transmit. "Enter," he said, and the cabin door opened. Lily walked in, in her usual black pants and blouse, dark pink this evening. He kissed her in greeting and palmed the lock on the door.

"I got my exam results back," she said excitedly. "Ninety-four percent. Only three more to go."

A tiny shard of pain sliced through Rian. Only three more exams for her to write before she left him. He pushed that thought away. Whatever he had with Lily wasn't a military operation. He wasn't even sure if he had the right to ask her about how he fit into her plans.

Too soon. He didn't want to frighten her off. There had been too much upheaval in her life already, with more to come.

"Besides all your conferences, what happened today?" she asked. "Some security grunts were talking about a smuggler being picked up."

"Not a smuggler," Rian corrected. "Just a freight ship with illegal weaponry and communications upgrades that showed up on our sensors. That indicates potential criminal activity, but they didn't have any cargo or known criminals aboard."

"So what happened?"

"Their modifications were disabled and their illegal torpedoes confiscated. We fined them, too, and now we have their ship on our watch list." He shrugged. "It wasn't a big deal." He poured two glasses of wine and held one out to her.

She tasted it. "So not a lot happens here, then." She sounded disappointed.

"That's a good thing, Lily," he pointed out.

"I'm on a spaceship for the first time. I was hoping there would be more action." She barked out a short laugh. "I mean, seeing aliens besides the Nym."

"There aren't a lot of non-humanoids in Commons or Kurran space. If we were on a battleship closer to the Sorkan border, maybe. Sorkans are tall and scaly."

Lily waited for an explanation. "The Sorkans have been pissed off at the Commons for years. Border dispute. It's a long story, but they don't invade our space, they just take shots at any ship that shows up on their sensors. Patrols along that border use battleships just in case. I spent some time on one when I was a lieutenant."

"And?" She sat on one of the chairs around the kitchen island and leaned forward expectantly.

"And nothing. The shields deflect their cannons and we don't fire back. They do it just to remind us they're there." He sat down next to her and changed the subject. "We're docking at Kevnar Station in fourteen days, after we drop off the science team."

"What's at Kevnar?"

"Fuel and fresh water, and we're swapping a few officers. Not Steg, unfortunately." He was babbling. When the hell had he turned back into an awkward adolescent?

She caught it and was looking at him like she knew something. He reached for her, fighting his impulse to crush his mouth against hers and drag her off to the bedroom like an animal. But there wasn't a scary vid playing, just the two of them in his kitchen. He was out of ideas.

She framed his face with her hands, a small smile quirking her lips. She leaned up and kissed him gently, no more than a light brush of her lips against his, and that did him in. His arms locked around her waist and pulled her off the stool as he stood up.

He knew he was in trouble, that Lily was trouble. She was

becoming an addiction, someone he could never get enough of.

She arched into him as he kissed her neck, her breath hot in his ear, urging him on. His hands slid under her shirt and drifted over the bare skin of her lower back.

An alarm wailed through his cabin, and the lights began flashing red. He let her go abruptly. "Shit!" he yelled.

"What's happening?" she shouted over the noise.

"Red alert. I have to get to the bridge." He saw fear in her eyes and, despite the din around him, a corresponding ache at the sight of her.

His comm badge trilled at his collar, and his first officer's voice sounded. "Kostin to captain!"

He slapped at it and strode for the door of his cabin, Lily behind him. "Marska here."

"Get on the bridge!" Rian could hardly make out the commander's voice over the alarm's blare.

"Status?" He rushed into the corridor and saw a few other off-duty officers heading for the lift.

"Unfriendlies." The officer's next words were muffled as Rian ran under a screaming speaker for the lift. The lights along the corridor flashed the same ominous red as the ones in his cabin. Lily ran alongside him, and he grabbed her hand and pulled her into the lift. More red lights, but the alarm was marginally quieter.

"What is it, godsdamnit?"

"Nym!" Kostin repeated.

Damnation. What the hell was a Nym ship doing there? Blood pounded in his ears, and his stomach turned over.

Were they looking for Lily? Had they figured out she was aboard a patrol ship? He gripped her hand tighter, not caring about the other crew around them. They were barking into their own comm sets.

The doors opened at the bridge. His office was off it, down

a small corridor. "Go," he ordered, and pointed to it. She obeyed and took off.

Commander Kostin, on bridge duty for the night, moved over at the command console. The enhanced viewport at the front of the ship showed a distant outline of a sleek rectangular box of a ship gliding straight for them. He didn't need to check their coordinates to see that.

Rian took the helm. "How far out are they?"

"Eleven minutes, sir," replied the commander.

"Why wasn't an alarm raised when they showed up on the long-distance sensors?"

"They didn't. We didn't pick up anything until they were fifteen minutes out."

"Six minutes," said a voice from behind them.

Rian could see that, and their increase in speed actually scared him.

"Advisory's already been sent out," Kostin said. "*Bishop's Pride* is twenty-nine minutes out, going at top speed." Rian knew Captain Jena would be double-timing her ship to make it in time, but he wasn't going to count on their help.

So the *Defiant* was on her own. "Shields," Rian barked and pulled up their status as someone yelled across the bridge.

"Shields at one hundred percent," Kostin confirmed.

Rian pulled up the weapons array and saw that Kostin already had the torpedoes primed and ready to fire. The sensors told him that the enemy ship's weapons were inactive, but he didn't trust that. A green light flashed in the corner of the console. They were hailing the *Defiant*.

The Nym never did that. They didn't explain or negotiate.

Everyone else had picked that up, too. "Sir?" Kostin asked.

"Open our link," Rian ordered.

"Are you sure? This could be a trap."

"They can see our torpedoes are ready. Open the link, Commander."

Kostin gulped but did so. Another beep on the console indicated that *Bishop's Pride* was now twenty-two minutes out. They would never make it in time.

Terror flowed through Rian, but he kept himself steady. The viewport's image changed from a rapidly-growing ship in deep space to the Nym, standing on its bridge. There was a group of them, all with deep-set black or green eyes, bulgy heads, wearing grey coveralls topped with black coats.

"Commons," barked one, showing its jagged teeth. Its accent was thick and nearly indecipherable. "Patrol ship. You are captain?"

"I am," said Rian, in a voice that sounded far calmer than he felt. "Your presence here is unacceptable. Commander." He nodded discreetly to the executive officer, who was ready to fire a torpedo.

"No," said the Nym.

"The *Pride* is nineteen minutes out," Kostin said quietly.

"We want Commons," said the Nym.

"You won't get it."

The Nym captain turned away and said something in his language to one of the others, his thin lips barely moving. The *Defiant*'s sensors couldn't pick up the muttering. "Fleet has what we want," the Nym finally said.

Lily. Oh, gods. Rian didn't reply to the Nym captain, but addressed the bridge directly. "Cut the comm link. Fire the torpedo."

A torpedo was launched at the Nym ship, rocking the *Defiant* and undoubtedly tossing a few unprepared crew into their consoles. The torpedo smoothly glided in the starfield towards the Nym ship. Under Rian and Kostin's skilled hands, the *Defiant* withdrew as the weapon sailed to prevent any debris from ricocheting back to her hull.

The Nym ship exploded, pieces already floating out to the reaches of space. Rian checked the sensors and was relieved to see that the debris was real and the enemy hadn't faked its destruction.

Kostin watched Rian do the scan. "Sir, we all saw the ship get hit."

"If this were any other ship, I would believe my own eyes. This is the Nym, Commander."

"Noted. Apologies, Captain." Kostin silenced the alarms, and data flowed into Rian's console screen. He felt some tension ebb from his body. Everything indicated that the *Defiant* had just blown up a Nym ship.

"Incoming from *Bishop's Pride*," Kostin reported. The viewport's image switched from the wreckage to the *Pride*'s bridge. Senior Captain Ursuline Jena was seated at the helm, her short white-blond hair awry and her tawny face flushed with rage.

"What the hell is going on?" she shouted.

"Nym interference," Rian replied automatically.

"I got that, Marska. I mean, what the hell just happened? All we saw was an explosion."

"Standard procedure, Captain. A Nym ship is to be fired upon if it refuses to leave."

"Where the fuck did it come from? We're scanning for an energy trace and nothing's shown up." Captain Jena was well-known for her formidable reputation and profanity-laden tirades, and Rian had an idea he was about to be eviscerated when she spied the comm traces. "You opened a godsdamned comm link with them? Are you fucking crazy?"

"They hailed us. We responded. I'll be detailing that to Fleet right away."

"Who talks to the Nym? You blow the fuckers up!"

The initial feelings of shock and terror had given way, and Rian was nearly giddy with relief. He tried to keep a smile off his face and failed. "Look around you, Captain. I did blow them up, and I even did a scan to check for other ships."

"Don't get smart with me."

She had relaxed a little and was now just pissed off rather than infuriated. Rian noticed now that she too was out of uniform, wearing a light blue tracksuit, its fabric printed with —were those *daisies*? That definitely didn't fit the image of the captain known for forcibly removing a meddling admiral from her bridge single-handedly. He grinned in spite of himself.

Jena caught it and glared at him. "Don't look at me like that, Marska. I was in the gym when I got your SOS." She sighed and leaned back in the captain's chair. "All right. I'm going to send in my report and alert Fleet again that those fuckers are breaching our space. We need more than patrol ships out here for the time being."

Rian agreed. "I'm going to my office to file a report as soon as I sign off."

"I'm retiring in a few years. All I wanted was a nice, quiet assignment where I could fine freighter captains with illegal weapons," she groused. "Instead I get the Nym."

Jena was gearing up for one of her epic tirades, and Rian sympathized with everyone in earshot. Not enough to listen to it, though, and he interrupted with his thanks. "I'll stay in touch, Captain," he promised, and they signed off.

He gave the overnight crew orders to alert him for any more activity and headed for his office to file his reports to Fleet. He had anticipated being up late, but not in the vicinity of the bridge. The lightheaded, almost carefree euphoria he had felt after saving his ship evaporated, and a familiar ball of dread formed in the pit of his stomach. He knew what the Nym were looking for, and so would the admirals.

He found Lily in his office, crouched on her knees and peering out the viewport. She didn't turn at the sound of the door cycling open.

"Lily," he said softly.

She screamed and toppled over, landing on her ass. "Shit!"

she exclaimed. Her face was reddened from weeping, her expression wide-eyed and panicked.

He helped her up and held her to him. She was shaking like a leaf, and he felt her heart beating frantically against his chest. He guided her to his chair and she sank into it and gripped his hands for dear life. He perched on the desk, facing her.

"Did you blow up that ship?" she asked.

He nodded slowly. "I issued the order."

"Tell me," she urged him hoarsely.

"That was a Nym ship," he began, and hesitated. How much should he tell a civilian?

Everything.

CHAPTER 14

Lily returned to her cabin with reluctance and more than a little fear despite Rian's assurance that nothing could hurt her. He had told her quickly what transpired on the bridge before apologetically turning to his office computer to file a report with Fleet. He promised to see her when he could, whenever that would be, and tell her more.

It was now four-thirty in the morning, and she had given up on seeing him for the rest of the day, but she wasn't disappointed. She would have been concerned if he *hadn't* spent the night in contact with Fleet. Seeing that torpedo launch into the Nym's ship had served as a terrifying reminder of the danger she was in.

She felt like an idiot. She had prided herself on adjusting to her new home and making a life for herself, accepting the chances of getting back to Earth in 2017 were next to none. And then she had conveniently shelved the whole reason she was here in the back of her mind. The Commonwealth Space Fleet was determined to protect her, and she had lulled herself into a false sense of security. She had believed everyone who said that the Nym couldn't get to her again. And what defenses did she have? She could fire a laser weapon, and that was it.

Taz had dropped by at 0500 hours, shadows under his eyes from lack of sleep. He had been roused from his bed by the red alert sirens and arrived at his station in communications right after the Nym were fired upon. He was pissed off to have missed out on the action. He came by with breakfast from the mess for both of them, but Lily didn't feel like eating.

"You could've given me some warning," she complained when she let him in her cabin. She threw a sweater over her pajamas.

"Relax. I've seen women in less," he replied cavalierly. He rummaged around her kitchenette and found a couple of forks for the fruit salad he brought, and produced some coffee from the replicator. They sat down at the tiny dinette table clipped to the floor. "I wish I'd been there earlier. I sleep like a rock. The alarms were going for about ten minutes before I woke up." Most soldiers slept lightly after going through training. His ability to sleep deeply at any time was one more thing that drove his commanding officers nuts, he explained. "But it's getting better. A year ago I would've slept through the whole thing. Have you heard from the captain?" he asked her around a mouthful of fruit.

She shook her head.

He swallowed and avoided her eyes. "I should tell you something," he said. "Promise you won't get mad or worry."

"If it's about the Nym, I promise I will get mad or worry."

"It's not the Nym," he assured her. "Um, I have to send in all comm logs and traceable movements to Fleet. I did it right before I came here."

Lily nodded, wondering where this was going.

"Fleet isn't taking any chances with the Nym and every-thing, and they're checking everyone's movements." He was trying to hint at something.

Lily finally understood. When they reviewed Rian's movements and communications, they were going to draw some accurate conclusions. "Oh, no," she breathed.

"You were wearing your badge in his cabin last night," said Taz.

"Is he going to be fired?"

"I assume you mean disciplined," Taz clarified. "Probably not. Fleet doesn't care if crew has personal relationships as long as it doesn't interfere with their duties. And you're a Commons civilian, which is usually even less of an issue."

"But I'm not just a Commons civilian," Lily pointed out.

"Right. They may take whatever's between you and the captain into consideration when they evaluate his performance as acting captain. They could find some technicality to slap him back down to commander and stick him on a station as an executive officer or a first officer on another ship. Also, remember this is Rian Marska we're talking about." He shrugged. "Maybe I'm just worrying you unnecessarily. If this were about you and any other captain, they'd be getting ideas."

"A captaincy is what he's always wanted," Lily said quietly.

Taz held up his hands, as though in defense. "Look, I'm just telling you what all of that is going to look like to Fleet. You and the captain are going to have to come up with your own explanation. I'm guessing he was boring you with Fleet history lessons."

"Huh," Lily mused.

"Well, the crew talks a little, and Lieutenant Steg thinks something more is going on, but Rian has his reputation to uphold as Captain Stick-Up-My-Ass, so the word is he's teaching you everything to know about patrol ships."

"Um," said Lily pathetically.

"You must be pretty bored by now."

"No."

Taz eyed her fruit salad. She pushed the bowl across the table to him and he dug in.

Lily burst into tears. She sniffled and wiped her eyes with her sleeve. "He wants a captaincy and I'm ruining it for him," she sobbed.

Taz put down his fork and calmly regarded her. "How can you ruin it for him? It's not like you can sabotage his career. You still look for buttons in the lift." Realization dawned on his face. "Oh my gods. He *hasn't* been giving you history lessons."

Lily shook her head.

"So you and the captain…"

Lily nodded. Taz's eyes widened.

"Damn. So he isn't a really high-tech cyborg after all."

"Taz, *please*."

"No wonder he's been less of an ass lately."

"Shut up, this is serious."

"Lily, you haven't ruined his career," he tried to assure her. "Fleet really won't make that big of a deal out of whatever you and the captain have going. Like I said, they know him well enough so that idea is furthest from their minds. If he loses out on a permanent captaincy, it'll be because he did something they didn't like. And he has. The whole ship knows it, even though he was right about a lot of things. We all would have died if he tried to run away from that star going nova with the shields down."

"But I want him to do what he wants," she protested.

Taz threw up his hands. "Oh, for gods' sakes!" he snapped. Lily flinched. "You got kidnapped by the Nym and dropped off almost a thousand years out of your time, and by some miracle you're not losing your mind. You meet Rian Marska, who if I'm going to be honest here, didn't seem to know what to do with a woman if she cornered him in his cabin and took off her clothes, and I know that actually happened on his birthday when he was a lieutenant and his friends in engineering hired a stripper for him. So he meets you and for the first time in his career he finds a distraction that as far as I can tell hasn't affected his leadership—except he's less of a micromanaging know-it-all." He took a long swallow of coffee. "Turns out Marska is actually human after all."

"Anything else?" Lily asked acidly. She sipped her coffee.

"Yeah. You're in love with him."

Lily throat constricted and she spit out some coffee back in the mug.

"Well, that's just charming." Taz made a face.

"How the hell would you know that?" she demanded.

"Is spitting an acceptable thing to do in public on Earth? Because here it's considered disgusting."

"No, I mean about your thinking I'm in love with him." She rolled her eyes. "How do *you* know?"

"Three reasons. Well, one of them is a theory, anyway." Lily waved her hand, urging him to get on with it. "First, you want what's best for him. You want him to succeed."

"Of course I do!"

"Second, I told you I'm from Vu'saar, remember?" She nodded. "I may be a half-assed empath, but I can still pick up strong emotions. It's like an aura."

Lily was confused. "How can you see that?"

"I'm not completely defective. Lots of inferior Vu'saarns can sense when someone's broadcasting emotions, and you're yelling loud and clear." He leaned back and crossed his arms over his chest, a satisfied grin on his face.

"And what's the third reason?"

"I've been in love before." He gave her a hard stare. "Don't tell *anyone* I told you that."

"With who?" she asked sarcastically.

"Many, many women," he said, dramatically placing his hand over his heart.

"Bullshit."

"It's the truth. You can be in love with more than one person."

Lily tried to process his talk about her being in love and his ability to see auras. She didn't want to talk about the former yet. "So you don't consider yourself psychic even though you can see auras?"

"Psychics don't exist."

She shot him a look. "You know what I mean."

"Lots of people have minor extra sensory abilities. It isn't special. I bet Mora does, too. She's part Kurran, and they can see them, probably more easily than I can. I only sense when it's a very strong emotion. That's not the mark of a telepath."

"I see." She took another swallow of coffee. "You know, Taz, I really would have preferred to have figured out the whole love thing on my own. It's a big deal to me, and I don't know if I feel it yet."

"Your conscious mind doesn't know yet," Taz replied sagely.

"Shit like this is why you get into trouble," she muttered.

He shrugged noncommittally. "What happens, happens."

"It's just—kind of weird, that's all. And before you ask, no one sees that where I'm from, and if they do, I didn't know about it."

"Maybe." Taz appeared unconvinced, like it was impossible for her to live among people who didn't have that ability. "If it makes you feel any better, Rian's aura never shows up when I'm around, even when he's angry about something."

"It doesn't, but thank you."

He stood up. "Don't worry about it. I'm sorry I said anything." He didn't sound sorry in the least, more gleeful that he had pulled something over her. "I have to get to communications."

———

AFTER HE LEFT, Lily turned on the last episode of *Lightning's Luck* but couldn't focus on it. She should be thinking about the Nym and what she was going to do when she eventually left the *Defiant*, but she kept mulling over Taz's pronouncement and fearing it was true.

She *was* falling in love with Rian. It had sneaked up on her without her noticing. After her disastrous relationship with Cameron, she had always thought if she fell in love again she would treat it like getting into a swimming pool: forever dipping in one toe and recoiling at the shock of cold water and then gradually easing in. She hadn't anticipated it being like luxuriating in a bath.

She had already been thinking about Rian's inclusion in her new life in whatever way she could have him, whether it was by video phone calls or they were assigned to the same station or ship. She couldn't see herself living in the Commons without him. She needed him.

She leaned back against the cushions and let her eyes drift closed as the *Lightning's Luck* crew battled a huge space lizard. She needed some sleep, too.

The doorbell pinged, rousing her from her nap. "Enter," she commanded, and bundled her sweater around her.

Rian stepped in, looking exhausted and stressed. She shot to her feet to greet him. He was paler than usual, and his blue eyes had half-circles beneath. The door slid shut behind him. She paused a couple of feet from where he stood, frozen by the look on his face. His expression was a mix of fear, anger, and desire.

"Rian," she whispered. "What happened?"

"They're talking about a court-martial," he said, his voice low and angry.

Shock slammed into Lily's chest. "Why?"

"I responded to their hail. I opened a comm link. I should've just fired."

"They can't be serious. They can't court-martial you for that."

"They can," he said. He took a step closer to her. There was an unfamiliar, almost feral look in his eyes, one that made Lily's heart skip a beat, but she stayed put.

"But it's just talk, right?" she asked.

"No," he said. "There's more." He took a deep breath. "The *Defiant* is being taken out of service. We're changing course for Kevnar, and the crew is being reassigned. A battleship is going to patrol our territory until the Nym is dealt with."

"Where will you go? You'll be the captain on the battleship?"

"No," he said and looked away for a moment. "I'm being reinstated as a commander. I've been posted to Kevnar, and I'll be taking an executive officer position."

He was being demoted, and he wasn't even going to be on a ship. Lily's hands balled into fists and she fought back tears of guilt and anger at this new injustice. "That's not fair," she protested. "They're wrong. You had the guts to talk to them and you actually managed to destroy their ship. You should still be a captain."

"Fleet doesn't see it that way. It's not just the Nym. They don't like how I handle certain things. They refuse to see that you can't look at everything in black and white when you're in the space lanes these days. Things have changed since the admirals were out in space." He relaxed a little, some of the tension easing from his shoulders. "Lily, the Nym—I had to find out what they wanted, even though I already knew."

"Me."

He shook his head. "Not just you. I won't let that happen."

Rian wouldn't let that happen. Not Fleet. Him.

"I think they're planning an invasion into Commons space," he continued. "I told Fleet, and they said they're always planning an invasion. But this is different. I *know* it is. They don't believe me." He moved a little closer to her.

"I believe you," she said.

He closed the short distance between them and gathered her in his arms, pressing a kiss to her forehead. "And they're figuring out what's going on with us," he said, his voice strained. "Technically, they can't punish either of us, but Admiral Kentz said I should 're-examine my personal relationships with others.' He saw my comm logs."

"I'm sorry," she whispered. "I didn't know I was going to cause so much trouble for you."

He tilted her face up. "Don't be sorry," he said firmly. "Any trouble I get into is worth it. *You're* worth it. And you'll be on Kevnar, too, so this isn't all bad news."

She debated whether or not to tell him she was falling in love with him, but something held her back. This wasn't the right time—not with his career in jeopardy, largely on her account. "Rian," she started.

"Mm?" he said against her hair.

She pulled away slightly so she could face him. "All that's happened—" She bit her lip. "I don't want to go back. I mean, I know I *can't*, but I don't want to, anyway. There's nothing left for me there. I want to be here." She took a deep breath. "With you." That was as close as she could get right now to confessing she loved him.

He seemed surprised, then pleased. "I don't want you to go, either." There was a palpable ache in his voice. A wistful sigh ruffled her hair. "Lily—I've told you how important my career is to me. It was the only thing in my life that kept me going." His grip tightened around her. "But all that's changed since I met you." He looked down at her and raised a hand to brush away a tear Lily didn't know was sliding down her face. "Why are you crying?"

"I don't know," she admitted hoarsely. "It's a lot of things. The Nym. Your demotion."

A hint of a smile ghosted across his lips. "Technically I was never a captain. I'm just being reassigned to a position that was available to me before. It'll be an adjustment, not being in the star lanes, but I'll get used to it."

"Fleet should have given you a chance," Lily protested.

"They did. They don't like how I run things. I can't change that, and I'm—well, I'm not fine with it yet, but..." He drifted off and pressed his lips to her forehead, and despite its chasteness, Lily couldn't suppress a shiver.

"I'd rather be with you," he finally finished. "I don't know what we can call what we have, but I want it to continue." His hands slid under her pajama top and caressed the small of her back. "I need you." He softly kissed a trail down her cheek to her neck. "I want you."

Lily's eyes closed, her breath catching when Rian's lips found the sensitive spot under her ear. She angled her head to kiss him, but he stiffened and loosened his hold on her.

"I'm sorry," he said. "I didn't mean it that way."

The words yanked Lily back to reality. Her body protested at his stepping away and it took a few seconds for her brain to form a cohesive response. Irritation at the interruption, followed by amusement, colored her words, and she couldn't help but roll her eyes. "I know," she affirmed. Taking a fistful of his shirt, she pulled him back to her. "And you're going all beta male on me and overthinking this." She stood up on her toes and kissed him fiercely. He immediately responded, lifting her off the floor. "My room," she gasped. "It's that way."

Her bed was unmade and there were some clothes littering the floor, but he didn't notice. He stripped off her pajama top and tossed it on a pile of laundry near the bed. He pushed her to the bed and slid her pants down her hips before kneeling over her. She felt exposed and a little self-conscious under his heated gaze.

"This is hardly fair," she protested, her fingers on his shirt seal. It slid open, revealing the expanse of lean muscles beneath.

"I like how you look," he replied simply. He tossed his shirt to the floor with the rest of his clothes. He kissed her, and she arched her body to meet his. His mouth drifted over her face and neck, his teeth lightly grazing her skin. *Marking me,* Lily thought, a shiver of excitement running through her. Branding her, claiming her for his own.

Her hand traced a line up his thigh to the erection that strained against the front of his pants. She wanted them out of the way and clumsily fumbled with the placket for a moment until they were open. He sucked in a harsh breath at her touch and helped her push them off.

He positioned her over him, and she raised an eyebrow. "I insist on my crew sharing the work," he whispered, and she couldn't help but giggle at that. It changed to a sharp gasp as he slid into her and grasped her hips, urging her to move along with him. With each thrust, she felt herself being taken higher and higher until she shattered, the force of her climax tearing a cry from her throat.

Without missing a beat, Rian smoothly flipped her on her back. He slowed down enough to kiss her neck and let her catch her breath for a moment. He pressed his mouth against hers and teased her lips open, his tongue tangling with hers possessively, sending another thrill through her. He hooked his arm around the back of her leg and started again, his strokes harder and deeper this time. Lily felt another climax building and whimpered. He slowed down again perceptibly. "Don't stop," she murmured against his neck.

His thrusts became more intense and she held on to his

back, her nails digging in his skin. He moved faster and his body shuddered his release as she cried out again, both of their bodies spasming.

His breathing was ragged in her ear when he finally sagged against her, his face buried in her neck. Aftershocks still twitched through both when he rolled on his side and pulled the sheet over them. He pulled her against him, spooning her perfectly against his chest as though their bodies were made for each other. Oh, hell, Lily reasoned, they *were*. His breath tickled the back of her neck, and he pressed a kiss to her shoulder.

She debated whether or not to tell him she loved him, and didn't. Declarations of love post-sex—no matter how spectacular, how *necessary*—seemed false to her, even though she meant it.

Instead, she rolled over to face him. "Hey," he said softly. He brushed a few strands of hair off her face.

"Hi," she whispered back. Her arms circled his chest. Their breathing was almost in tandem, and soothing. All of her fears from the night before were fading, a soon-to-be-distant memory. They would be on station soon, the Nym stopped, and she and Rian could...continue what they had started, as he put it, she thought sleepily. Make a new life with the man she loved at her side.

"Lily," he said and nudged her back awake.

"Mm-hm?"

"Was it that boring?" She heard the grin in his voice, but her eyes still flew open.

"God, no," she assured him. "I'm just..." She fumbled for words. *I'm in love with you, and all I can do is wreck your life.* "Very comfortable," she finished. Her earlier sense of safety fell flat. They were still aboard the *Defiant*, still in the Nym's sights.

"Me, too."

He settled her back against him, but Lily was wide awake again. "Rian? Don't you have to go to work?"

"You're trying to get rid of me already? You're breaking my heart." But there was a lightness in his voice. He kissed her, a slow, lazy kiss that was over far too soon.

"I don't want you to get into any more trouble on my account."

"None of this is any of your fault, and I'm off-duty until 1200 hours." He ran his fingers over her back, eliciting a shiver from her.

"Then what?"

He sighed. "I have a vidconference with Fleet, and I have to run a diagnostics on security patches that were downloaded into the ship's sensors. Fleet's transmitting the program now. Are you worried?"

"Yeah, a little." *A lot.*

"Don't be." His hand moved to trace her breasts, and his fingers teased her nipple until she gasped. His mouth covered hers, and he shifted his body until he was above her, supporting his weight on his elbows. "We'll be okay," he murmured and kissed her neck. Lily felt something in her respond, and she locked her fingers around his neck and brought his face down to hers, echoing her hopes. "We'll be at Kevnar Station in a few days, and this worry will be behind us."

LILY HAD SET the cabin alarm for eleven, but she woke up early. She gently slipped out of bed and tried in vain not to wake him.

"Going somewhere?" he asked sleepily.

"Go back to sleep," she said softly. "You have another half-hour. I was just going to get a drink. Do you want anything?"

"No, thank you." He watched her leave the bedroom, still naked. A small smile played over his mouth at the sight. He ordered the illumination on, the lights set to low. She returned to bed with her juice and took a few sips before setting the glass on the nightstand. She chewed on her lower lip, and he knew she was concerned about something. "What is it?" he prodded.

"The usual," she replied. "Exams, moving, evil space aliens."

He didn't want to have this conversation right now, which surprised him. Ordinarily he was willing to discuss military theory and strategy any time, and he had in the past, while he was in bed with a long-ago lover. He didn't want to talk about the Nym, not when she could make him forget everything except hunkering down in the covers for as long as they could get away with. But she seemed set on discussing it.

"Rian, we both know they were after me," she said.

"Yes." He sat up, the blankets bunching around his waist. "Some of the Fleet higher-ups think there may be something on this ship that's broadcasting our business to unfriendlies, but damned if we can find it. Some kind of energy trail we're not aware of."

"You said the Nym's technology outdoes yours."

"It does," he confirmed. "We could still pick up evidence of its use, though. Everything leaves a trail, even if we don't know exactly what the device is."

Lily nodded, understanding. "Could someone communicate with an unfriendly and erase the transit logs?"

That was what had woken her up—she was worried. Of course. So was he. "No. Well, theoretically, yes. But trying to make that kind of adjustment would lock down external communications, and the culprit would be caught. Also, no one on this ship, including me, has that kind of knowledge or training. We just look out for smugglers and haul science teams across the galaxy." He gave a small, mirthless laugh. "You really pick good pillow talk."

"You'd rather I tell you we should kick everyone off the bridge for an hour and play 'Good Captain, Bad Captain'?" Some of the sparkle was returning to her eyes.

"I've never heard of that, but yeah, I would." He crawled back under the blanket. "Come here. We both need sleep."

CHAPTER 15

All was quiet in the *Defiant*'s airspace this evening, something that ordinarily would have pleased Rian if he wasn't pissed off at losing his captaincy and paranoid about Nym activity. He was handling the former better than he would have a few months ago and found himself looking forward to the transfer to Kevnar. He could admit to himself now that there were upsides to essentially being a secretary to an admiral. He wouldn't be a captain, but he wouldn't have to deal with the *Defiant*'s crew either. As for the Nym, *paranoid* wouldn't cut it. *Scared shitless* was a better term, but he'd be damned if he let anyone know about that.

At least Fleet had stopped talking about a court martial for the time being. He and Senior Captain Jena had had a private vidconference earlier in the evening. She, too, had been threatened with a court martial after firing on the disappearing Nym ship a couple of weeks earlier. "You're damned if you do and damned if you don't," she pointed out. "The rules about the Nym change depending on who's pissed at you. They can't control the Nym or predict their next move, so they control us instead. It's fucked, Marska."

He was finding that was true, but Rian Marska wasn't Ursuline Jena. She terrified most of Fleet, including half the admirals. Hell, she would be an admiral herself if she had stopped referring to them as "a bunch of shit-brained no-nuts" about twenty years ago. "Don't worry about it," she had assured him. "Tell them the truth about what happened. The only way to deal with the Nym is to blow the fuckers to pieces on sight. If anything, they should be promoting you for having the balls to talk to them."

He checked on Lily frequently, sometimes just her location, other times to say hello. It was out of fear, and he couldn't help it. Despite Fleet's assurances that all the scans conducted on the ship proved the initial suspicions otherwise, the possibility of a traitor aboard was something that weighed on his mind. He had been accused of being too analytical in the past, too paranoid, and after more thought, he tended to agree. Not this time. Something just wasn't adding up, and he couldn't put his finger on it. It was driving him crazy.

The Nym *knew*. They had figured out which patrol ships had stopped by Rubidge Station around the time Lily was found in the cargo hold: *Bishop's Pride* five days before the *Defiant*, and the *Shelian* two days after the *Defiant*. *Bishop's Pride* and the *Defiant* were older ships, the *Shelian* had taken her maiden flight out of the shipyards two years ago. The *Defiant* was equipped with a generously-sized cargo hold and was notorious for its constant repairs; the *Pride* had a single unused fighter bay and was a reliable old ship. Someone had put two and two together and possibly mistaken the *Pride* for the *Defiant* and tried to attack her first. Fleet had waved away his theory, but that didn't deter him. He was going to find out how the Nym knew and how much they knew. This was the first time in his life he wasn't doing something for the sake of his career. This was about Lily, pure and simple.

From his office, he ran every scan filter authorized by Fleet and an unauthorized one developed by his brother-in-law, who used it in the shop where he worked. Nothing unusual had shown up.

He was missing something.

Maybe Lily had a tracking device on her. *In her*, he corrected himself. From his office computer he pulled up the files from her last exam, administered by Mora Kharn. She had had three Fleet-approved vaccinations that day, guarding against Coll particles and venereal disease, and an immuno-booster. She had also had a contraceptive transderm implant. All standard vaccinations for everyone aboard.

He looked more closely at the file. The drugs' manufacturing stamps were recorded, per procedure, and nothing looked out of place.

A mediscan wasn't out of the question, just to be on the safe side, but Rian had no intention of asking anyone in the infirmary to do it. He just had to get his hands on a unit and scan Lily. For the first time, Rian was glad he was forced into taking field medical courses during school.

Mora Kharn may be an admiral's daughter, and her psych profile didn't fit that of a traitor, but Rian wasn't placing his faith and the lives of Lily and his crew on those criteria. Just because the profiling program hadn't failed in the past didn't mean it was infallible. There was a first for everything.

He checked the computer in his office to see who was scheduled for duty in the infirmary, and by a stroke of luck found it was Dr. Bekri and a lone nurse on the evening shift. Bekri would be too absorbed in the latest installments of the vid serials to care if the captain strolled in and helped himself to a mediscan unit, and the nurse was fresh out of school and still had a healthy fear of authority.

He slipped out of his office and took the lift to the infirmary. He strode in the doors, setting off a chime. Bekri stayed in the glassed-walled office, a datatab in his hand and his eyes glued to his computer screen. He offered the barest of nods to Rian in greeting and didn't say a word. Someone would have to flail around a severed limb to get the man's attention.

Under ordinary circumstances, Rian would have upbraided Bekri for his lack of attention, but this was far from a regular day. He offered a silent prayer to the gods, thanking them that Ashford wasn't on duty as he rummaged around the storage room in the back and helped himself to a mediscan unit. He slid the palm-sized device in his pocket and left the infirmary without speaking to the doctor. He passed the nurse on his way out. Gods knew where she had been.

Where did Fleet find these people, and why were they always assigned to the *Defiant*? It didn't matter that in a few days' time they wouldn't be his to deal with anymore. A work ethic was still important.

He forced himself to wait until he was off duty at 2300 hours before doing an impromptu check-up in Lily's cabin. He declined a cup of tea from the replicator and held out the mediscan.

"What's this?" she asked.

"I'm going to scan you for a tracking device," he said, flicking the unit on. He calibrated it to a deep scan setting. "It's more thorough than the ones you've already had. Take off your clothes."

"Usually you kiss me first," she muttered, but complied. She stripped off her T-shirt, dropping it on the floor.

In spite of their predicament, Rian smiled and felt lust roil inside him. "I will later, I promise. But I have a theory that you were implanted with something that doesn't protect against Coll particles and pregnancy." He still couldn't stop his breath from hitching as she pushed her pants down her legs and kicked them off.

A stricken look overcame her face. "No," she whispered. "Mora wouldn't do anything like that."

"How long have you known Mora?" he asked, holding the mediscan over one of the vaccine's entry points in her hip.

"Almost as long as you have," she shot back.

Ouch. "Good point," he replied tersely.

The deep scan took ten minutes to complete, and Rian knew Lily was pissed off about his suspicions. She glared at him as he held the unit over her back and hips and asked for every detail of her appointment with the nurse. He could live with that. Lily alive and mad was better than her dead. No matter how much he loved her, her well-being was most important to him.

The unit beeped in his hand and he dropped it. He picked it up with shaking hands and tried to focus on the report scrolling across the screen. *You love her* echoed through his mind.

"Rian?" Lily said, exasperated. She pulled her shirt over her head. "What does it say?"

"Nothing," he said and flicked off the unit. "That's the problem." She pulled on her pants.

"I told you so," she said.

"I know," he sighed. "I'm sorry. I know you and Mora are friends. But right now I don't trust anyone."

"Even me?"

"Except you," he corrected. "Come here." She closed the short distance between them, and he held on to her for a moment, taking in the scent of her hair, acutely aware of her breathing. He felt the tension ebb from both of their bodies, and he dropped a kiss on her forehead.

"Have you had dinner?" she asked against his shoulder.

"Not yet."

"Neither have I. I'll make something." He let her go, and she fussed with the replicator, producing some soup and tea, and he sat down at the table. "Do the apartments have kitchens on Kevnar?" she asked.

"They do."

"I told you I'm a good cook," she said. "When we get there, I'll show you."

He felt heartened at that prospect. Maybe she was thinking about their future together, too, and felt something beyond physical attraction. He tested the waters further, bringing his own ideas in the open. "I was thinking I could teach you to fly a shuttle," he said cautiously. "Kevnar has them available for personal use. It's a helpful skill to have."

"Really?" She set down bowls of soup and took the seat across from him.

"The station is within flying distance to a few residential and commercial planets," he continued. "I was thinking when all this is over...I still have furlough available." Far more than he should, he thought ruefully. He had a few years' worth of leave he hadn't taken.

"You mean vacation time," she translated. He nodded.

"We could take a vacation?" She laughed. "God knows we both need one."

He took a deep breath and tried to stop himself from shaking. He wanted to tell her he was in love with her, but it wasn't something he was accustomed to confessing. He had nothing to go on; he'd never said it before.

"Where would we go?" she asked.

"I have a few places in mind," he answered noncommittally, but now he couldn't think of them. Furlough seemed so far off and would be until a war with the Nym was diverted and Fleet was happy with his work at Kevnar. "Lily," he said urgently. *Damn, that came out wrong.* Now she looked worried. He forced himself to relax. "Lily, I have to tell you something."

"Is it the Nym?"

"No! It's just something I have to tell you. And you don't have to say anything; I just want you to know." He was handling this badly, and he didn't want to hear a response if she didn't reciprocate—not yet. But Rian was well-known for tackling problems and for examining things too closely. Better to just get on with it. "You're very special to me," he managed.

Just get to the point.

"More than that," he continued. "You mean more to me than anything, including Fleet, and I never thought the day would come where I would say that to someone."

She had an odd look on her face, a combination of hope and caution. He took that as a good sign and continued. "I don't have any right saying this because if you get the chance to go home I want you to do what's best for you and not think about my feelings." He took a deep breath. "I think I'm in love with you." *Think*—there was the understatement of the century. He would kill for her—had killed for her already.

She closed her eyes for a moment, absorbing the information. "That's good," she said, a smile spreading across her face. "Really good."

He breathed a sigh of relief. He hadn't scared her off. "Well, I don't think I'm in love with you. I *am*."

But she wasn't finished yet. "I love you, too," she said quietly.

He hadn't been expecting that. He wanted to hear it but didn't think he would. "You do?" he said hoarsely, unable to contain his surprise.

"Why are you so shocked?" she asked gently.

"I hadn't thought about your response too much, actually. I just wanted you to know." He gazed across the table at her, not caring that he looked like a lovesick kid. The words he wanted to say flowed out of him. "I want us to be together. I want you in my life for as long as I can keep you."

"I'm going to be," she promised. She stood up and skirted around the small table, her dinner forgotten as she settled in his lap and twined her arms around his neck. "I don't want things any other way."

————

LILY'S EYES FLEW OPEN, her heart pounding, and for a few seconds she was disoriented. She checked the clock inset in the wall—four-fourteen in the morning. There were tears drying on her face, but that wasn't unusual when she dreamed lately. Beside her Rian slept, his breathing steady and calm. She kept her cabin lights on the dimmest setting at night, still unaccustomed to sleeping in the total darkness afforded by deep space. She had expected that the stars would offer some light, but they didn't. She had never known true night until she came here. On Earth, there was always something, be it the moon or streetlight shining through her bedroom window. She touched his face, and he stirred slightly but didn't wake. She smiled. He had been exhausted from the prior day's stress, and had looked terrified when he told her he loved her. She would never forget that.

She lay back on the pillow and tried to think about what had woken her. She had been dreaming about something, and for the first time it hadn't been a nightmare about the cryonics lab or Dr. Zadbac chasing her. She closed her eyes and forced the memory to return.

The dream had revolved around her first week in Toronto, moping and wandering around the Dufferin Mall, buying things for her new apartment. She had known she was dreaming and felt frustrated that instead of sinking into a fantasy involving Rian, she was stuck in a crowded mall. She saw the other shoppers pushing past her, clutching brightly colored paper bags bearing store logos, and smelled the odor that permeated every shopping center she had ever been in: that mix of fast food, perfume counters, and air freshener. She had just left a cell phone kiosk, a top-of-the-line smartphone and twenty-page contract in a little bag in her hand. She was fuming a little after listening to the sales clerk's spiel about the phone's satellite technology, and she had interrupted him and told him not to bother; it was the phone's superior memory capacity she was after. She had a bunch of her father's e-books she wanted to load on to it and keep with her all the time. She had done that when she got home that afternoon.

Someone ran into her with a baby stroller and didn't notice her, merely angling it and her horde of wailing children into Old Navy, where the storefront proclaimed a back-to-school sale. This was what Lily hated about Toronto, and what had drawn her to it to start over: the invisibility. No one noticed her existence, no one knew her father had died and her fiancé and best friend left her for each other. There wasn't a tree farm to struggle with or a house with a dying furnace to worry about. No strings here, no attachments.

She passed Victoria's Secret and considered going in. But she had no one to wear sexy lingerie for, and she had already spent a boatload on the new phone, which all but came with a guarantee that it would erase her misery and give meaning to her life once again.

Her father had loathed cell phones.

Her father, who was sitting on a bench in front of the store, where he most certainly had not been when she bought the phone. Daniel Stewart was wearing dirt-streaked jeans and a goofy Spinal Tap T-shirt under a beat-up denim jacket he'd had since his college days. His grime-streaked hands held a ceramic mug of black coffee, the same cup he drank from for years. He looked like he had just come off a day of tree planting. He and the crowds around him were oblivious to one another.

"Hi, sweetheart," he said and smiled.

Lily's heart caught in her throat, and tears sprang behind her eyes. "Dad?" she said. "What are you doing here?"

He shrugged. "Wanted to say hello." He patted the bench. "Have a seat."

Lily was about to tell him how badly off the rails her life had gone, but he held up a hand to silence her. "I'll make this quick," he said. He pointed to the bag holding the phone. "I hate those things."

"I know." Tears slid down her cheeks. She hadn't dreamed about her father since before she left for Toronto, and he had never spoken to her in them before.

"They have their uses, though." He took the phone out of the bag and thumbed over the touchscreen, and Lily saw it was the way she had last seen it. The wallpaper was set to the photo of the orange cat that used to skulk around their farm, and he flipped through the pictures and e-books. "Good uses and bad uses," he added cryptically. He handed it back to her.

"Dad..."

"I have to go. I love you, Lil."

Then Lily had woken up. She wiped away fresh tears, remembering the sound of his voice and his odd commentary.

Her cell phone. That outrageously expensive bit of genius with its Internet browser, eight megapixel camera, and *Undead Uprising* mobile app in addition to making calls guaranteed never to drop on her wireless provider's network. The one remnant of technology from her time she hadn't seen since she woke up in the cargo hold of a spaceship, whisked away to be decontaminated in sick bay. The phone that was equipped with a GPS feature, should she ever lose it in her home, at work, or the side of a highway. The kiosk's sales clerk had assured her she could look up the phone coordinates on her computer, whether it was turned on or off. It was one of the few like that on the market.

Lily slipped out of bed and dashed to the living room, her

footsteps muffled by the carpeting. There was a big viewport in here, and she stared out at the starfield. A satellite from the old days drifted a few thousand miles away, a tiny metallic cone among the stars. They were remnants from an old era that no one had seen fit to dismantle.

Realization hit her like a bucket of ice water, then fear.

She bolted for the bedroom and shook Rian's shoulder. "Wake up," she commanded. He stirred, mumbling. "Lights!" she barked, and the cabin illumination switched on to full power. Lily's eyes narrowed against the brightness.

"The hell?" Rian muttered.

Lily was already dressing. "I know how the Nym found us," she said. "And you've got a traitor on board."

―――――

LILY EXPLAINED as much as she could about her theory in the elevator ride to sick bay, where, Rian told her, her purse and belongings should still be in a decontamination locker. Rian had insisted on stopping by his cabin so he could pick up his laser pistol and an extra charger clip, and it was holstered at his hip. The sight of it made Lily even more nervous.

"Is there still a GPS satellite orbiting around Earth?" she asked.

"There are a lot of satellites around Earth," he admitted. "There are a lot of them around their galaxy and surrounding areas from the first days of intergalactic travel and trade. The Commons doesn't use them anymore. We have our own network of communications beacons."

Lily remembered seeing an abandoned satellite her first trip to the mess. "You have your own network now."

"Yeah. Our beacons are smaller, cheaper, more secure, and mobile." He rattled off their attributes like he'd be programmed with them. He was reverting back to his captain mode, but Lily could tell he was nervous.

Her mind raced. The first Global Positioning System satellite had been in use since she was a little girl, the Russian GLONASS installed by the time she was in university. By the time she had been kidnapped, the Galileo satellite, controlled by the European Union, had recently been launched. And of course smaller cone-shaped versions still littered civilized space.

The memory of the news reports she had half-listened to in her car ride to work that morning and on her phone on her lunch break came flooding back. "There was a UFO orbiting Earth on and off for a couple of weeks before I was kidnapped," she told him. "I completely forgot about it until now. It showed up and disappeared near our satellites."

"What did it look like?" he asked brusquely.

"I don't know. I never saw any pictures. I didn't really follow that story at all. Just silver," she recalled.

"Like a Nym cruiser," Rian guessed. "We can check out wormhole and vortex activity later. Fleet will need to know that."

"I'm sorry," she said. "I should've remembered."

"It's okay. No reasonable person would blame you for forgetting."

"The Fleet higher-ups will."

"We'll worry about that later."

Sick bay was deserted this early in the morning. "Where's Bekri?" Rian whispered. "He's the overnight doctor. He should be here."

"It's probably a good thing he isn't," Lily said. Rian nodded in agreement and led her to the storage area at the back of the infirmary, to a wall of sealed lockers. He palmed open the lock on one and flicked on the mediscan he had pilfered the night before. Carefully, he removed a clear plastic cube from the lockers. Inside, Lily recognized her black corduroy purse and the things spilled around it—her keys, the contents of her wallet, crumpled receipts, and a twenty-dollar bill.

Rian quickly scanned the cube. "No toxins," he announced, and opened it. "This could have come out of decon a long time ago." Lily reached into the bag and felt around for the smooth rectangle of her cell phone but came up with nothing.

"It's not here," she said bleakly. "Shit. Where did it go?"

"I don't know," Rian replied darkly. "There's only one person who would."

They turned around to head for the corridor to wait for the ship's chief doctor to arrive in the infirmary, but froze. Dr. Ashford blocked the doorway, holding a very large, very lethal-looking laser pistol in his hands.

Lily screamed. Rian automatically drew his own weapon.

"Put it down, Commander," Ashford said softly. "This is a Rikto-Four."

The name meant nothing to Lily, but Rian's glare told her it was significant. His voice was low and cold with fury when he spoke. "That's a Nym weapon."

"It is," Ashford confirmed calmly. He kept it trained on Rian while he pulled something out of his pocket: Lily's phone, turned on, the screen glowing brightly. "You're smarter than I gave you credit for," he told her. To Rian, he said, "You're a lot dumber."

"The satellites," Lily squeaked.

Ashford nodded. "They're everywhere, and this lazy galaxy never thought to take them down. Your Global Positioning System was one of the smartest inventions your people ever came up with."

Lily couldn't believe Ashford's utter calm, as though he were telling her about the latest in mediscan units. "Why?" she said.

"Nothing you ever needed to worry about."

Red alert sirens blared around sick bay. "That's a Nym ship in orbit," Ashford said over the din. He tossed the phone on the floor, and Lily heard a faint snapping sound as its pink case cracked. He closed the small distance between them and grabbed her arm roughly. She struggled and shrieked as Rian raised his weapon to fire at Ashford. But the doctor held his gun to Lily. "If you move, I'll kill her," he shouted over the noise. Rian didn't lower his weapon. The doctor took a small, unfamiliar comm badge from his pocket. "Say goodbye to the commander," he ordered.

"No!" Lily screamed and tried to wrench away. "Rian, shoot him!"

She saw a streak of laser fire hit Ashford, whose grip loosened. But she felt herself being lifted away and the air sucked from her lungs, then everything went black.

CHAPTER 16

Bright light flooded Lily's eyes, and she greedily sucked in mouthfuls of air. Nausea slammed into her, and she doubled over on an unfamiliar floor and gagged, sure she was going to be sick. She gasped for a couple of minutes, but nothing came up. Pain ratcheted around her skull like a ping-pong ball, and she tried to stand up.

She looked around and saw the metal gridwork that made up the floor, and the smooth, sterile metal walls of the room she was in. It looked like a cleaner version of the *Defiant*'s cargo hold. A bulgy-headed Nym guard stood sentry at a large set of closed doors. But that wasn't what made a scream rise to her throat.

Dr. Zadbac stood before her, his bulbous face wearing a triumphant expression.

"*Minsa* Stewart," he said and held out a hand, as though he made to help her off the floor. She ignored the gesture and unsteadily climbed to her feet.

"You are not used to transport unit, no?" he asked. "Lots of people get sick the first few times. Especially one like ours.

It's much stronger and faster than the Commonwealth Fleet's."

"What the *fuck* is going on?" she demanded, hoping he didn't detect the fear in her voice.

"We're not going to hurt you," Zadbac assured her.

Lily didn't believe that for a second.

"We have to kill you, but it won't hurt," he continued.

Lily would have given the bastard points for honesty if she believed him. She felt her gorge rise again and forced it back. Going into hysterics wouldn't help at all, and she had no doubt Zadbac had painful ways of shutting her up if she started screaming.

"Where's Captain Marska?" she asked.

"On his ship, I presume."

"Dr. Ashford?"

"Still on the patrol ship."

The nausea was fading, and she thought quickly. There was no way she could take down three people, especially without a weapon. She and Taz had covered only the basics in hand-to-hand combat, and she had never anticipated having to take on a Nym. At the very least, she could try to get something out of Zadbac about what they were doing. They owed her that much.

"Why?" she asked. "Why were you on Earth in 2017?"

Zadbac's mouth compressed into a thin line. "If you had stayed where you should have, you wouldn't be here today."

"Why did you kill Andrew Claybourne?"

"He fought back. My colleague was merely attempting to defend himself."

"From what?" Shit, the hysteria was creeping back. She tamped down her fear and stared him straight in his black eyes.

"He attempted to leave our office. My colleague tried to stop him. They fought." Zadbac's face twisted in disgust. "He did not return with me."

Andrew Claybourne hadn't died in vain. Lily would dwell on that later, when she got out of here.

At least Zadbac wasn't reaching for a weapon. The guard looked straight ahead, as though she and the doctor didn't exist.

"Why was your ship orbiting around Earth's satellites?"

The guard called out something in the Nym language. Zadbac snorted. "I do not like humans either," he replied in English, keeping his gaze pinned on Lily. "They talk too much. Earth was a mistake."

"What do you mean, 'Earth was a mistake'?"

"If you are not quiet, *Minsa* Stewart, I will have to quiet you myself."

"You're going to do that anyway." Her voice rose to a shout. "At least have the fucking courtesy to tell me what you're up to!"

Zadbac sighed and removed a transdermal unit from the pocket of his black coat. He wore a utility belt full of medical apparatus around his waist. She recognized some of them from her pharmacy text files and the *Defiant*'s sick bay.

Sick bay. *God*. Dr. Ashford. Whatever Rian did to Ashford, it wasn't brutal enough. For the first time, Lily saw the logic behind Fleet's mind-wipe policy, but a mind-wipe was still too merciful for that bastard. She could only pray Rian was okay.

Zadbac held out the transdermal spray but didn't move to apply it. "We don't like the Commons," he said simply.

"No shit." She deliberately kept her eyes away from the unit and on his oversized head.

"The Nym are dying. We need more space and a new planet, and we have nowhere to go. If we start over, we can rebuild our empire from the ground up. From the beginning of interstellar travel. Prevent Earthers from ever expanding in their galaxy and the one beyond."

It was ridiculous, and far too simplistic for Lily's imagination. "That's it? You wanted a new empire?"

"So did Earth. That's why they migrated."

"The Kurrans wouldn't have allowed you to do that," she spat.

"We would have dealt with the Kurrans, I assure you."

"I don't believe you," Lily shot back. "Your ships can move through Commons space undetected. It happened twice, with the *Defiant* and *Bishop's Pride*. What's to keep you from taking over space that way?" She had to keep him talking until she figured a way out of the room.

"We don't have enough ships to do that. That's part of what we were doing on your planet in your time. We were, as you say, evaluating resources. We miscalculated the time travel equation. We should have landed in 2217, three solar years before the Commonwealth formed. Our ship left us on Earth and didn't return for us for four of your solar months. We tried out a new cloaking device in your space, and your ships destroyed both of ours."

"One," she corrected. "The *Pride* fired, but your ship disappeared."

"It was hit," Zadbac said darkly. "It disintegrated on the other side of our wormhole."

Wormhole? She knew that a wormhole could be detected and tried to make sense of what Zadbac was telling her. She filed the information away to tell Rian and Fleet later, and she would. She *had* to get off this ship, if that's where she was.

"Enough," Zadbac said and held up the transdermal spray. With his other hand, he grabbed Lily around her throat, leaving her pulse point exposed. She struggled and tried to breathe, her hands uselessly tugging at Zadbac's grip. She covered her bare skin with her hand, trying to prevent contact. Zadbac cursed in his native tongue but didn't give up.

She thought back to Taz's instruction. Without the time

to give it any more thought, she kicked Zadbac as hard as she could, her booted foot meeting squarely with his upper thigh. It was a little off the mark, but the impact had startled him enough to let go of his grip on her throat. She kicked him again, but he didn't go down, merely doubling over. He dropped the transderm spray, and she snatched it before it could hit the floor and held it to the first patch of exposed skin she could find, on top of his bald head. She pressed the plunger as hard as she could and prayed that whatever was in there adversely affected the Nym.

He looked up at her, shock in his face, unable to stand upright. An angry red welt was forming on his scalp where she had sprayed him, and his features were slackened. She kicked him again and he went down on the floor, gasping.

Laser fire streaked through the cargo bay. Lily screamed and threw herself to the floor next to Zadbac, who was now seizing and uttering wordless, guttural cries. She grabbed the oversized laser pistol clipped to his belt and fumbled with the only switch on it, hoping it was the safety. A charge from the guard's weapon seared the floor a couple of inches from where she lay, and she held up hers and fired. A scream of shock and fury echoed through the room, and the guard was slammed against the wall, his scorched hand dropping his weapon to the deck with a clatter. That had been a lucky shot. She didn't expect to get another.

Zadbac lay the floor, curled in a fetal position. She kept her belly to the ground and slithered behind him, using his body as a makeshift shield. He made no move to relinquish the gun, and his mouth opened and closed like a fish out of water. Across the room the guard dropped to his knees and groped for his weapon with his uninjured hand. Lily angled up on her elbows and aimed her own weapon at him, resting it on Zadbac's waist. He ducked out of the way and with a shaking hand picked up his gun and trained it on her. Lily took a deep breath and fired one last time.

The charge hit him squarely in the chest, exiting through his back and spraying black blood along the back wall. The guard's eyes rolled back and he dropped to the floor with a heavy, sickening thump.

Lily took a few deep, shaky breaths, forcing herself not to panic. The nausea had returned, and she leaned over and threw up on the floor next to Zadbac's body. He had stopped clawing the air and was laying perfectly still, his eyes wide open in disbelief.

She had just killed two people and wasn't going to kid herself. That had been due to sheer dumb luck, and she doubted that when the bodies were found any remaining Nym would underestimate her. She had to get out of here. She took a few deep breaths, and the nausea faded.

Adrenaline surged through her. She reached for the comm badge clipped to her collar and paused. If the Nym could track her down through an ancient cell phone, they could certainly track and hear her words to the *Defiant*, if she could even get through to the crew.

She was on her own.

She stepped to the door, pressed her ear against it, and heard nothing. The palm pad wasn't shaped for a human hand, so she didn't try pressing it. Too large, and designed for clubbed, webbed fingers. The status light on the gun on her hand was still green, and miracle of miracles, it had an indicator on the side. She had hardly used any juice.

Still, she wasn't going to waltz out of here with just one weapon. She looked down at the guard's body in disgust. He and Zadbac were soaked in black blood that gave off a horrible stench. She held her breath and reached for the body, taking the weapon that had fallen to the floor next to him. She shoved it awkwardly into the waistband of her pants. The movies made it look so much easier.

She stepped back and fired on the doors, praying the charge would penetrate through them. Charred indentations appeared, and she cut out a square large enough for her to crawl through and kicked out the metal after a couple of tries. Pain reverberated through her body, and she gave the door a mighty smack with the barrel of the gun. The metal gave, and she forced it out the other side. She stuck out her head first and looked down an empty hallway on either side.

Good. She crawled through, the jagged edges of the hole slashing at her clothes. She ignored the sting of a few cuts on her arms and tried to pick a direction.

One end of the hallway ended in a wall, and the other had a few doors that looked like they could house more cargo bays. There was an elevator at that end, too, but she didn't want to take it unless necessary. *Stairs*, she thought. Preferably ones that would lead her to an empty office with a comm console so she could figure out how to send an SOS. Or an unmanned control panel. Maybe she could take over the ship and steer it to friendlier skies.

Like that was going to happen. She wouldn't know a Nym control panel if it were right in front of her.

The ship shimmied and tilted to the left. *Oh, God, what next?*

She eyed the elevator and forced herself to stay on her feet. She was well and truly screwed, but she wasn't going down without a fight to save the universe as it was supposed to be.

———

RIAN'S LASER pistol had been set to stun, and he woke Ashford with a kick to the ribs. The man sputtered and sucked in a labored breath. Rian wanted to beat him until he was nothing but a pile of bloody pulp on the floor, but instead he aimed his weapon at the doctor's head.

The ship sharply jerked upwards, and Rian stumbled. Ashford made a feeble grab for his weapon, but a security officer pressed his foot against the doctor's neck and kept his own weapon aimed at him. Medical instruments that hadn't been securely strapped down clattered to the floor.

Steg, roused from sleep, was in charge of a security detail that Rian had ordered to sick bay. The ex-prizefighter made a move to pound Ashford into oblivion, but Rian didn't want that to happen just yet and held up his free hand. Steg shrugged a little and strapped the doctor's hands in plasticuffs.

He had to find Lily, and this bastard knew where she was.

He entrusted bridge duty to Commander Kostin. He felt a rumble and a series of heavy thumps throughout the *Defiant* as the ship's tractor beam activated. His first officer deserved a commendation after this; it took a great deal of skill to steer the ship directly above the Nym cruiser that had appeared out of nowhere.

Rian tapped his comm badge. "Captain to Kostin. Status!" he barked.

"Tractor beam engaged."

"The ship?"

"Our sensors indicate it's trying to cloak, but it can't even under our traction." He heard the commander's glee through his badge. "We've got it locked for the time being, but we're keeping our shields up as a precaution."

Rian understood. Most ships were rendered immobile and defenseless by a tractor beam, but he wouldn't put it past the Nym to develop a craft that could fire through that. It looked like they hadn't, though. They probably hadn't anticipated a Fleet ship—an antiquated patrol ship no less—to ever take them hostage.

"Hold the beam, Kostin," he said. "What's the ETA for help?"

"Thirteen minutes for *Bishop's Pride*, twenty for the *Magna*."

Well, praise the gods for that. The *Magna* was a battleship, the kind of craft Rian had once dreamed of commanding.

Ashford coughed. "You can't hold the Nym much longer," he wheezed. Rian leveled his weapon at him. "They'll get through your shields eventually."

"We'll destroy them before that."

"She's on there."

Rian wasn't surprised to hear that; it was the most logical place for Lily to end up, and a team was trying to break into the Nym's systems to find her. "Start talking," Rian said.

"I want amnesty."

"Start talking," he repeated through gritted teeth.

"I'll tell you everything I know if Fleet gives me amnesty."

"I can't offer you that. I'm only a commander."

"You can help talk them into it."

He was wasting time. Rian resisted the impulse to shoot him. "I'll consider it," he said.

"I want your word."

Killing him wouldn't get Lily back. "I promise to do what I can," Rian lied. "Tell me where she is."

Ashford hauled himself up to a seating position. "That's your problem, Commander," he spat. "You've been letting your emotions get the better of you."

"Quit stalling."

"You should be worried about Fleet and the Commonwealth. You should be worried about the Nym." He struggled for breath and held his ribs where Rian had kicked him.

"I am. Lily is part of that."

"You're an idiot," he spat.

"Fuck you."

There was a buckling under their feet. "Shields holding," Kostin reported over his comm link. Rian had deliberately kept it open, and Kostin could hear every word of his exchange with the doctor. He half-listened to the bridge crew as they scrambled to keep the tractor beam and shields engaged.

The device Ashford had used to transport Lily beeped. It was a few inches from his hand, and he made a grab for it. Rian kicked it out of his reach.

"They didn't want her, you know," Ashford said. "She was an accident. She's no use to anyone, dead or alive." He winced as he shifted his bulky frame on the floor. "She's probably dead by now. If she isn't, she will be soon. Nym ships are set to auto-destruct before they can be taken prisoner. You know that, Commander."

An icy chill gripped Rian's heart, but he didn't lower his weapon. He would not—could not—believe Lily was dead. He had to believe that she had found a way to stave off the Nym to get through this. *Had* to.

"Amnesty," Ashford snapped.

Steg was overseeing the security detail and heard Ashford's demand. The security chief muttered something damning in his native tongue before uttering a sarcastic, "Sure."

———

ENSIGN TAZ SHRAFT had been forced away from his communications panel by higher-ranking crew members. He relinquished his post reluctantly and followed the security team to sick bay, listening to snatches of conversation. The Nym were back; they were under their feet, and they had one of his friends in their clutches. He wanted to help and could, but no one would listen to him. Captain Marska hadn't noticed him, and Taz's frustration felt insurmountable. He felt his stomach turn over at the mention of the Nym's auto-destruct sequence.

He hated feeling powerless.

Unless...

He ran for the transport bay. There was a tertiary access panel there, and he knew it probably wasn't in use. Unbeknownst to his superiors, he wasn't a total idiot, and had gone into engineering in an effort to direct his fondness for hacking and tweaking code into something positive. Reprogramming equipment was supposed to alert his superiors about design flaws. Fleet just didn't see things his way and forced him into a boring desk job in communications as punishment for things that didn't warrant it. He knew he would have been an asset as an engineer.

He was right about the shuttle bay and was relieved to find it was abandoned. He logged into the ship's systems using a senior access code he ripped off from a former commanding officer he had in his first days in Fleet. He was lucky, and the computer read the code as if Captain Flitt were actually on board. Data flowed through the console, information a mere ensign wouldn't ordinarily have access to.

The data on a vessel held in traction could be accessed by the holding ship, and he pulled up the Nym's primary systems interface. Other crew members had been doing the same, and he saw that they were focused on the auto-destruct sequence that was going to go off shortly and trying to override it in time. They were doing it incorrectly; the better way was to find out where that command was hidden and disable it from the inside. A vessel built in almost any shipyard could be taken out using the methods they were trying, but they had forgotten that this was a Nym ship.

He found a pathway another officer had opened on the enemy vessel. It looked like the coding for a transport beam. If they had been able to get a hold on Lily, they could have used that bit of code to hack into the transporter and bring her back here, but they couldn't get a lock on her. There was a shield of some kind hiding all life forms on the ship.

Taz stared at the Nym cruiser's data. The only way to get Lily back was to shut down the entire ship by hacking into their primary systems interface, rendering the life form shield and auto-destruct useless. It would also shut off the air, and if Taz were more familiar with Nym-built hardware he would have tried it anyway. But this wasn't a Commons or Empire ship, and he had no idea how long the emergency air circulated, or even if the Nym utilized such devices. Under ordinary circumstances, he would have welcomed the challenge, but he had to get this done in a bare few minutes, without anyone on board the *Defiant* noticing. They would certainly find a way to stop him.

The line of code for the transport unit was linked into communications and security aboard the cruiser, which was good. The pathways that branched off each program began with the same string of numbers, and he memorized them. That likely indicated the beginning of the PSI's coded address, buried deep in the computer systems. He searched along other lines of data, looking for a link beginning with that sequence, and came upon a cluster of them. He followed the line of code with his hands on the console's smooth surface.

There it was. That had to be the controls for the PSI.

All he had to now was circumvent around the PSI and knock out their defense systems without shutting off life support or blowing up the ship. When he did that, he could link the *Defiant*'s PSI to the Nym's, essentially turning the latter into an extension of the Fleet ship. If the tractor beam could hold on long enough to successfully worm his way into the enemy ship, he could control it remotely. Like a bunch of cargo bots.

If this weren't a life or death situation, this would be fun.

CHAPTER 17

Lily held her weapon at the ready and pressed a button next to the elevator. Its doors opened; she stepped in, and it immediately began to ascend. *Damn it!* She examined the smooth walls for an emergency stop button to no avail. A short ladder was built into the wall that reached the ceiling, which gave her hope. Even a group of people as arrogant and advanced as the Nym had to have emergency protocols in place for something as simple as an elevator.

She heard a series of barked commands over an intercom panel near the ceiling. She didn't understand a word of it but had no doubt that the ship's crew was on to her.

There was a single, tiny button near the floor. She pressed it and prayed. The elevator ground to a halt.

Relief coursed through her, but it was short-lived. She whirled around the elevator but couldn't find any means of escape. She hoisted herself up the ladder and pounded at the ceiling panels with her fists. One gave way an inch or two, and she slammed the butt of her gun against it. A small burst of energy jolted her arm and seared a black spot on the floor. Oops.

She hit the panel with her fist again and it loosened. Her hands aching, she forced it aside just enough to wiggle her body through and sit on the roof of the elevator.

She looked around. "Holy shit," she breathed softly. She could see a network of metal beams, cables, and the stark bodies of other elevators around her, arranged in a semi-circle. She looked up and saw the floor above her, about fifteen feet. She would have to climb to the next deck and pray that her luck would hold out.

Her gun in one hand, she grabbed onto one of the support beams hugging the elevator's body and wrapped herself against it. She forced herself to remember climbing ropes in high school gym class. She took in deep breaths and concentrated, inching up the support beam, made more awkward by the weapon in her hand and another in her waistband.

An elevator on the other side of the half-circle whirred into action and stopped on a deck two levels below her. A new fear gripped her: What if the elevator she had broken out of started moving? She hurried her pace, picking up a rhythm that would have made her gym teacher proud. Finally she approached the metal decking of the next deck and held on to the beam. She let go of it with the hand gripping her gun and thought quickly about how to get through the doors without drawing attention to herself. If she shot through them, someone would notice before she could get through. She'd have to launch herself at the doors and push her way through.

She had one chance to do this.

She could. She would fall through and roll.

Lily's toes touched the floor's edge and she swayed slightly, gripping the beam beside her. She threw all of her weight against the doors and crashed through them to the floor. She crouched down on her knees, grateful for the solidity beneath her. Then she saw the pair of black boots a few inches away.

She looked up at the stunned Nym soldier. Without thinking

further, Lily fired her gun upright and scrambled out of the way as the body fell face-first to the decking with an ungainly thump. Black goo seeped from its body and splashed on her clothes. She looked around and saw no one else, but that was going to change soon. The blast from her weapon had been loud and had sliced cleanly through the Nym, leaving a smoking crater in the wall behind him. She could see a comm badge winking through the black sludge on his chest. She ripped it off his uniform and stuck it in her pocket. That could be good for something.

She was in a small foyer. There were a few doors lining the walls, nothing labeled in her language, of course. She would have to pick one and brave whoever and whatever was behind it. If she stayed here, every door would open, and she would have far more Nym than she could handle.

Well, she already did. She picked a set of doors and fired her gun. There was a hollow sawing noise, and she kicked them in.

She saw a viewport looking out over space. Then two shocked Nym sitting at consoles, strapped into chairs.

Dear God, she'd picked the cockpit. She fired two quick charges to the Nym, who slumped over in their seats, leaking black blood everywhere. She held her breath—did they ever *stink* when they died—and pushed against one with all her might. He fell over to the floor, and she took his seat.

She looked at the console in front of her. Red symbols blinked in an angry staccato across the screen, a clock next to it. No, a countdown. It was counting down minutes and seconds.

It was down to eight minutes, twenty-eight seconds.

Whatever was supposed to happen in eight minutes, it couldn't be good. She tapped the console and found it unresponsive to her touch.

No.

She tapped her Fleet comm badge and prayed. "Stewart to Captain Marska," she said. "Stewart to the *Defiant*—anyone!" *Please, please let someone hear me.* She had no idea of the kind of range these things had.

A familiar voice replied, and she nearly wept at the sound of it. "Lily!" said an incredulous Rian.

"I'm on a Nym ship. I can't get out. Help me!" The fear and panic she had kept at bay had overtaken her. She was in danger of having a complete meltdown, and she couldn't afford that.

"I know," Rian said. "We have a tractor beam containing the ship. Lily, I need you to listen to me very carefully. Where are you?"

"A cockpit or a navigation room, I think. I think I killed the pilots. I mean, I know I killed them, but I'm pretty sure they were the pilots."

"Starboard or portside?"

"I have no fucking idea! I just crawled through an elevator shaft! Can't you find me?"

"We're trying."

Lily heard some static, and the link went dead. She heard voices nearby, the angry growl of the Nym.

No.

It would not end this way.

She looked around the room for a place to hide and found nothing. She would have to go back into the corridor. She could get back and hide in the elevator shaft.

She chanced a peek outside. There were at least two voices, and they sounded like they were around the corner. She bolted for the broken elevator doors and looked up and down the shaft. She could climb another deck and cut her way onto another deck. It was her only option. She teetered on the edge of the deck, willing herself not to look down, and jumped gracelessly for the support beam. She clutched it for dear life. Tears blurred her vision, but she soldiered on.

I didn't tell him I love him.

"Lily?" said a hoarse voice from her comm badge.

She kept herself wrapped around the beam and tapped it. "Yeah?" she whispered.

"It's Taz."

———

RIAN'S COMM BADGE TRILLED. "Shraft to the captain," he heard.

"Captain here."

"I'm in the Nym's PSI," the ensign said proudly.

"What?"

"I hacked into the PSI. I've almost figured out how to shut down the ship. I'm in their computers right now."

Rian looked at Lieutenant Steg, who glowered at the doctor as he demanded answers from him. "Watch him," he ordered.

"Yes, sir."

"Shraft, what have you done?" he demanded.

"I've unlocked their transport code," Shraft replied. "I've got a lock on Lily's DNA. I know where she is, approximately. I can't bring her here using our locks, though. I can't get through that part of the ship's shields."

Rian looked around the floor and spotted the badge Ashford had been holding. He grabbed it. "What if I use a Nym badge?" he asked Shraft. "If I have one, I can transport to their ship, get Lily, and use it to bring her back, right?"

"Sure. Where do you have a Nym badge, though?"

"Right here. I'll explain later. Ensign, can you do this?"

"Yes," came back the confident reply. "I just need to have

the data on the badge. Can you plug it into a port and let me look at it?"

Rian raced to the doctor's private office and unplugged the computer perched on the desk. He jammed the badge into the vacant port and relayed the location to Shraft.

"I see it," the ensign said. "It's showing up as invasive, but…" He heard some taps, Shraft's fingers flying across the console. "Contained. Lily is on deck four or five; it's hard to tell through the shield. I'll transport you to deck five."

"Affirmative." Rian removed the badge from the port and held on to it, his weapon in the other and primed. He braced himself for the transport.

He was a little unsteady on his feet when he materialized on metal gridwork, but quickly regained his equilibrium. He looked up and down the foyer he was in and saw the dead Nym lying not two feet away. Beside him, a set of smashed-in doors. He blanched and crept forward to a set of doors decorated with black scorch marks. Inside was a cockpit helmed by a pair of dead Nym.

Lily had done this. He couldn't help but feel pride.

He left the cockpit and tapped his badge, calling for Lily. A soft voice issued out of it. "Rian?" she said.

"I'm on the ship," he whispered. "I can get us back. Tell me where you are. We've got to get out of here."

"The elevator," she replied. "I'm in the elevator shaft. Where are you?"

"The bridge. I just found some dead pilots. Good work."

"Go back out in the hallway. You'll find a set of broken elevator doors. I'm climbing up another deck."

He slipped out of the cockpit and into the corridor, where he found the broken doors he had passed earlier and two Nym peering down the shaft. He fired off two blasts from his pistol and they dropped heavily into the shaft, muted thumps sounding many decks away. He heard a very frightened and feminine scream from somewhere in there. He looked down the shaft and his stomach turned over.

"Up here," came a hoarse whisper.

He looked up and saw Lily clinging to a support beam. He had never been so glad to see anyone in his life. "Get up here," she hissed. "They know I escaped. Come on."

He jumped for the support pole she was holding on to and shimmied up the cold metal until her feet were almost level with his eyes. "We have to get out of here," Rian said.

"I'm going to the next deck," she said and kept moving upward.

"No, the ship is set to auto-destruct in a few minutes. I have a Nym comm badge that will let us bypass their shields and get back to the *Defiant*. If the auto-destruct goes before we unlock the tractor beam, the *Defiant* will be blown to pieces." He hoisted himself up a few feet, twisting around Lily's body wrapped around the support so he could face her, his legs holding her in place. In the dim light offered in the lift's shaft, he saw the tears on her face and the reeking Nym blood staining her skin and clothes. After all of this was over, he would never let her go again. He wrapped an arm around her, kissed her temple, and fumbled in his pocket for the Nym badge. He slipped it out and it slid from his grasp, down the shaft.

Lily stared down, horror on her face. "Shit!" Rian snapped. He forced himself to remain calm and keep his grip on the support beam. "Lily, we have to move. Now!"

The lift below them whirred to life and began going up. Lily screamed.

"Go!" Rian shouted. If the lift got to them... he stole a glance at Lily. He would not think about that.

The lift vibrated along the supports, now three decks away. He could see a ragged hole in its top. "We'll have to kick in those doors," Rian yelled over the noise, and he looked up at another set of doors half a deck above them.

"We won't make it," Lily shouted back, and she tossed her weapon down the shaft, freeing both of her hands. She felt around her pocket for something and pulled out a flat square streaked with black gore. Another Nym comm badge. Rian didn't have time to ask where she got it.

The lift was a deck and a half away. "Hang on to that," he said. She nodded. "When I tell you, we're going to jump." She nodded and clutched the badge in her hand until her knuckles went white. He wriggled his body around the support until he was behind her and clasped his hands around her waist. Her spare Rikto-Four dug into his stomach, but he ignored it. He kept his eyes the rapidly ascending lift. "Let go!" he shouted.

She obediently released her grip on the beam as he pushed them off it. They landed with a thump, the lift's ceiling cracking under their weight. Rian instinctively crouched down, and Lily followed and immediately reached for the laser pistol in her waistband. Rian already had his ready, and he slammed his weapon at the lift's ceiling. Pieces rained down on its occupants, a pair of Nym, who turned shocked green eyes to the sight above them. Rian put short, quick charges through both of them before they could react. He motioned to Lily. "Jump in," he said. "I'll be right behind you."

She didn't argue or hesitate. She dropped through the hole and landed on a body oozing black blood. "Fuck!" she said in disgust. "They stink!"

Rian grimaced and jumped in after her, blood splattering his clothes. His nostrils constricted at the smell. The gods only knew what that lift would smell like after an hour or two, but they didn't have enough time to find out. "The badge," he said. "Do you still have it?"

"Yeah." She opened her hand, where the badge had made indentations in her palm.

Rian tapped his comm badge. "Shraft," he said. "I've got her."

"Thank gods," said the ensign. "You're down to two minutes, forty seconds."

"I lost the first badge. We have another one. Will that work?" He held his breath.

"I cleared more code after the last time we communicated. I've got your DNA, Captain, and a bunch of Nym comm badges in the vicinity." There was a pause. "Got the transport lock."

The lift stopped, and its doors opened.

A battalion of Nym soldiers stood at the doors, weapons at the ready. Rian grabbed Lily and she clung to him, but further reaction was halted by the sensation of being turned inside out. Neither could say anything as the air was sucked from their lungs.

Today marked the first time Rian wanted to be pulled through a transporter.

Their bodies coalesced on the *Defiant*'s bridge. The impact from the transporter knocked them both off their feet, and Lily's Rikto-Four skittered across the floor. They both lay on the decking, breathing heavily, before Lieutenant Asmo jumped up from her post at navigation to help. Rian forced himself to sit and tried not to throw up. Transporters delivered a hell of a wallop.

Lily lay on her side, weeping. Asmo talked to her, murmuring soothing things and urging her to take deep breaths. Rian crawled over to her on hands and knees and helped her sit up. She swayed a little, taking in her surroundings in disbelief. "Rian," she said simply.

"We made it," he replied.

"I think I'm going to throw up again." But instead, she slumped to his chest in a dead faint.

The *Defiant* shuddered violently as the tractor beam was

disengaged. "Captain," Kostin shouted. "Shraft couldn't disable the auto-destruct. Hold on. This is going to be bumpy."

Rian slapped at his comm badge. "Shraft," he said sharply. "Are we disconnected from the Nym's systems?"

"Yes, sir. Forty-five seconds to auto-destruct."

"Thank the gods." He eased Lily off him, and Asmo crouched down to hold her up. Rian ran to the nearest console and quickly took in the situation. Kostin had disengaged the tractor beam. He and Kostin banked the ship to the starboard side and brought up the engines to their full power. He activated the shields and watched the image of the Nym cruiser displayed on the forward viewscreen. They weren't going to get far enough away to completely avoid the explosion, and he doubted their shields at their current state would protect the ship from the impact. He recalled the last explosion the *Defiant* had to ride out, that star going nova. He had nothing to lose; his method had worked before, and Fleet was already pissed off at him. "Cutting power to the engines," he announced to the bridge. Kostin sputtered a laugh.

"This is why I like working with you, Captain," said the first officer.

With the power reserved from the engine shutdown, Rian bolstered the shields. "Ten seconds," said Shraft through his comm badge, and Rian relayed that information to the bridge. He and Kostin activated the ship's manual controls. It veered sharply to port, and a few people on the bridge were knocked over by the impact.

The Nym ship exploded cleanly on their viewscreen. Debris rained on the *Defiant* before floating away, and the red alert sirens began wailing again. Rian cut the noise, and the red lights kept flashing silently.

"Damage?" Rian asked the crew.

"None," said Kostin proudly. He and Rian corrected the

ship's angle, and Rian did a quick check of the ship's systems to be sure. There were certainly going to be reports of injuries, but the life form sensors told him everyone on board was alive. He powered the engines again, and the ship jolted and began its familiar thrum beneath their feet.

"Captain," said Asmo from behind him. He turned around. Lily was awake. He bent down and helped her to her feet.

"I'm really here," she said.

He nodded.

"You got me out," she said.

"I had a lot of help."

"What the hell just happened?" She rotated her shoulder. "I was slammed into the floor and then everything went dark." Tears formed in her eyes and spilled down her cheeks. "I killed some of them," she said.

He motioned to wipe away some of them, then saw the Nym blood dried on his palms and lowered his hands. "I know," he said. "You did the right thing. I was amazed at what you did."

"*I'm* amazed I did that," she said and scrubbed at her eyes with the back of a grimy hand. She looked at the blood congealing on her skin and made a sound of disgust. "God," she sighed and sniffed the air. "We both stink." She looked around the floor and picked up the Nym badge.

Rian remembered dropping the first one and felt like an idiot. "I'm sorry," he said quietly. "I completely fucked up back there. I should have pinned that thing to my clothes. If you hadn't had that one..." He didn't want to contemplate what could have happened.

"We would have taken one from one of the soldiers in the lift," she said.

"We wouldn't have had time." She had nearly died because he let a badge slip from his fingers.

"But it's over," she said. "I had one that I took from a Nym I killed." She took a deep, shaky breath. "It's going to take me a long time to get past that." She wrapped her arms around his neck, not caring that they were on the bridge or surrounded by crew, and neither did he anymore. "Rian," she said. "I love you."

The crew discreetly turned away. He whispered his next words against her mouth. "I love you, too," he murmured before pulling her up against him in a passionate embrace. He kissed her, lifting her off the floor as though his life depended on it. It did. He needed her.

"Incoming from *Bishop's Pride*," said Kostin.

"What the hell?" sniped a voice from the viewscreen. "Since when is *that* acceptable behavior on a bridge, Marska?"

Rian released Lily and turned to the formidable Senior Captain Jena, who was glowering at him. "Captain," he said respectfully. "We appreciate your assistance."

"What assistance? I saw a big fucking explosion almost right next to your ship. What is it with you and big fucking explosions, Marska?"

"That was a Nym vessel, Captain," Rian explained patiently. "It auto-destructed. Me and Lily were transported off just in time."

"Who the hell's Lily, and what were you doing on a Nym ship?" Jena leaned forward in her chair. She actually seemed intrigued.

Rian gestured to her, holding on to his arm and cowering under the captain's fierce glare. She raised her hand tentatively. "Hi," she said.

"This will be explained later, Captain," Rian said smoothly. "I certainly owe you an explanation, and so does Fleet."

"I'll be seeing you on Kevnar, anyway. I'm being transferred there. They're taking my ship out of service," she spat. As an afterthought, she added, "Fuckers."

"Incoming from the *Magna*, sir," Kostin said.

"I have to respond to that, Captain," Rian said. "Thank you, and I'll be seeing you shortly."

They signed off. Lily brought his face to hers for a kiss as the screen changed from Jena to the *Magna*'s senior captain. He let her go, then took his seat in the captain's chair.

———

LILY HOVERED by the bridge's elevator doors, staying out of the way. Should she leave? She desperately wanted to take a shower and change her clothes.

Her comm badge pinged, and she jumped. "Sick bay to Stewart."

She tapped it. "Mora!" she exclaimed. "Are you okay?"

"I'm fine, but all hell's broken loose in here," she said. "Taz is here. He broke his wrist when the ship went ass-up. Did you sustain any injuries?"

"Nothing serious. Just cuts and bruises, and my shoulder is sore."

"Get your ass down here," Mora said. "That's an order. I can do that, you know."

Rian was deeply engaged in a conversation with the captain of the *Magna*, and Lily wasn't about to bother him now. She slipped into the elevator.

Sick bay was full of crew, some dressed and others in civvies or pajamas. Mora and a few other off-duty nurses bustled around the area, checking bone regenerators and taking scans. The ship's other doctor, Bekri, held court from the waiting room in a wrinkled Fleet uniform. Mora spotted Lily and offered a tentative smile. Her short hair was mussed, and she wore a nightshirt and Fleet-issued pants under a too-large lab coat with bulging pockets.

"Stand still," she commanded. She held out her mediscan unit.

"Here?"

"The rooms are full," she explained. "We have four concussions, a broken pelvis, and two broken legs. Since you're still upright, you're getting checked out here." She eyed the unit's screen critically.

"How am I doing?" Lily asked.

"Very well considering, and I want to know every detail of what happened," Mora said. "Your rotator cuff is torn, but that's not going to kill you." She removed a big pair of shears in a case from one of her coat pockets. Sliding off the case, she said, "I'm going to put on a bone regenerator, and it'll be as good as new in a couple of hours. Don't raise your arms; you'll make it worse," she added, exasperated. "That's why I have scissors. Are you really attached to that shirt?"

"No, and if I was I'd be out of luck, anyway." She wrinkled her nose at the stench wafting off her.

"Good point." Mora cut through the fabric a few inches to expose her left shoulder and applied a small bone regenerator, a piece of flexible material that felt like silicone. Mora made some adjustments to it remotely from her mediscan. "It'll fall off when it's done its work. Do you want a painkiller or anything?"

Lily shook her head. "I'm not in any serious pain."

"I gathered that. I just thought you might like to be a little fucked up after what happened," she muttered. "The back storage area is being guarded by a security detail. Ashford's still in there." She stood back and regarded Lily, awe in her face. "I can't believe you and Captain Marska survived a visit to a Nym ship."

"It's never been done before?"

Mora shook her head. "Not that I know of, but mere nurses don't study that." She sighed. "If you want to talk, I'm here."

Lily nodded. "Thank you." She looked around sick bay. "But you're busy, and so's Rian." Mora raised an eyebrow, a knowing smile on her lips. "Before you say anything, it's..." She fumbled for words. "I hope it works. And I need to find Taz. He got us out of there."

Mora pointed to the doorway, where a wild-eyed and disheveled Taz had run in. His left arm was in a sling, the wrist wrapped in a bone regenerator. "Lily!" he exclaimed. "Thank the gods. Are you and the captain all right?"

"We are. He's on the bridge, talking to the *Magna*'s captain and then a bunch of Fleet suits."

"I figured as much." Taz eyed the bone regenerator quietly humming on her shoulder.

"I'm okay, Taz. What about you?"

"I'm fine, just worried. I was listening in to everything on the bridge. I held on to a console when the ship tipped over. I'm just a little stressed, you know?" He looked at Lily again. "You're really all right?"

"I really am, and it's because of you," Lily replied. "We never would have gotten out of there if you hadn't hacked into their ship." For what felt like the hundredth time that morning, Lily felt tears in her eyes again. "'Thank you' isn't enough. I don't know what else I can do to tell you how grateful I am."

Taz opened his mouth to respond, but Mora cut him off. "For gods' sake, Taz, she already has a lover."

Lily couldn't help but laugh. "Is that what you call them? It sounds so old-fashioned and scandalous."

"You have a better term?" Taz asked.

"I can't believe this is up for a debate right now," Lily said, just as Mora turned to Taz and demanded, "You knew about this?"

"A Kurran nurse didn't?" Taz shot back, reminding Lily that plenty of humanoid races had minor empathic talents.

"I'm mostly human," she retorted. "I only have the Kurran aversion to sunlight. I can't invade peoples' minds."

"Neither can I, but…"

"Boyfriend," Lily interrupted. "'Boyfriend' is sufficient. This really isn't the time to argue over who's psychic and who isn't."

"Psychics don't exist," Mora corrected. "Anyone who says they do is scamming you. And 'boyfriend' is juvenile."

Lily looked around the waiting area, hoping to see someone in need of a nurse, but everyone was talking into comm badges or checking their bone regenerators. Her own comm badge pinged. "Marska to Stewart," said a familiar voice. "I need you in my office. Admiral Kentz is on our vidlink."

Lily motioned to hug both of her friends but paused at the smell emanating from her clothes. Mora rolled her eyes. "It's just a coat." She embraced Lily, towering over her smaller frame. She stepped back, and Taz enveloped her in a hug. Lily planted a small kiss on his cheek. "Thank you," she whispered.

She waved a goodbye and headed for the bridge.

CHAPTER 18

"It's not as nice as the ones assigned to a captain or an admiral," Rian sighed. "But at least it beats the *Defiant*. It'll have to do."

"What do you mean, 'it'll have to do'?" she replied. "This is twice the size of my place in Toronto, and the hallways smell a lot better." She heard Rian's sharp intake of breath at the mention of Earth, but she pretended not to hear it. "What's so special about a senior captain's apartment?"

"They get a study, and the admirals get housekeeping service."

He and Lily were arranging their belongings in the executive officer's apartment on Kevnar Station. It was a spacious two-bedroom unit with a proper kitchen, large windows, and a bathroom that had a real tub and not a human-sized hairdryer. A small apartment had initially been assigned to Lily, but she had scarcely seen it before Rian offered to help her carry her meager duffel to his suite. Rian had already set up an office in the second bedroom, and Lily downloaded the premiere of *Lightning's Luck,* Mora's party having been postponed and the location changed to Lily and Rian's new home. The *Defiant*'s crew was awaiting new assignments on Kevnar and badly needed some distraction from their Nym encounter. So did she, and had avoided talking about it with Rian until now.

He had spent hours in meetings since their arrival at the station four days ago, and under his urging, the admirals weren't forcing her to talk yet. She knew she would have to give them her version of the events soon and had acquiesced to a meeting the following morning. Rian hadn't told her much about his dressing down by the admirals but knew she had been a part of the reason.

She liked Kevnar Station, though. It was more austere than Lily expected after the constant noise and rush of Rubidge. In between meeting locals and other officers, she had managed to take in some of it. It had a serenity garden she knew she would be spending lots of time in, full of beautiful, unrecognizable plants, and a library that had a modest collection of bound books in addition to millions of files available for download. She would enjoy her new home.

"I don't know if I'd want a housekeeper," she said in response to Rian's lament. "I don't like the idea of someone else washing my clothes."

"Lily..." He drifted off. She knew what he was thinking about, what issue was at the forefront of his mind.

The vortex. Dr. Ashford had told Fleet about the artificial vortex technology that the Nym developed, about the open one that currently hovered in a galaxy neighboring the Milky Way. The route the Nym had taken on their mistimed mission to twenty-first-century Earth.

The technology was unstable, hence Zadbac and Pitro's stranding in Toronto. It couldn't be used too often lest it rouse the suspicions of the locals, which their cruiser did in the days before Lily was kidnapped. The Nym had managed to get in and belatedly realized they were two centuries too early to begin rewriting history.

Their miscalculation in time travel made Fleet think positively. The Nym and their science were fallible, and already Fleet was working on developing a device to detect manmade vortexes and wormholes. They could finally keep step with the Nym's plans.

"Did Ashford ever say why he did it?" she asked, evading him.

"The Nym made the usual promises," Rian said. "Money. Access to living test subjects. Lily, you have to tell Fleet sooner or later."

A vortex could be replicated long enough for Lily to go home. Files pertaining to the creation of them had been found in Ashford's personal effects, and the science team aboard the *Defiant* jumped at the chance to reconstruct some of the debris from the Nym ship.

"And how did the newshounds figure out there was a time traveler?"

"He had a friend on Rubidge who told someone, also for money." Rian's blue eyes were shadowed and worried. "Pelly Bhackhar. She's been taken into custody, too."

Pelly. Lily remembered being introduced to a curator by that name on station. She nodded.

"She was involved with the historical society when you were found on Darcan-2," he explained. "The Nym contacted her when you were moved into a traveling exhibit. She was supposed to keep track of your whereabouts and deliver you to the Nym so you could be killed." His expression darkened, and Lily's hands involuntarily formed into fists at her side. "She and Ashford were involved personally, and they followed your movements. She had herself transferred to the museum at Rubidge when she found out you were going there permanently. Ashford joined the *Defiant*'s crew only a couple of days before you woke up. Apparently he was quite insistent on that transfer. She admitted to digging up news clips for you to find in the library at Rubidge. Zadbac and Pitro brought some of your media back."

"And they figured out how to use my phone to communicate our location in space."

"Yes."

"I guess they're going to undergo mind-wipes?" It sounded gruesome, but still not enough punishment for the doctor.

He nodded. "The trial is scheduled to start next week, but the evidence is pretty damning. Did I tell you that this morning they've assigned four teams to dismantle the old satellites in Commons space? It's a big job, but they'll have it done within a few months."

Lily snorted softly. She likely had the one device in existence that could respond to one of those old satellites, but the Commons was now worried about their being used for other nefarious purposes. Her cell phone was being held as evidence, but Fleet had promised to return it. She wanted it back for her father's books.

Rian made as if to reach for her, but pulled his hand back before making contact. "Lily, what are you going to do?"

She had already made up her mind but was under orders to give the opportunity serious thought. "I can't believe you're worried about my answer," she said softly. "I told you weeks ago."

"Are you sure? You didn't think it would ever come up. You had a life on Earth."

"I have a life here, a happier one," she insisted. "Do you want me to leave?"

"Gods, no," he said.

He clutched her in a hug that squeezed the breath from her lungs. "Rian," she squeaked. "My ribs." He released his death grip on her and held her loosely, as though he expected her to turn away.

"I'm staying," she said. "You're stuck with me forever."

"Good." He kissed her, his tongue flicking her lips apart. He guided her to the couch and didn't stop, his lips tracing a path down her throat while his fingers fumbled with the buttons on her sweater. "My sister is taking a trip to meet you, gods help us."

"I want to meet your family," she said.

"I think you'll get along. And I have furlough arranged, but not for another seven weeks." He sat down and pulled her in his lap.

"Rian," she gasped. His hand slid under her blouse. "Are you sure—but don't you have another meeting soon?"

"I have three hours," he said. He laid her back on the couch and kneeled over her, making short work of the sweater's buttons. "I'm meeting with an arms developer over new weaponry in this quadrant. Arms developers are easier to deal with than Admiral Brynon." One of his new bosses.

Lily's hands took on a life of their own and unsealed his shirt. "This isn't the behavior of a captain," she admonished him.

"I was demoted, remember?" he said against her skin. "Mere commanders get away with a lot more."

She giggled and then turned serious. He angled himself up on his elbows, concern across his face. She didn't want to see him look worried anymore. "Rian, there's nowhere else I want to be than here," she assured him. "I want my life to be this way. I love you, and I'll be telling you that every day for the rest of our lives."

For the first time in days, he relaxed and gave her a genuine smile. "I love you, too," he said.

His hands threaded through hers, and he kissed her again.

ABOUT THE AUTHOR

Jessica Marting is a sci-fi and paranormal romance author, art enthusiast (not quite an artist, despite all that time in art school), an avid reader, and makeup collector. She lives in Toronto.

Sign up for her newsletter at jessicamarting.com/newsletter for pre-order alerts, sales, freebies, and more.

ALSO BY JESSICA MARTING

Magic & Mechanicals

Wolf's Lady

Sea Change

Bound in Blood

Dragon's Keep

Spellbound

The Searchers

Blood Ties

Blood Moon

Blood Virtue

Zone Cyborgs

Haven

Paradise

Oasis

Safe Harbor

Sanctuary

Refuge

The Commons

Supernova

Celestial Chaos

Standalone Novels & Novellas

Spindle's End

Trade Secrets

Neon Vice

Dead Ringer

Rapture

Escape From Europa 10

Castaways

Demon's Favor

Her Perfect Match